The Unhappiest Boy in America: A Novel

Ralph Oppenheim

This is a work of fiction. All the names, characters, businesses, places, events and incidents in this book are either the product of the author's imagination or used in a fictitious manner. Any resemblance to actual persons, living or dead, or actual events is purely coincidental.

CHAPTER 1

Myrtle Wright, Jan Pancake's roommate, once went off on one of her rants, this time swearing that she would never patronize any business whose marketing strategy relied on people sliding flyers under her windshield wiper. "It's annoying, I don't like strangers fiddling with my car; besides, it's not much of a way to gain a competitive advantage, is it?"

Jan didn't see what the big deal was. Besides, she didn't own a car, so it didn't really pertain. She was okay with flyers under windshield wipers, didn't mind pizza menu door hangers, and she had no problem with flyers on bulletin boards. Which was a good thing because that's how she found out about the Alistair MacNaughton Internship at the Akron Sentinel-Herald. From a flyer tacked to the bulletin board in the lobby of the School of Business building. Because she was a few minutes early for her "Ethics in Modern Journalism" class she had the time to pull a notebook from her backpack and write down the details of the internship and the website for the Alistair MacNaughton Foundation. After class she bundled up for the raw February weather and returned to her dorm room.

Myrtle was lying on her bed studying organic chemistry. She looked over to greet her roommate. "Hey."

"Hey," Jan answered back. She shed her winter coat and hung it up in the closet. Tidiness is important when you're living in a double room that is eleven feet by twelve feet. In fact, if you aren't lying on your bed or sitting at your built-in desk then your options are limited to standing or being elsewhere. Myrt studied on her bed because that's what made her comfortable. Listening to old tunes through earbuds while she studied made her comfortable. Singing along also made her comfortable. Right now she was listening to an old cowboy song by Bob Wills and His Texas Playboys.

Jan settled into her desk, went online and after checking her email, went to the Alistair MacNaughton Foundation website. She downloaded and printed out the internship guidelines and an application . She told Myrt about the internship.

"How'd you learn about it?" Myrt asked.

Jan always made a point of being truthful so, even though she knew what was coming, she told Myrt.

Myrt looked aghast. "You're charting your life's direction based on a flyer you saw on a bulletin board? Are you mad?"

Jan was ready for her. "In my communications class we did a unit on ephemerata and other fugitive sources of information. I don't remember the exact name for it."

"You mean like the flyers on the ride board? Or Chinese restaurant menus? That sort of thing? That's ridiculous."

Myrt got off her bed. She made air quotes: "Needed – ride to Myrtle Beach for spring break.' Now there's Ph.D thesis material if I ever saw any."

Jan placidly asked, "So, what do you think? The deadline is March 1."

"Akron, huh? Did you know Akron used to be known as the City of Assassins? Beware!"

Jan laughed. "Akron'll be fine and I'll be lucky if I get it. Sounds really great to me," said Jan. She couldn't help sounding a little excited.

Sensing that, Myrt said, "Then go for it." Then she added, "Besides, it could be worse. It could be Gary, Indiana."

"Don't be a snob," Jan said.

Myrt walked the few steps it took to cross the room to look over Jan's shoulder at the application. "I can't believe they don't have you fill it out online. That newspaper must be really backward." She snatched a couple of the pages Jan had been reading from Jan's desk.

"Myrt, please don't discourage me. I've got my family for that." Jan thought of herself as pretty good natured, but her roommate could sometimes be a little annoying.

"I'm sorry. You're right I should be encouraging you." Myrt put her hands on Jan's shoulders and swiveled her around in the chair to face her. "Look at me, Jan," she said in a mock serious manner, "You should go for it because it could be an important step in your career. You deserve the chance."

"Thanks." Jan smiled at her roommate."

"In the whole wide world you are the most qualified person for this internship."

"Don't overdo it, Myrt."

Myrt flung her arms out. "Why, spotting that flyer on the bulletin board was fate. It was no accident. It was like when Alexander Fleming discovered penicillin. Or when Madame Curie discovered curiosity."

"Okay, that's enough," said Jan. "You should be a drama major."

Myrtle read from one of the pages of the application she had snatched. "'In your own words, tell us why we should choose you for an Alistair McNaughton Internship.' What a stupid question! Who else's words should you use – Percy Bysshe Shelley's?"

Jan laughed. "I always loved that guy's middle name."

"That's why I use it whenever I can."

Jan got up from her desk holding the application aloft and began pacing around the small dorm room. Myrt's critical spirit was contagious. "You're right; some of these questions are dumb. How about this one: 'Why do you think you should be selected?' I don't know. They're asking me to put myself in their place and tell them what they should do and why. That's impossible. I'm not in their position; if I were, I wouldn't be applying for their internship; I'd be running their program!"

Myrt cheered her on. "That's telling 'em, girl!"

"They might as well ask me whether they like chicken fricassee. How am I supposed to know?"

"I like the word 'fricassee'."

"Me, too." She paused. "They just want me to say flattering things about how great their newspaper is."

"Some nerve!"

"Like, 'The Sentinel-Herald serves as the vital, indispensable heart of the Akron community.' How's that?"

Jan sat back down and began scribbling on a yellow legal pad.

"I like it!" Myrt enthused. "I wish I knew what 'fricassee'

means. I guess I can Google it."

"And I'll put something in about 'supporting the democratic ideal'. This girl can play their game…and beat them."

Myrt returned the pages she was holding to Jan's desk and resumed her place on her bed. "Fracas, that's a good word; a real newspaper kind of word." She paused a moment. "Is it fracas or fracas?" She pronounced the word first with a hard 'a' then with a soft 'a'.

It made no difference to Jan. She ignored the question and concentrated on the application.

"Okay, here's another," Jan read. "In your own words, tell us why you seek a career in journalism?" Jan turned to Myrt. "Well?"

They were both silent for a minute. Then Jan tentatively suggested, "Because it's a noble field that plays a vital role in the democratic processes of this country?" She chewed on the end of her pencil. "Naw, I'm already using 'democratic'."

Myrt asked, "What do you mean by 'noble'? Tell me how noble it is when a reporter asks a grief-stricken mother who's just lost her family in a house fire," - here Myrt raised an imaginary notepad in one hand and an imaginary pen in the other – "'So, ma'am, what are you feeling now?' Just playing devil's advocate, okay? It's just that I don't see you asking some grieving woman that question. I don't know if you have it in you…and I don't think that's a bad thing."

"It's bad manners and hurtful. I wasn't raised to hurt people."

Jan thought back to an interview she'd conducted a few months before for the school newspaper. A professor at a local medical school, a member of the Army Reserves, had recently returned from a tour of duty somewhere near the Balkans. Jan asked him where he had been stationed. The colonel answered, "I can't tell you that. And even if I could, I wouldn't."

Jan had been taken back by his response. Being truthful is one thing; being gratuitously rude seemed unnecessary.

But a real reporter would have asked a follow-up question like 'Why not', she thought at the time. She ignored his response and went on to ask the next prepared question on her notepad. Later, she rebuked herself for her timidity. She had taken his remark personally. She had to admit to herself that she hadn't conducted herself in a professional manner. Maybe she wasn't ready to be a real reporter?

Jan frowned. "Myrt, am I kidding myself by thinking I might be able to make a real contribution to the field of journalism?"

"Probably," was Myrt's answer.

"Myrt, why was Akron known as the City of Assassins?"

"Consider yourself lucky if you never find out."

Jan raised her eyebrows. "Hmm."

Chapter 2

Discovering that flyer on the bulletin board may not have been historic, but it was fortunate that she discovered it when she did. Less than an hour later a student named Brooks Watt spotted the same flyer, pulled it off the board, folded it up and stuck it in his pocket. A competitive lad by nature, Brooks figured he'd improve the odds of his winning the Internship by limiting the number of applicants. Brooks was the kind of guy who'd race over to the library right after class to check out all the books on an assigned topic. Everyone else was just out of luck. He was the kind of guy who carried a briefcase to school when he was in the eighth grade.

Jan's doubts about her reportorial skill were rebutted by the glowing letter of recommendation Jan submitted as part of her application for the Alistair MacNaughton Internship. There it was in black and white:

"Jan Pancake has the makings of a fine journalist," Professor Coleman had written, along with other laudatory pronouncements. It embarrassed Jan to read the whole letter. Humility was a guiding force in her upbringing. She read it reluctantly, by closing one eye and squinting through the other. After a while she worked up to the point where she could read it with both eyes open.

Well, I may have fooled Professor Coleman, Jan thought to herself, when she read the letter, *but now I have to fool the internship committee if I get an interview.* Shaking her head, Jan corrected herself. *Convince them, not 'fool' them.*

From across the dorm room Myrt said, "Jan Pan, hello, you're talking to yourself."

Jan was at her desk. "Huh? Oh."

Myrt was studying. It may not have looked like she was studying; she was lying on her bed listening to music through earbuds. But Myrt had the gift of being able to absorb organic chemistry or Greek history or most any other subject while engaged in other tasks. She had a photographic memory. Unlike other pre-med students she had lots of time for things other than studying; things like music and dancing.

Jan, by contrast, could only study while sitting at a neat and orderly desk. She kept her keyboard covered when not in use. She needed quiet in order to concentrate. Her memorization skills worried her and she spent time working on them by memorizing poetry. Other students learned not to ask her to recite 'Hiawatha'. Still, in the future Jan probably won't remember the names of most of her classmates. Myrt, on the other hand, will remember their names and even the names of the janitorial staff that cleaned the dorm's common areas.

Some roommates get along so poorly that they divide their dorm room into geopolitical areas: spheres of influence, demilitarized zones, extraterritorial jurisdictions. Though they were quite different people, Jan and Myrt had been roommates for three years and got along so well that they considered one another best friends. Had she wanted, Myrt could have had a single room or rented an off-campus apartment. Jan was a scholarship student and had to live in a dorm. Myrt chose to room with Jan.

Jan was a quiet person. Myrtle was not. Right now she was dancing around the room and making weird noises.

Oh no, not again, thought Jan. "You're doing that awful throat singing thing again. You sound like Popeye after he's swallowed a set of bagpipes."

"I intend to become a master of Tuvan throat singing," replied Myrt. "Nothing can stop me."

"The problem is that Tuvan throat singers are from Mongolia and you're from Lexington, Kentucky. There isn't much of an audience for that kind of thing around these parts."

"I'm not looking for a fan base."

"That's just for starts. It also sounds weird. Why would you want to sound weird?"

Because it's fun!"

Myrt was a big fan of world music. There was a period when she tried her hand at Portuguese fado singing. During another period – all of sophomore year, actually – she imitated Edith Piaf. She sang like the Little Sparrow, smoked Galoise, wore a beret and a tragic expression. Closer to home, she considered becoming a blues singer like Big Mama Thornton, but decided that she wasn't prepared to do the necessary suffering. Of all Myrt's different phases Jan preferred the Piaf.

"Want to go folk dancing tonight?" asked Myrt, interrupting her throat singing…and not a moment too soon for Jan.

Jan shook her head. "Tim's coming over. We're going to study together."

"Suit yourself," said Myrt. She began to mambo.

Chapter 3

An Alistair MacNaughton Internship – named for the late prominent Owner/Publisher of the Akron Sentinel-Herald– was one of the best internships available to college juniors.

It is only a slight exaggeration to argue that many internships can be described as Dickensian. (How Dickens might have described them we'll leave to the English majors out there.) Often unpaid, these internships give students the chance to gain class credits in exchange for workplace experience. That, at least, is the idea. But it is often an unfair exchange because students pay for the class credits and often get stuck doing meaningless tedious tasks. Conditions in a Victorian blacking factory may have been grim, but children at least received a few pence for their labor plus all the blacking they could carry home in the back pockets of their threadbare trousers. (What they did with all that blacking was their business.) It's enough to turn an ambitious student into a slacker. The internet is full of internship horror stories. You can look them up.

Students who receive MacNaughton Internships get class credit paid for by the newspaper. Even better, they receive a housing allowance and are paid a salary commensurate with that of an entry level journalist. They are assigned mentors with whom they are supposed to work closely in order to learn the practice of journalism. Unless they make a complete botch of it, interns who have done well often receive firm job offers contingent upon the successful completion of their senior years.

Interns are required to submit progress reports at the mid-point of their internships and at its' conclusion. It was a smart move for Jan Pancake to have Professor Coleman write her letter of recommendation. Professor Coleman had been local news editor of the Sentinel-Herald for many years before retiring from the paper. If not one of the legendary editors, Coleman had been a respected one. He had served on the selection committee when he worked for the paper.

CHAPTER 4

The air in the Student Union room where folk dancing was taking place was stuffy and gamy. The men's locker room in the school's field house smelled better, even on game day. A study conducted by the Cultural Anthropology Department at Philander College showed that on average folk dancing enthusiasts use underarm deodorant 40% less often than non-folk dancers. This study was of no use to anyone, especially the folk dancers. Most were already aware of the situation, or proud of it, or willing to ignore it.

"Deodorant is an unnatural social construct; the result of prosperity. Third world inhabitants can't afford deodorant, see no need for it, and we stand in solidarity with them," explained one dancer. "I'm sure Frantz Fanon didn't use deodorant."

Myrt was unable to see the issue in political terms. So, she occasionally adopted the identity of Dora the Deodorant Warrior, decked out in a little red cap adorned with small deodorant tubes. She got the idea for the red cap from the beer helmets that the fraternity guys wore on game days. Around her waist she had a pouch apron like the ones peanut vendors at baseball games wear. Myrt dispensed samples of deodorant from her apron that she purchased from the travel size bins at CVS. No one seemed to resent her handouts because college students love to get anything for free. (That's why you'll often see students patiently waiting in line at Costco to get free samples of food so miniscule they fit on the end of toothpicks.)

Anyway, Myrt was Dora the Deodorant Warrior and handed out little deodorants. That ran into some money, but Myrt thought it was worth it. Fortunately, she came from a wealthy family. She enjoyed folk dancing because it was a way to meet people and get some exercise. There were only two things she worried about. One was a group of Morris dancers over in a corner of the room who were always ready to stir up a little trouble. Myrt was keeping an eye on them as she wiped some perspiration from her brow.

Myrt's other concern was a girl named Anna Romanovsky, nicknamed 'Anna Pavlova', who always showed up for folk dancing.

She usually danced by herself. Her idea of dancing was to whirl around with arms and legs flying, spinning and flailing around in an uncontrolled manner that caused untold havoc on the floor. At the commencement of this folk dancing session Myrt had posted an updated list of names - Anna's past victims - and their injuries. The length of the list gave testimony to the near-lethality of her limbs. Myrt wisely posted the list anonymously. To do otherwise would risk arousing the Pavlovian temper and her buzzsaw legs.

Myrt was headed for the lemonade table when she spotted Jan and her sort-of boyfriend, Tim, entering. She went over to her roommate and asked, "I thought you were going to study?"

Jan quietly said, "I'll tell you later." She clearly meant, *when Tim isn't around.*

So Myrt waited until Tim had gone over to talk to a friend. "What's going on?"

Jan said, "We were studying and Tim got fresh. So, I suggested we come here. I don't think he's happy about it."

Myrt smiled. "Hearing somebody use an old-fashioned phrase like 'getting fresh' is so refreshing! I'm so tired of that expression 'hooking up'. Well, welcome. Just stay away from Anna. She's already hospitalized one dancer tonight."

"Because she's an art major she thinks it's okay to endanger lives," Jan grumbled. "I heard she's calling it 'performance art' and wants to get class credit by having herself recorded and uploaded and turned into an NFT video."

Myrt could only shake her head in disbelief.

By now, Tim had finished greeting classmates and joined Jan and Myrt. Myrt noticed that he made no attempt to put his arm around Jan or show any affection.

"What's going on?" he asked.

"We were talking about sending Anna to wipe out a few Morris dancers," Myrt said seriously.

"What have you got against Morris dancing?" Tim asked.

"It's the bells, the ribbons, the sticks, their big clunky legs, the whole thing," Myrt answered. "They give me the creeps."

"Me, too," agreed Jan. Directing her gaze at Anna, Jan said, "I never thought of folk dancing as a contact sport."

"Sweep his legs, Anna!" yelled Tim with what sounded like a hint of admiration.

Myrt grimaced as Anna's ferocious flying feet claimed another victim.

It had been a computer in the Housing Department that determined that Myrt and Jan should be roommates; more specifically, an algorithm designed to maximize the diversity within the student body. Philander was a small, expensive private college. Having a scholarship student room with a student from a prosperous family would, it was felt by the college administration, broaden the outlooks of the students involved in this act of social engineering and improve student life as a whole. Sometimes it worked out. Myrt and Jan got along well. The previous year Jan had spent the mid-term break at Myrt's family's home outside Lexington, Kentucky. They'd both had a good time. Myrt invited Jan home again this year, but Easter was going to fall during vacation and Jan knew she would have to return to West Virginia for the holiday. Mid-term break was a couple of weeks away.

"You can come home with me," Jan said.

Myrt shook her head. "You know my family. It's important that we be together at the holidays. They're talking about going to our place in Georgia, and they want me along."

Myrt had shown Jan photos of the family place on Little Saint Simon Island off the coast of Georgia. It was a picturesque white beach house, small unlike the family's home in Lexington which was surrounded by acres of lawn. Jan couldn't help but feel a pang of jealousy. She brought herself up short almost immediately by her memory of Pastor Linger's admonitory words: "Jealousy is the one vice that imparts no pleasure."

Still, it was difficult. When she first beheld the elevator in Jan's family's house her jaw dropped in amazement.

"It's just a small elevator," Myrt said apologetically. She didn't know why she should have been made uncomfortable. But she had been. "It's not like those elevators on aircraft carriers. Now those suckers are big."

Jan said, "Well, sure, they have to lift airplanes."

There wasn't any point in Myrt mentioning her father's airplane, which, too, was small, at least compared to Howard Hughes' Spruce Goose.

Myrt was sincerely sorry she couldn't go with Jan. The disparity in their families' circumstances didn't matter to her.

"How will you get home," she asked.

Jan drew her lower lip in then exhaled, shaking her head a bit. "I don't know."

"You could invite Tim," Myrt suggested.

"Just because he has a car?"

Myrt smiled. "No. Because you want his company...and he just happens to have a car."

"You should be the one who's pre-law, not Tim," Jan returned the smile.

CHAPTER 5

Tim said 'sure', he'd go to Jan's home for the mid-term break. "I'm curious about how your family lives."

Great, we'll be the objects of curiosity, like animals in a zoo, thought Jan. She cast him a dirty look.

Tim caught it. "What'd I say?"

She didn't answer.

They were walking down the campus's Main Path on a beautiful early spring day.

"We can leave Friday. I've got an 8:30 French for Poets class. We'll leave after that. Okay with you?"

Jan said that worked for her, too.

"Is there anything special I should bring?" asked Tim.

"Sears, Roebuck catalogs," said Jan in a grave tone. "Mom says we're running low."

"Huh?" Tim thought for a minute. Then he stopped in his tracks. His shoulders hunched up. "Oh, no," he said. "You can't mean…"

Jan began laughing. "No, no, no! I'm kidding. Besides, if Sears has a catalog anymore it's online."

Tim gave a sigh of relief. "Why can you poke fun at West Virginia but I can't?"

Jan shrugged her shoulders.

Trying to sound casual, Jan said, "By the way, don't mention dancing to my family. They're still a little funny about it."

Dancing was no longer forbidden to members of Jan's church and hadn't been for some years, but many of the older, more strait-laced faithful held fast to old practices. Jan and her brother and sisters knew that their parents didn't exactly approve of their going out dancing and such from their tight-lipped expressions and the way they'd turn silent whenever those topics came up. So, while they never overtly expressed disapproval, Jan knew enough to be cautious.

CHAPTER 6

Before they left for break Myrt asked Jan if she wanted to go to the local salon and get gussied up. She knew that Jan's religion forbade her from cutting her hair.

"You can still get your hair done up, right? You have such beautiful thick hair. And you can have a fingernails re-do, some toe work and a facial. That's not verboten, is it?"

"I don't think so, but.." said Jan. She made a convincing show of reluctance, but she actually was eager to be pampered.

Myrt shook her head. "Come on, we went through this last year, remember? There's nothing wrong with making yourself look good, Jan. It's not all vanity."

"Not all, just enough," replied Jan sardonically. "Okay, I'm game."

"And it's on me," said Myrt.

"Even better. Thanks," said Jan. She had learned that people often get pleasure from giving things to others. She used to be quick to turn down offers of gifts, fearing that their basis was some form of pity. But experience had taught her to distinguish the different varieties of charity. Now saying thanks came easily. Especially with Myrt.

Jan was slender and of average height. She had a fair complexion. When she was in the ninth grade a classmate named Les Marcum had declared that Jan was not overly 'repellent', a word he had just learned from that week's chapter in <u>Word Wealth</u>. 'Not repellent' became his highest compliment. In the years since, Jan had grown even less and less repellent. A few months back a classmate had called her 'fetching'.

Myrt, too, was not overly repellent. She was larger than Jan. She was bosomy, had green eyes, a smile that was a wonder, plus red hair. Not that carroty color but real red. She could turn heads and knew it.

At the appointed hour they marched into the fanciest salon in Mount Olive. When it was determined that they had been groomed to the max, Jan and Myrt looked at themselves in one of the salon's floor to ceiling mirrors.

"What do you think?" said Myrt.

"I think you look pretty good."

"What about you," Myrt demanded. "How do you think you look?"

Jan smiled. "I look good, at least good enough for most normal purposes. That's from <u>Our Town</u>."

"I thought where your parents live is called 'out county'."

"They do. I'm talking about the play by Thornton Wilder."

CHAPTER 7

After a few hours of driving, Tim and Jan passed the overhead sign announcing "Welcome to West Virginia – Wild and Wonderful."

"Welcome to the land of fried bologna sandwiches, opioid addiction, snake handlers and bad teeth," chortled Tim.

Jan glowered. "I thought we agreed not to make fun of West Virginia."

Tim apologized but couldn't help himself. "I still don't get the fried bologna."

Jan turned to face him. "What don't you 'get' about poverty, Tim?" she snapped.

Tim looked sheepish. Jan quietly said, "Sorry, I don't mean to be self-righteous, but sometimes, Tim, you can be such an…" She paused to search for the right word. "Such an apple!"

Tim wondered, *"An apple?"* but wisely remained silent for a while. It was easy enough to see the poverty as they drove into the heart of Appalachia. It may be a fact that West Virginia has the highest percentage of home ownership in the country, but an awful lot of those homes are in dire need of repair.

It was a pleasant spring day. The woods were full of redbuds and dogwoods in bloom. Once they left the interstate Tim had to keep his eyes on the road. Roads were narrow, curving every which way up and down the mountains. Huge logging trucks and coal trucks barreled along forcing other drivers to pull to the sides of the road to make room for them. No matter which way you turned there seemed to be mountains looming over the roads. The car's GPS was of no use in these mountains. Neither were cellphones.

Driving was so treacherous that Tim concentrated on the road and forsook telling the city slicker/country bumpkin jokes he had worked up for the trip.

It was late afternoon when Jan directed Tim onto a gravel road leading into the hollow where the Pancake family's farmhouse sat. It was a good-sized old white house surrounded on three sides by hills. A barn stood out back along with a number of sheds. There were chickens and ducks in the yard. A pen held sheep and goats. As soon as they pulled up in front of the house her family tumbled out to greet them. One after the other they hugged/kissed Jan while Tim stood to the side. Once all the greetings were exhausted Jan introduced Tim. Jan's sisters and brother – Sissy, Mary Lou, and Josiah – were friendly towards him. Jan's father, Charlie, mother, and grandparents were more reserved. They doled out smiles to strangers sparingly.

While the older generation chattered, remarking on the appearance of Jan, and covertly sizing up Tim, Josiah and Sissy conveyed Jan's bags to her old bedroom on the second floor. Lugging his own bag, Tim followed Sissy upstairs.

"You'll have my bedroom," she said. "I'll be bunking with Mary Lou."

Tim made the appropriate noises apologizing for the inconvenience. He dumped his bag on a plain wooden chair. A towel and washcloth lay on the bed. There was a bureau and mirror. An unframed reproduction of Jesus giving a sermon to a group of Judeans was it for décor. There were none of the magazine clippings from popular magazines that teenage girls usually decorate their rooms with. No photographs of classmates smiling, hugging and mugging at water parks or the mall or the beach.

Sissy, a large, somewhat ungainly girl, smiled at Tim.

"I hope you'll be comfortable here. I guess you'll be wanting to clean up and take a nap before supper," she said before leaving the room and closing the bedroom door.

After a light supper and a little chitchat the family turned in early for the night.

CHAPTER 8

It was obvious that Jan was the apple of the Pancake family's eye. They hung on her every word. She was the first member of her family to go to college. The stories she told about campus life – she was careful in the selection of stories to tell – were as exotic to the Pancakes as would be The Tales of the Arabian Nights to an Eskimo. And for Tim, a guy from Williamsburg, Virginia, the Pancake family was fascinating and as exotic as the Native Americans were to the Jamestown settlers, though slightly friendlier. He liked Josiah, who was the friendliest of the bunch. Josiah was a big, good-looking guy in his late twenties with a mop of brown hair and a big smile. He helped manage the farm and worked on farm machinery for extra money.

After breakfast their first morning at the farm, Josiah invited Tim to help him work on some vehicles that needed repair. Tim was of little use, having very little knowledge of such things, but he could tell that Josiah had good mechanical skills. Josiah was focusing on a tractor that had a rusted out exhaust system that was dragging on the ground.

"I think we can save Mr. Heater some money here," he said to Tim.

Tim followed Josiah into a barn/workshop to a large pile of scrap metal. Josiah put on some leather gloves, got on his hands and knees and began digging through the pile.

"What are you looking for?" Tim asked.

"There should be some large tomato cans in here somewhere," said Josiah.

Tim poked around. "Why a tomato can? Wouldn't a pineapple can work just as well?"

Josiah ignored the question. He got up, found another pair of gloves and tossed them to Tim. He went back to digging in the scrap pile.

Tim laughed. "You look like a mole burrowing in the dirt."

"Just help me look and knock off the remarks," said Josiah. "Have you ever seen a mole burrowing in the dirt?"

Tim looked sheepish. "Well, no," he admitted.

After a while Tim called out, "Here's one." He raised a can in triumph.

Josiah shook his head. "Sorry, honey, not big enough. Keep looking."

Eventually Tim turned up the right sized tomato can. He tossed it to Josiah.

Josiah examined the can. He scowled. "Sorry, this is Del Monte; I prefer Libby."

Tim was flummoxed. "What possible difference can it make what brand it is?" he asked.

Josiah laughed. "It doesn't. Can't you tell when your leg is being pulled? Bring me those tin snippers" Josiah commanded, jerking his head in the direction of the tool bench. He returned to the tractor.

Tim went to the tool bench and tried to figure one which one of the hand tools looked the most like something that would be used to snip tin. He brought it to Josiah, who took the tool and thanked him. Apparently, Tim had chosen correctly.

Josiah used the snippers to fashion a large patch for the muffler. He welded it in place.

"We've just saved George Heater around nine hundred dollars," he said. "Thanks for the help." He got up from under the tractor, went over to Tim and gave him a friendly slap on the shoulder.

Tim bobbed his head modestly. "I enjoyed it."

"You like Jan," Josiah said, more as a statement of fact than a question.

"Sure."

Josiah went, "Hmm." He gestured to Tim to follow him. Walking towards the house he said, "You can feed the chickens now."

"Are they cage-free?" asked Tim

Josiah looked at him askance. "Do you see any cages?"

"You have cattle, too?" asked Tim.

"Also cage free," Josiah said. He shared his father's dry sense of humor.

CHAPTER 9

Jan laughed. "That's a West Virginia thing. You'll hear men call other men 'honey' and sometimes 'sweetheart'. I know it's weird. It doesn't mean anything."

"Josiah does have a girlfriend, right?" asked Tim.

"I told you, it doesn't mean a thing. Yes, he has a girlfriend. You just met her." She pointed toward the young woman sitting next to Josiah at an adjoining picnic table. "That's Lally." Jan winked and elbowed Tim in the ribs. "But it's you Josiah really likes." Jan laughed. "And he calls you 'honey'."

Jan was sitting next to Tim at the main picnic table. The entire extended family was at the farm, and many others besides, so dinner was being held out in the barn which was illuminated by lanterns. The food was all carried out by the women.

The blessing was made by Pastor Linger who was sitting at the table next to his wife, with Jan, Tim and Jan's parents and grandparents arrayed near the Lingers. After the customary invocation he made a special blessing: "And we thank you, Lord, for bringing Jan here tonight to share this meal with us." He smiled at Jan, then noticed Tim. He added an appendix to the blessing: "And for bringing..," He hesitated and looked over at Tim.

"Tim," contributed Tim.

"And thank you, Lord, for bringing Jim, too. Amen."

The assembly responded, "Amen."

"Close enough," grumbled Tim.

Dinner was bountiful. Chicken - fried, not fricasseed -, macaroni and cheese, celery sticks with cream cheese, green beans with bacon, fried green tomatoes, and biscuits, of course. Apple and blueberry cobbler for dessert. Lemonade or sweet tea.

Zero fried bologna.

During dinner Pastor Linger turned to Jan. "You look well, Jan. College seems to be agreeing with you."

She smiled.

"I like the way you're doing your hair," said Mrs. Linger.

Pastor Linger asked, "Will you be around long enough to give a talk to my youth group in two weeks? You can tell them what college is like."

Jan said she doubted whether she'd be home that long. That was when she shared with the table the possibility that she might get an Akron Sentinel-Herald internship. She hadn't disclosed this news to her family. She described the job and salary and how it could lead to the opportunity to do some real reporting. "I'll be able to make a difference in the community."

"Which community," asked her father. "This community?" He sounded a bit sour.

Jan reminded her father that there weren't many newspapering opportunities in the region. There was a local weekly and the throwaway that was distributed to the grocery stores.

Her mother's parents were seated at the table and were listening. Her grandfather frowned and mumbled something to his wife.

"Grandpa?" Jan asked.

To Tim it sounded like he said something about raisins in a West Virginia accent. Whatever it was it got Jan's hackles up. "I'm sorry, Grampa; I'm sorry, Gammy, but I intend to make something of myself."

"What does that make us - nothing?" asked her grandmother.

"But Akron – it's so far away," Jan's mother said, with more than a trace of anguish in her voice.

"Akron, and maybe New York or maybe Los Angeles or even London, England," Jan said in a defiant tone. "But wherever I go, a part of West Virginia will go with me. And it's not like I won't come home as often as I can. And with a good salary I'll be able to do that a lot."

That seemed to comfort her mother. She smiled. Her grandparents couldn't bring themselves to smile.

Later, after dinner, Tim and Jan strolled down to a little pond and watched the polliwogs.

"I don't get that bit about raisins," Tim asked. "Why did dried fruit get you so worked up?"

For a few seconds Jan was puzzled. Then she figured out what Tim was talking about. "Raisin', not raisins," she said, shaking her head. "'Don't go above your raisin'. That means if it was good enough for your grandparents, and good enough for your parents then living here and doing the same things they did should be good enough for you. To aspire to anything loftier would be considered…" she searched for the right term.

"Hubris?" offered Tim.

"Unrighteous," said Jan. "My grandparents think it's going above my raisin' for me to think about making a success of myself in journalism. Even though some good journalism could put a stop to some of the abuses that have kept so many of the people around here poor."

Jan's voice took on a tone that mixed anger and frustration.

Tim said, "Your parents seem supportive."

They sat down on a bench by the water. It was getting dark.

"My parents have made some amazing adjustments; I'll say that for them. I'm proud of them. You wouldn't believe how many parents around these parts won't allow their kids to even consider going to college."

Tim took Jan's hand. "Being here with your family has made me understand a lot of things. I think you're pretty amazing."

"Thanks, said Jan, "but we'd better get back soon. Otherwise…" Using her spare hand, she zipped her index finger across her neck.

"Right. Just one more thing: if you get that internship you'll be gone a long time."

Jan stood up still holding his hand. She yanked Tim to a standing position and led the march towards the house.

"You're right. I'll be a long time gone."

After attending Easter Sunrise Service and a picnic with the entire congregation of Pastor Linger's small church Tim left for Williamsburg. He thanked the Pancake family for their hospitality, said he'd pick Jan up in a week then used a carefully drawn map to make his way to parts of the country that have GPS, internet, and cellphone service.

As he drove around he took note of all the artifacts people displayed in their yards and gardens. He saw lots of brass bed stands and large rusty pots, old plows and threshers, wagon wheels and other farm implements. He figured it had something to do with a yearning for a simpler agrarian past but wondered whether there was more to it than that. After all, these people were living in a pretty simple agrarian present which must not be all that different from a simple agrarian past. He had been reluctant to ask Jan, fearing that she'd get overly defensive about her culture. He was trying to be as supportive as he could. He decided that instead of asking, "So, why do West Virginians put all that junk in their yards? Is it their idea of landscaping?" he'd be sensitive and ask her to "Please share your insight into the cultural significance and history of this unique tradition." Yeah, that would be better.

CHAPTER 10

On the agreed upon day Tim returned to the Pancake family home. They were friendly enough towards Tim. Josiah loaded Jan's bags into the car, she kissed her family goodbye, and off they went. The family watched from the porch until Tim's car went around a bend and disappeared.

"My mother made sandwiches for lunch," said Jan.

"That's nice."

"Don't you want to know what she made?" Jan teased.

"Don't tell me. Fried bologna?" Tim asked.

"That is correct!" Jan chortled. "I requested it especially for you."

Tim smiled and shook his head. "You're too much."

"Do you know why it's called bologna?"

Tim confessed he didn't.

"I don't know either," said Jan.

While they were driving back to Philander College (and while Jan was yelling at Tim for calling those artifacts "yard junk") the committee appointed to select the next interns for the Akron Sentinel-Herald was holding its meeting in the fourth-floor boardroom in the newspaper building. They sat with identical file folders in front of them. At the head of the table was old Mrs. MacNaughton, the retired publisher of the paper who had inherited the paper from her late husband, Alistair. She was a handsome old woman, although quite frail. She wore a simple blue wool suit and three strands of pearls around her neck. Sitting across the table from each other was Jeremiah Murphy, the Managing Editor, and Jack Tweedy, who would be the interns' mentor.

They had examined all the applications that had been submitted on time. They read the personal statements and responses to questions. They looked at the academic transcripts and the letters of recommendation. They had pretty much made up their minds.

Except for Terence Gallier, the president of a large insurance company. He flipped through his folder and said, "Well, let's not be too hasty. I'd just like to go over them again."

A couple of the committee members groaned.

Gallier acknowledged the groans. "You know me; I don't like to rush things. I'd like to make sure that we've done a thorough job."

"We have, Terry," said another member.

"But, say, what about this Brooks Watt fellow from Philander? Class President. Good grades."

Jerry Murphy shook his head. "Did you see his letters of recommendation? One of them called him a weasel in so many words. Besides, we asked for one letter of recommendation and he sent us four. The sign of a classic bootlicker. We don't need any more bootlickers."

The other members nodded in agreement.

Gallier could see he was beaten. Murphy was probably right.

"I think we've selected two really strong candidates," said Mrs. MacNaughton.

That settled it.

Jerry Murphy said, "If they interview well then we've got our interns. If not, we'll revisit the list. Jack, you'll contact them for interviews?"

Jack Tweedy nodded.

Jerry Murphy, using both hands, raised up his file folders a few inches then dropped them back onto the table. "That's it then."

He got up from his chair, walked around the table to help Mrs. MacNaughton out of her chair and the meeting was over.

CHAPTER 11

When Jan returned to her dorm room from mid-term break Myrt was already there. They hugged.

"I brought you a present," said Myrt. She pulled a fancy gift bag of soaps and shampoos and other grooming aids from out of her closet and casually tossed it underhand to Jan from her side of the room. She did that so it wouldn't seem like any kind of a big deal that it was from an expensive Atlanta store.

Jan thanked her and asked about her vacation.

"Pretty good. Hey, you got a telegram," Myrt said. "Came this morning."

"A telegram? I didn't think there was such a thing anymore."

"Neither did I," said Myrt, "I thought it was just in old movies. But you got one. Here."

Myrt handed her the telegram that she had earlier placed on Jan's bed. "In the movies telegrams are usually bad news. Jimmy Stewart was always getting telegrams."

Jan didn't know who Jimmy Stewart was. She opened the telegram and read its contents. She smiled placidly. "Well, I've got an interview for that internship. That's good news. Maybe telegrams are for good news and registered letters are for bad news."

Myrt wasn't about to let this news pass placidly. "Wow! This calls for a dance." She grabbed Jan and began dancing a samba. "Shall we try the Anna Pavlova mystical dance of death?"

Jan whooped and tossed the telegram in the air.

Shrieking and laughing, they followed the samba with an impromptu two-person conga, snaking around the little room. When they were exhausted from their dance they fell on Jan's bed. Once she had caught her breath Jan looked at the ceiling and said solemnly, "I prayed I'd get this internship."

Myrt asked, "Is it wrong to pray for an internship?

"You mean because it's self-serving? I don't know."

"What would your pastor say?"

Slowly and thoughtfully Jan answered, "Maybe 'Do nothing from rivalry or conceit'. Philippians."

Jan climbed off the bed and picked the telegram off the floor and looked at it again.

"I have to call someone named Mr. Jack Tweedy to arrange an interview. I'll do that tomorrow morning." She paused. "Jack Tweedy, that's a nice name."

Still lying supine on the bed Myrt said, "Yes, very tweedy. Wow, Jan Pan, intrepid girl reporter."

Jan corrected her. "Intrepid woman reporter....maybe"

Myrt got up and gave Jan a high five. "It's as good as yours!"

CHAPTER 12

Jan called the Akron Sentinel-Herald the next morning and got through to Mr. Tweedy. She identified herself, talked with Tweedy about the internship for a few minutes and made an appointment for an interview Tuesday of the following week at one o'clock. Jan would have to miss her Shakespeare class but that would be her first absence of the semester for that class.

After thanking Tweedy and hanging up Jan composed a thank you letter to Professor Coleman for writing such a complimentary letter of recommendation and dropped it in the mail. It seemed like a good idea. Good manners, too.

Jan and a group of students were having lunch in Thomas Hall.

"What if they ask you, 'how did you prepare for this interview?'" a student named Todd asked.

"I'll tell them that I rented a copy of <u>All the President's Men</u> and watched it three times," answered Jan.

"Really?" he asked.

Jan laughed. "No, Todd. I'm a journalism major. I studied. That's how I prepared for the interview."

Tim asked, "What if they ask you who your hero is?"

Jan had an answer for that. "I'll tell them: Diogenes, the ancient Greek who went searching for an honest man. Searching for honesty is searching for truth and that's the journalistic ideal."

"Ooh, that's a good one," said Myrt. Everyone agreed: that was a killer answer.

Because Myrt and Tim had classes Tuesday neither would be able to drive Jan to her interview. Instead, Myrt offered her the use of her car.

Monday night they put together Jan's interview outfit. They chose a white blouse and a simple plaid skirt with black low-heeled shoes. Jan tried it on in front of the mirror. It met with Myrt's approval. An altogether sensible look. Not high fashion; more Lois Lane than Brenda Starr. Myrt gave her a penny to put in her left shoe for good luck.

"Good mojo," explained Myrt.

Looking at herself in the mirror Jan got close and examined her teeth. "Maybe I should've bleached my teeth."

"Never a bad idea. You might end up a television reporter. All you need for that is white teeth and a big head."

Jan asked, "A big head?"

Myrt nodded. "The successful ones all have very large heads. You must've noticed."

"We couldn't get television at our house."

"Yup, big empty heads."

"So, you think my teeth are bad?" asked Jan.

Myrt couldn't resist a cheap shot. "Jan, you are from West Virginia, after all."

Jan hid her head in her hands and groaned.

"Your teeth are fine. Don't worry," assured Myrt, once she'd seen the effect of her words, proving that she wasn't a cruel person. "And you've got freckles. Nobody can say 'no' to someone with freckles."

CHAPTER 13

The next day Jan left Philander early. It was another pleasant Midwest spring day. After being mislead by the GPS at least three times, forced to backtrack the same number of times, she finally made it to Akron by noon. The first thing she did was locate the Akron Sentinel-Herald building. The building faced a square that enclosed a small park. Features of this park were a statue of a Civil War hero with pigeon epaulets, two park benches, some shrubbery and a few plants struggling to survive. In the middle of the park was a fountain, which gave its name to the square. A few years back the streets around Fountain Square were torn up and turned into a pedestrian mall. It didn't take long for the mall to become a gathering spot for drug dealers and other urban pioneers. Within days of the mayor witnessing a man bathing in the fountain, civic action was taken: paving, striping and parking spaces returned. The modern sculptures that had been placed around the mall were distributed to other parks in the city.

Across the park from the Sentinel-Herald building was City Hall, an impressive neo-Romanesque brick building that harkened back to a time when the City fathers dreamt of a glorious future of non-stop growth for Akron. Most of the buildings on the streets surrounding the square were three-and-four-story structures also of neo-Romanesque design. Small businesses such as Gelsenleiter's luggage and stationery store ("In Business Since 1957") occupied ground floor storefronts. One block north was the Courthouse. Bookending the Courthouse were bail bondsmen's storefront offices. One displayed a window sign that was a kinetic masterpiece of neon artistry: a jailbird– portrayed as a Monopoly game-style villain wearing a striped uniform – sprouts wings and flies away leaving behind the neon bars that hold him. The bail bonding business must be doing well to afford such a sign. Not as fortunate apparently were some of the other businesses on that block. Some storefronts gave the appearance of long-term vacancy. One large store, Yount's Appliances by name, had tattered signs posted in the plate glass windows announcing a closing sale that must have taken place years before. One of its windows was boarded up, making the store look like a missing tooth in an unhealthy mouth.

Having located the Sentinel-Herald building Jan could relax a bit. Since she had some time before her interview she drove around to get an idea of what Akron looked like. She got an idea and was back at the Sentinel-Herald at fifteen minutes before one. She parked in an adjacent lot. She noticed that the building had a cornerstone that read '1923'. It was a substantial five story building of limestone and brick with double-hung windows. Pigeons perched on the ample windowsills. The wood frame windows could still be opened. The sign identifying the newspaper spanned the breadth of the fifth floor. It was in Gothic Bold and at night it was illuminated, except for the 'a' in 'Herald' which had burned out and not yet been replaced.

Jan presented herself to the receptionist who dialed Mr. Tweedy's extension and announced Jan's presence. The receptionist, an older woman with frosted hair, smiled and pointed toward the elevator.

"It's a little slow. Or you can take the stairs." The door to the stairs was adjacent to the elevator. "When you get to the newsroom just ask for Jack Tweedy." She seemed friendly enough.

By the time Jan elevatored to the third floor Jack Tweedy was waiting in front of the elevator door to greet her. He identified himself and shook her hand warmly.

"Welcome to Akron, Gateway to Dayton," he said with a chuckle. He asked whether she'd had a good trip.

Jan smiled and said she had. (That was the truth: the elevator ride was smooth, quiet and uneventful. The ride to Akron had been another story thanks to the GPS device.)

They were on the main newsroom floor. It was a large room filled with people working at computers on grouped desks. It was not a noisy room like in the old black-and-white movies, with people smoking stogies, wearing baggy grey suits and fedoras, banging on black Remington typewriters and yelling "Copy!" The sound of keyboarding was the room's overriding thematic tone, but it was a muted clackety-clack. Tweedy led her past some desks and a few cubicles to the back of the room, up three steps to a tiny alcove. There was enough room for a desk, desk chair and opposing guest chair. There were no framed photographs on the desk or walls. Tweedy invited her to sit down. He had a folder with her information on his desk in front of him. He twiddled his fingers on the folder and pursed his lips.

Tweedy was an older man with thick, curly white hair. His half-moon glasses constantly slid down his nose, requiring frequent adjustment. He was of medium height and medium girth. He was impeccably dressed in a gray suit, a white shirt, a blue bowtie and a sweater vest. He wore well-shined black bluchers. This was the look he had adopted decades ago. It suited him and he had maintained it, with slight variations, since then. His face reminded Jan of the beloved teddy bear she had carried around everywhere as a child and still owned. Like the teddy bear, Tweedy showed his years.

"Would you like some coffee or tea?" Tweedy asked.

Jan smiled. A younger host these days would have offered coffee, tea (perhaps herbal), or bottled water. She declined his offer.

She was prepared for a barrage of questions. She was ready for the inevitable "Tell me a little about yourself."

To her surprise, Tweedy asked, "Do you have a favorite Beatle?"

The question threw her for a loop. "Wasn't that a rock group from the nineteen sixties?" she asked.

He chuckled and said, "Yes."

"Uhm, Stinko?"

Tweedy laughed. "There was no Stinko. Maybe you're thinking of Ringo."

Jan apologized. "I'm sorry; I didn't listen to a lot of pop music growing up."

Tweedy nodded. "No need to apologize. Lots of chores around the farm, I'll bet."

"Yes."

"I can't think of any more questions for you. May I call you Jan?"

Jan agreed to this.

"And you can call me Jack, if you'd like." Tweedy responded. "Now let me tell you a few things about this paper and your job." He got up. "There'll be two interns. Come on, I'll show you around."

As he guided her around he explained, "You will be an intern but you will be an employee. It won't be make-work. You'll be on the news staff, so you'll get assignments from the local news desk and anyone else. I may be your mentor, but you won't be shadowing me, understand?"

Jan nodded. She was a little confused. Did this mean she'd gotten the internship? Despite not having a favorite Beatle? It sort of looked that way.

They stopped at an office that was mostly windows. Jack knocked. Jeremiah Murphy was at his desk. He motioned them to enter.

"Jerry, this is one of the new interns, Jan Pancake. She'll be starting once school lets out." Turning to Jan, Tweedy said, "This is Jerry Murphy, the Managing Editor."

Murphy smiled and reached over the desk to shake Jan's hand. "Philander College, right? Good school. I worked with Phil Coleman when he was here. An excellent journalist. An excellent teacher, too, I'll bet."

"He's teaching one of my classes. I think he's really good."

Jerry Murphy was a peppy sort of guy. "You've got Jack Tweedy here. You have any questions he's the man to see – knows everything and everyone, especially the way to the men's bathroom."

Tweedy smiled wryly. Murphy came from behind his desk. He put his arm around Tweedy. He whispered something in his ear that made them both smile. He turned to Jan.

"I'm sorry, I know that's rude, Jan," Murphy said. He didn't seem sorry. "It's been a pleasure meeting you. I hope everything goes well for you"

He returned to his work. Tweedy ushered Jan out of the office.

"Let the tour continue," he said, leading Jan in the direction of the desk belonging to the sports editor, Bob Greene.

Jan was confused again. Did Mr. Murphy just give her the kiss off? It sounded that way from his words of farewell. They sounded like those rejection letters that end, "Good luck with your future plans."

It had been her good fortune that Jan wasn't directly familiar with that sort of letter. Still, she'd seen enough of them through family and friends. She thought she'd better get this cleared up right away. Though she was supposed to be accompanying Tweedy, she slowed down her steps.

"Mr. Tweedy?" she stopped and called to him.

Tweedy stopped, turned around and discovered Jan a few steps behind him.

"Yes?" he asked.

"Did I get this internship?" she asked hesitantly.

Jack Tweedy seemed surprised by the question. "Why, of course!" he answered, putting that issue to rest. He looked around. "I don't see Bob Greene around. I think it would be a good idea for you to meet one of our current interns." Tweedy looked around for the intern. He went over to someone working at a desk and asked, "Have you seen Arnie Stavis?"

"I think he's in the morgue."

Tweedy thanked him and clapped his hands together.

"This is a good opportunity to show you the morgue," Tweedy said to Jan and motioned for her to follow him. Jan had learned enough journalism lingo to know that the morgue was a newspaper's archives, its library of clippings. She followed him down the steps to the mezzanine and opened the door to a room that was empty but for one young man who was flipping through a file cabinet. Arnie Stavis was an elfin guy with short brown fringy hair, wearing large round tortoise shell spectacle frames.

Tweedy called to him, "Arnie, this is one of the bright young people who'll be starting as intern this summer."

Arnie smiled and walked over, putting out his hand to Jan. "Hey."

Jan shook hands, said 'hi' and identified herself.

"Where are you coming from?" Stavis asked.

"Philander."

Stavis nodded. "Good school." He pointed to himself, "Antioch. I hope you have as good a time here as I've had. It's been a great experience and I've learned a lot." Out of the side of his mouth he said to Tweedy, "That'll be ten bucks. You can pay me later."

Tweedy laughed. "We've really liked having Arnie here."

Arnie asked, "But will you miss me when I'm gone?"

"Not for a second!" Tweedy shot back. They laughed. Tweedy had a jovial laugh.

Stavis said, "Seriously, if you have questions please call me. I'll give you my number. Of course, I've still got a few weeks left here so I'll see you around."

Stavis fished through his pockets and located his business card.

Jan thanked him and filed the card in her pocketbook. Tweedy thanked Stavis and told Jan, "I want you to meet the folks on the local news desk. Then we'll go upstairs and see the Circulation and Sales people. After that I'll leave you to H.R., what used to be called 'Personnel'."

They said goodbye to Stavis and were making their way back to the third floor when suddenly Tweedy stopped in his tracks, scratched his head and said, "Wasn't there a rock group called The Policemen? They had a member called Sting."

Tweedy seemed pleased and a little surprised that he was able to pull this fact out of his memory morgue. Jan didn't know how to respond.

"You could be right," she said, not knowing whether this was true or not.

Back on the third floor she met the members of the local news desk and immediately forgot their names, darn it, but they were friendly and she'd meet them again in a few weeks. The Metro Editor gave Jan a copy of the Associated Press Style Manual. She owned a more recent edition, a requirement of one of her journalism classes, but it seemed rude not to accept one from the Metro Editor. At the last station, H.R., Tweedy said, "Well, I'll let you deal with Doris. And I'll see you in a few weeks. Have a safe trip home."

With that Tweedy waved and departed.

Jan didn't have time to say, "Goodbye...and thanks!" to his face, so she said it to Tweedy's back as he was walking to the elevator. Maybe he heard; maybe not.

On the ride back to Philander, Jan sang along with the songs on the radio that she knew. She stopped off and treated herself to something called a "Grand Slam" at a chain restaurant. It was a breakfast plate; Jan recalled that her grandfather had often said that breakfast was the most important meal of the day and this was an important day. It was a new beginning and breakfast seemed like a good way of greeting it, even if it was already late afternoon.

When she got back to school it was time for dinner. She went to the dining hall and spotted Myrt and Tim eating together. She joined them. She smiled but didn't say anything. Jan had learned from Myrt how to create dramatic tension.

Myrt said anxiously, "And?"

"And I nailed it!" squealed Jan.

Jan and Myrt jumped up and down on their chairs. Had they been males, they would have made those apelike 'hoo, hoo, hoo' sounds and pumped their fists in the air. The only male in this trio was Tim, who wasn't the 'hoo, hoo, hoo' type. He smiled.

Jan returned Myrt's car keys, thanked her, and described the day's events. Myrt seemed excited; Tim less so.

"That Beatles question must've been some kind of trick. You handled it well," said Tim.

"You're going to have to get a car," said Myrt. "I can get my father to lend you the money. You can pay him back once you've got an income. We'll have to find you a cute apartment. Then we can decorate it. What else?" She turned to Tim.

"What else, Tim?"

Tim shrugged his shoulders. He couldn't think of anything so he said, "I've always liked the chocolate pudding they serve here."

Myrt said, "You know, Tim, sometimes you're a pretty mysterious guy."

CHAPTER 14

The rest of the semester was uneventful. Maybe Jan studied for her journalism classes a little more intensely; or maybe she would have studied just as hard if she hadn't gotten the MacNaughton internship. She did well on her finals.

One afternoon she ran into Brooks Watt as he was leaving the student union. From the way his eyes were darting around, Jan could tell he was looking for a way to avoid her. Realizing that he couldn't, and not wanting to appear as though he were snubbing her – he was, after all, Class President and every vote counts - he gave her a weak smile and said, "I guess you got that internship." He paused before offering a begrudged, "Congratulations."

Jan smiled. "I was lucky."

Brooks said, "I wasn't. They must've been looking for diversity."

Jan wasn't sure what he meant by that so she just smiled and said, "Must've."

. A week or so before it was time to leave campus Jan and Tim took a walk down Middle Path and into the rose garden. It was mid-afternoon and beginning to get warm. Rather than immediately talking about their relationship they talked about roses; giving life to the expression 'beating around the bush'. Tim said that his mother raised roses and was a member of the Master Gardeners in Williamsburg.

"Maybe you can visit some time this summer," Tim said with a forced enthusiasm. "You can see her roses. By then you'll have a car." He paused. "But you might not have accrued enough vacation time." He fell silent.

They sat down on a stone bench. Jan took his hand. Tim looked down at their hands and smiled.

"Do you think there's a future for us," he asked hesitantly, "I mean, as a couple?"

"Time and chance happen."

Tim wasn't sure what Jan meant. He was uncomfortable, wasn't used to talking about his relationships. A light sheen of perspiration formed on his upper lip. He wiped it with his free hand.

Jan said, "I guess it depends on what we want. Our lives are going to be very different very soon. You'll be going off to law school next year. I'm starting my internship. We won't know how we'll feel in the future."

Tim admitted that it was true.

"We really don't know what the future holds for us, you and me," he said. "Things would've been easier a long time ago. If we grew up in a village we'd stay in the village. We'd have stayed put."

Jan nodded. "Like West Virginians. People stay put. That's where family and church are."

"But not jobs."

Tim stood up and regarded Jan, still seated. "That's what I admire about you. You're like those characters in Robert Heinlein novels, the ones who are brave and bold enough to leave home."

Jan was momentarily speechless. Apparently Tim had given this some thought.

"Jan," Tim announced, "the future belongs to the brave and the bold and that's you!"

All she could say for a minute or two was, "Hmm." Then she recovered her powers of speech and said, with a tinge of sadness, "I've missed my home and I've missed my church and all the people I've grown up with. I've lost a lot. I know I can't go back now, but I'll hold onto 'my raisin' as much as I can."

Tim felt self-conscious, as though he had said something really stupid and said so.

Jan said, "No, what you said was true and very nice. And you're right: we're going to be apart for a long time no matter what."

He hadn't actually said that. But it was what they both knew.

Jan rose from the bench, tightened her grip on Tim's hand and began leading him out of the rose garden.

"Tim, I'm going to treat you to a meal at the Village Inn, what do you say? It may be the last good meal we share for a while."

CHAPTER 15

Myrt and Jan drove down to the Pancake farm for a visit and to find a car. Myrt had visited the Pancakes twice before and enjoyed being with them. For their part, the Pancakes couldn't figure out what to make of Myrt.

"Got lots of energy, I'll say that," was Charlie Pancake's summarization. Charlie was Jan's father.

Josiah made a few phone calls to acquaintances in the region who might know about a suitable car. An index card on the bulletin board at the front of the IGA provided one lead. Josiah called the guy, someone named Xander, who had a car for sale but insisted that he was only available to show it in the evenings. Following the directions this man gave them, Josiah and Jan drove to Xander's farm. It was dark when Xander came out of his house. He was an unshaven middle-aged man in dirty overalls.

"Out back," Xander said. It was more like a grunt. He led them way out into a field toward a car that they could make out vaguely in the distance.

"It's awfully dark out here," said Jan. She stumbled over something.

They had walked about one hundred and fifty yards before Josiah stopped.

"Come on, Jan, I don't like the looks of this," he whispered. To Xander, who was walking ahead of them he called, "Sir, I'm sorry, we've changed our mind."

Xander stood there in his field and scowled and muttered something.

Josiah and Jan hotfooted it back to Josiah's truck and drove away.

"What was that all about?" Jan asked.

"Don't know; don't want to know; want to be around long enough to wonder," said Josiah. "Don't worry, there are other places."

As they made their way back to the Pancake home Jan said, "I had kind of a bad feeling about that guy."

"That makes two of us," said Josiah. "I know the Xanders have the reputation of being a truculent clan. Don't see none of them at church ever. While back one of their kin got himself electrocuted."

Jan grimaced and asked, "What happened?"

"The usual. Sneaking into a mine to steal copper wire to sell. Bad luck for him: the electricity was still on."

The next day Jan and Josiah didn't have any better luck.

Myrt didn't feel like looking at cars. She couldn't see why Jan didn't want to simply go to a car dealer and buy a new car, especially since her father would lend her the money.

Jan and Josiah drove to a used car lot in town run by a guy named Herb, a man with ginger hair, a limp and a glass eye. Looking at him straight on Jan noticed that he wasn't entirely symmetrical, that is, one half of him was slightly smaller than the other.

"Josiah, I don't think this guy's on the level," she whispered. "Literally."

"His prices are bad, too. Let's go home."

As they were returning to Josiah's truck Herb trotted after them. He handed Josiah his business card that read "Herb's the name; used cars are the game."

"Tell them Herb sent you," he requested.

They climbed into Josiah's truck. Jan was a little discouraged.

Once home she related the experience to Myrt and her family. Mrs. Pancake was helping Myrt with a quilt pattern called Patch As Patch Can.

"Don't ya just love it?" Myrt said. "Who'da thought quilters would capable of such a corny pun?" She howled with laughter. "There's another quilt pattern called Bachelor's Dream. Only we'll make it Bachelorette's Dream, right?"

Mrs. Pancake, a very shy quiet person, nodded.

Myrt said, "Quilting is very hip now, you know. Movie people are quilting these days."

"Oh, yes, yes they do," agreed Mrs. Pancake.

Jan had promised herself she'd visit Pastor Linger and his wife, Diane, so the next morning she called over to the parsonage. Linger was delighted to hear from her and urged her to come over right then.

"Want to come?" Jan asked Myrt.

Myrt shook her head. "No, I'm happy here. You go, though." She pulled her keys out of her pocket and tossed them to Jan. Myrt began singing an old tune by Jelly Roll Morton.

Jan drove the couple of miles to the parsonage, a small brick house with green metal awnings over the front door and the windows. Pastor Linger answered, a big smile on his face.

Pastor Linger had a nice smile. Now in his seventies, he was still a handsome, slender man. Many of the women in the congregation harbored secret crushes on him. He had a calm, steady, mellifluous way of speaking.

"Welcome, welcome, welcome," he said, drawing her into the living room. It smelled delicious in the house.

Once they were inside and the door closed Linger called out to his wife, "Diane, Jan Pancake is here."

Since it was a one-story house it was no time at all before Mrs. Linger appeared in the doorway with oven mitts on both hands and said, "I've just made sugar cookies. We can have cookies and lemonade. How does that sound?"

As they munched cookies and drank lemonade Pastor and Mrs. Linger and Jan fell into a familiar, comfortable conversation. But things had changed since Jan was a little girl. As in the past, Jan talked about her classes, classmates and her plans. But Pastor Linger was aware that his end of the dialogue didn't weigh as heavily on giving advice as in years past.

"You're a grown woman now, Jan, or almost all grown up" Linger said. Then, with a touch of irony and rue he continued, "You don't need what wisdom and sagacity I have to impart anymore."

Jan disagreed. "Pastor, I think I'll always be needing your advice."

"I'll be there for you," he replied. "but, truthfully, I think you're about two years away from calling me by my first name."

Jan laughed. "You mean Pastor isn't your first name?"

They talked about some of the goings on in the community and county. Pastor Linger affirmed that things hadn't changed very much in their community.

"A generation goes and a generation comes, but the earth remains forever."

Jan smiled. "Ecclesiastes, right?"

"Correct."

Pastor Linger asked about "that young man you brought home at Easter. Jim, was it?"

"Tim."

"He seemed nice," said Diane Linger. "Has he made his commitment to Christ?"

"I don't know. We talk about cultural and secular things, not so much spiritual things. He talks a lot about pudding."

"Pudding?"

"Uh huh."

The pastor and his wife nodded, then let the topic drop. Pastor Linger said that Jan had put him in a pickle: he couldn't find a replacement for the upcoming VBS.

"Without you it won't be the same," Pastor Linger said. "It looks like Diane is going to have to take your old class."

Jan described the tribulations surrounding her search for a used car. Linger looked at his wife and said, "We've talked about getting rid of the second car. We don't really need them both."

Diane nodded. "I hardly use mine. Jon, why don't we let Jan have my car?"

Jan was stunned. "No, I can't take your car."

"Nonsense," Diane replied. "Why not?"

They trooped out of the house to look at the car, an old Ford Taurus.

Mrs. Linger looked at her old car and shook her head sadly. "It runs well, but it looks terrible. I keep running into deer and every time we get it repaired the parts that got fixed are painted a different color. That's why we call it 'Joseph'."

Jan immediately piped up, "Because it has a coat of many colors! I'll keep the name."

In the end they agreed to sell the car to Jan at an extremely fair price. Jan said she'd come back for the car and paperwork in the next day or two. Taking turns, the Lingers gave her a warm hug.

"We're very proud of you, you know," said Mrs. Linger. "We've known you for your entire life."

Jan corrected her. "Not my *entire* life."

That afternoon Jan and Josiah got the paperwork and registration/licensing of the Linger's car squared away. The car was now hers. Josiah gave the car a thorough going-over and declared it sound. After Jan seated herself in the car in front of the parsonage she rolled down the windows to say goodbye.

I'll take good care of Joseph."

The Lingers extracted a promise that she would come home again real soon.

As she drove away the Lingers waved goodbye. Diane Linger got a little misty-eyed. She was going to miss her car.

Misreading his wife's emotions, Parson Linger was puzzled. "Diane, we'll be seeing her Sunday morning,"

He wasn't much of a car person.

CHAPTER 16

All students had to vacate their dorm rooms by the second week in May. Myrt had already put her stuff in one of the storage spaces the school made available. She decided to stay with the Pancakes a few more days and leave at the same time as Jan. She was determined to finish her Bachelorette's Quilt and take it to Lexington with her. Her family planned to be at their place on Little Saint Simon Island by Independence Day. In the last few days Myrt had gotten into the swing of the daily household chores. She helped Charlie and Josiah with some of the livestock and showed enthusiasm when it came to working in the vegetable garden. She wore overalls over tank tops that somehow or other showed off her figure to good advantage. One day Mrs. Pancake looked out the kitchen window over the sink one day and saw Myrtle leaning on a spade and chatting with Josiah. "I'll allow as how she is bursting with good health and vitality," she said to no one in particular, as she rinsed some dishes.

But Sissy, who was shelling peas, heard.

"I think she's got her eye on Josiah, Mom," Sissy said.

Mrs. Pancake seems shocked. "Josiah? Pshaw! They have nothing in common. And he's got too much common sense. Besides, he's got Lally."

Sissy smiled. "Lally's nice, Ma, but she's like biscuits and gravy."

"What's that supposed to mean?" asked Mrs. Pancake.

"She's biscuits and gravy and Myrt's champagne and caviar."

Mrs. Pancake stared at Sissy. "Well, I've never had caviar and I've never had champagne and I like biscuits and gravy just fine," she said resolutely. "I don't see that Josiah's much different. And when's the last time you had champagne and caviar, young lady?"

"Never," sighed Sissy.

To Mrs. Pancake that proved some point or other. She pulled off the Playtex Living Gloves with a snap and hung them over the faucet to dry.

Sunday morning Myrt and the Pancake family went to sunrise service. Sitting on the bench with her family, Jan looked around at all the familiar faces. She had played with many of them as a child and had grown up with them. Sometimes it was uncomfortable, even stifling, to be part of such a small group. But that was in the past. After church the congregation had a picnic.

When it came time for the roommates to leave Myrt got teary and extended a heartfelt invitation to the Pancakes to come to Little Saint Simon's Island for a vacation. She asked them to promise they would. They refused, politely and sincerely, to make that promise.

While waiting outside for Mrs. Pancake to bring them bag lunches Myrt showed Jan her hand, palm up.

"What do you make of this?" she asked, scratching at her palm.

Jan said, "Myrt, you're pre-med. I'd think you could recognize a callous when you see one."

Myrt seemed pleased. "Well, how about that," she said dreamily, "a callous."

"We're now former roommates," said Jan.

They hugged and Myrt said she'd help Jan decorate her apartment once she had settled on a place. Myrt invited the Pancakes once more time to visit her family's summer house, but she knew it was futile: the Pancakes weren't a traveling family.

They rolled out of the gravel driveway, one following the other, honking their horns and waving at family.

Jan had to drive back to school to clear her stuff from the dorm room. She didn't plan to be returning to Philander as a student for at least six months. As she drove away from West Virginia all sorts of emotions surfaced: a bit of fear of what the future would bring; a bit of guilt for leaving her family; but mostly excitement at the opportunities that she hoped awaited her. She turned on the car radio searching for a song by the Beatles to see what all the fuss was about.

CHAPTER 17

Josiah and Sissy both offered to go to Akron with Jan to help find an apartment, but it was something she thought she should do herself. She had already called Arnie Stavis, the outgoing intern, for any leads. He couldn't really think of any, but urged her to avoid renting any place owned by his landlord. He described his landlord using a term Jan would never consider repeating. She drove around Akron to become familiar with neighborhoods. During her interview with Jack Tweedy he had suggested she contact Mary Karnes, the Classified Advertising Manager, if she needed help with anything. "Mary knows everything and everyone," Tweedy had said.

After spending two nights at a cheap motel and one day looking for a suitable place to live, Jan called Mary Karnes at the Sentinel-Herald. She identified herself and described the fruitless search she had conducted so far. The online apartment search websites were sometimes misleading. Sometimes the places weren't vacant; some hadn't been vacant for years. There were good reasons for the ones that had been vacant for a long time. Some were in bad buildings, but you wouldn't have known that from the pictures online. Not to generalize, but all the apartments in her price range were dumps.

"Tweedy recommended me? Hmmm. Well, you should've called me before, honey," said Mary Karnes. "How much do you have to spend?"

Jan told her how much the internship's housing allowance allowed.

"So, you ain't a trust fund baby, are you," Mary said

Jan assured her she was not.

"Say, where you from?" asked Mary.

When Jan told her Mary laughed and said, "I thought I detected a Mountaineer accent. I'm from MacDowell County. You wouldn't know the town."

"Try me," said Jan.

Mary tried her. True enough, Jan had never heard of the place.

"Near Welch. Only much smaller. A flyspeck. Like they say back there: smaller than a mine owner's heart," Mary said.

"Smaller than a mustard seed," Jan shot back.

"Smaller than a tick's turd."

Jan laughed. "Do you ever go back?"

"No point. The town's gone. Mine played out. Everyone's moved away."

It was the case with a lot of mining communities.

Mary sounded a nostalgic note. "Great place to grow up, though." Then, getting back down to business: "Is it just for yourself?"

Jan said yes.

"Look, honey, you go get lunch somewhere and call me back in a couple of hours."

Though she had left her family only two days before, Jan had begun to feel adrift. It was good to hear a friendly voice from near home. She went to a restaurant and had a fried egg sandwich and looked around at the other diners. She challenged herself to try to figure out a background story for each of the diners, starting with the skinny guy sitting alone at a corner booth. She thought this exercise would sharpen her journalistic eye.

The skinny guy? Clearly a small-time crook. Jan could tell from the way he hunched over his lunch plate, guarding it the way she imagined an offender would protect his meal in prison.

The next time she saw this man he was wearing a paper hat. He was a pressman at the Akron Sentinel-Herald named Leo Sanford and he was deacon at his church. Jan wasn't entirely wrong: Mr. Sanford had spent a good deal of time in prison...doing church outreach. Jan learned a lesson, though – a good journalist assumes nothing and sticks to the facts.

After two hours had passed Jan called Mary Karnes and got some good news. A few phone calls had yielded three possible apartments. Jan jotted them down and thanked Mary.

"What about tonight? Need a place to stay 'til you've got an apartment?" asked Mary.

Jan told her she expected to stay at a motel until she had an apartment. Mary asked her for the name of the motel. Jan told her. Even though they had yet to meet, Jan could visualize Mary wincing.

"The Centennial? That place is a dump! And pretty dangerous."

"It's okay," Jan assured her. She didn't think it was necessary to mention the spiders or the toilet that didn't stop running or the half-eaten jelly donut she discovered embedded in the green shag carpeting beneath the bed.

"Nonsense, you'll stay with us," Mary declared. She gave Jan her home address and dictated directions, ordering her to show up after she'd looked at the apartments.

"And I'm calling D.J. to make enough dinner for three. He's a real good cook, you'll see."

"But you don't even know me," Jan objected.

"Can you think of a better way to get to know someone than to have them stay under your roof?"

Jan couldn't. She thanked Mary, clicked off the phone and began making her calls. The first two places were okay, definitely better than what she had seen so far. They were both in small apartment buildings within the city. When she called the third place a man answered, "Dobbins Doggy Lodge." Jan was confused, not sure whether she had written down the telephone number correctly. She asked the man whether he had an apartment for rent.

"Well, I don't know," he said slowly. He seemed reluctant to answer the question. Then Jan informed him that Mary Karnes had told her about this place.

The man dropped his hesitancy and became friendly. He described the place and invited Jan to drive out to look at the cottage. He asked Jan whether she knew the area.

"Then let me give you directions," he said.

It was outside the city. Jan calculated that it would take at least twenty-five minutes to get from there to the newspaper if the place was suitable. But she liked being in the country. Following the directions provided by the man, who identified himself as Fred Dobbins, she ended up on a country lane and eventually to a driveway with a sign, "Dobbins Doggy Lodge." She drove in and was greeted by two collies. Mr. Dobbins came out of the house and greeted Jan. The dogs barked a couple of times, wagged their tails and nuzzled Jan. She began patting them.

"Scoot," Mr. Dobbins said to the dogs. The dogs reluctantly turned to go back to the house.

"I like dogs," Jan assured Mr. Dobbins.

The dogs seemed to understand. Granted a reprieve, they returned for more patting and followed Dobbins and Jan.

"Any trouble getting here?" Mr. Dobbins asked. Jan shook her head. "Okay, then, let's go." Dobbins led Jan out back and pointed to the kennel and its outbuildings.

On one side of the property sat a small cottage, white with green shutters and a green tin roof. There were window boxes that hadn't been tended to in a while. That was Dobbins' destination. He opened the door and ushered her inside. The collies didn't hesitate to enter.

"We've never really rented it before. We've always offered it to a kennel worker, but the gal we have now has her own family home. It's furnished, except for a bed, and you can use what you want. Whatever you don't want can go into the barn."

It was a small place: living room, kitchen, bedroom and bathroom. Out back there was a cement patio. Near the patio was a laundry drying umbrella set into concrete.

Jan said she'd take it.

Mr. Dobbins smiled. "Knowing Mary Karnes serves as your background check. I'll just need first and last month's rent."

"Can I move in right now?" asked Jan.

"Sure. Come to the house when you're ready. We'll sign a lease." Mr. Dobbins took the key out of the door and dropped it in Jan's hand. He left, clucked to the collies to follow, and closed the door behind him. Jan found herself suddenly tired. She flopped into a big ugly chair and fell asleep. She could unpack and call home late, but for now she needed a nap.

CHAPTER 18

Jan stayed with Mary and D.J. Karnes for two nights. That gave Jan time to buy a new bed and have it delivered, get kitchen essentials and get to know the Karnes. When Jan met Mary in person she was surprised how closely her mental image of the woman conformed to the actual Mary, who was a compact woman in her fifties. She had brown eyes, wavy gray hair that she kept pinned close in the back, and a complexion like weak tea with no more flesh on her face than was absolutely necessary. Her face went well with her no-nonsense attitude but didn't reveal her generous nature. D.J., her husband, was a laid-back guy who made his living driving a newspaper delivery truck. Jan liked both of them. D.J. gave Jan a tour of Akron. He showed her the best neighborhoods, where the industrialists built their mansions during Akron's better days, but his focus was mainly on the neighborhoods she should avoid.

"If you cover local news you'll be seeing a lot of this neighborhood," D.J. said about the Huntington Park area.

Jan filed that away in her memory. The next day, her first day on the job, she'd get the same warning from another half dozen staff members she met.

On the first day on the job Jan received valuable information like this, had her picture taken for her I.D., was given a parking sticker for her windshield, was shown the proper way to fill out time sheets, and signed some forms relating to retirement. Retirement seemed a long time away so she didn't pay too much attention to the H.R. person's explanation. Jan was more intent on getting to know the people she'd be working with.

Once she was through with the people on the fourth floor, she walked down to the third floor and made her way over to Jack Tweedy's little office. The door was open. Tweedy, sitting at his desk which had a window looking out onto Fountain Square, turned to face his visitor. "Yes?" he asked.

Jan could tell he didn't recognize her. She was forced to identify herself. Once he remembered who she was he seemed pleased to see her. He invited her to sit.

"The first thing you'll need is an <u>Associated Press Style Manual</u>," Tweedy said. He fumbled around the shelves in his office and found one. "It's our Bible," he said handing it to her.

"That's funny," Jan thought, *"I thought the Bible is our Bible,"* but she didn't say anything. She now had three A.P. Style Manuals.

"The next few weeks you'll be assigned to the Local News Desk, Pell Newcomb's desk. Come on, I'll take you to him."

On the third floor the news areas weren't divided up by rooms. Instead, desks abutted other desks so that reporters faced other reporters. The more reporters in a department the more desks were put together. Privacy was minimal on this floor. Reporters either learned not to scratch, learned how to scratch surreptitiously, or learned not to care if people noticed. From overhead the room looked like a game of Tetris.

"Pell, this is Jan," Tweedy said to a man sitting in what must've been the Local News Desk complex.

The Local News Editor, Pell Newcomb, stood and greeted her. Newcomb was a well-dressed man of around forty-five with round tortoise shell glasses similar to Arnie Stavis's. He had a medium build and blonde hair. He thanked Tweedy.

Tweedy said to Jan, "If you need me you know where to find me." He returned to his little office. Newcomb found Jan a seat and began explaining her duties.

"I'm sure you've learned at school that the newspaper business has changed. What's also changed is the way people read the paper. Forty, thirty, twenty years ago people bought the paper for national, then regional/local news, sports, community and lifestyle, in that order, more or less. Now, people get their national news from the internet. Same for lifestyle. The S-H can't compete with the big papers or the internet there. But people still read our paper because they want our local and community news and sports. That's why this Desk is so important. Remember what they say: all news is local."

Jan knew all this from school, but she wanted to show that she wasn't wasting his time, so she nodded.

"When does the other new intern start?" he asked.

"I don't know," she answered. "Maybe I'm the other intern. I just started." This was Jan's idea of a joke. Newcomb tilted his head like a blue jay looking at her and said, "I guess. At first you'll be covering community events like spelling bees and library summer reading programs until they're coming out of your ears. Can you use a camera?"

Jan indicated she could.

"Good, then we can fix you up with a camera. Stephanie can familiarize you with the camera you'll be using. She's the photography editor. Do you need a copy of the A.P. Style Manual?"

This time Jan said 'no', though she was tempted to see how many Manuals she could accumulate by the end of her internship.

So far the internship was shaping up to be a good experience. No one had asked her to go to their cobblers to pick up their shoes. She hadn't been told to go for coffee. But it was now lunchtime, a big test for interns. Would she be told she had to fetch peoples' lunches?

CHAPTER 19

"Would you like to go for lunch?" Arnie Stavis asked.

"Sure," said Jan.

"There's a Chinese place around the corner. It's cheap and I've never gotten sick from their food. It's called The Palace of the Red Death."

This was Arnie's idea of a joke. The actual name was The Imperial Golden Jade Dragon Gate. (Under previous ownership it was known as The Buddha Golden Dragon Gardens.) Arnie urged Jan to go with the $5.99 all-you-can-eat buffet and proceeded to give Jan a tutorial on the best strategy to use at an all-you-can-eat buffet.

"If you want to get the upper hand at this place don't waste time on things that fill you up or that you can make at home." He pointed to the rice dishes and made a face. "Avoid rice. It expands in your stomach. That's wasting space."

Jan would make a move to scoop something up, look for Arnie's approval, then replaced the serving spoon if he frowned or shook his head. Eventually she was able to fill a plate with a sufficient number of items that had won Arnie's seal of approved entrees.

Once seated Arnie began giving Jan career advice as he ate.

"Look, the future is in online gaming and drones. Reading is a nineteenth century technology. People aren't interested in knowing things anymore; they want to do things. Real sports are dying out; virtual sports are the thing of the future. First, because climate change is going to make going outside to play or watch sports impossible – too hot. So, drone sports in indoor race and obstacle courses will become the next big thing. Total involvement. And online massive gaming involving hundreds of thousands of people is where the money will move to."

"And newspapers?" Jan asked.

Arnie vibrated his lips and made a sound like "Phhtt."

Jan could only shake her head indicating consternation.

"Don't get me wrong. There'll probably always be online newspapers, but they'll be sort of like puppet shows."

"I guess that once you graduate you'll go into digital entertainment?"

"You betcha. Are you ready for a second round?"

Jan could hardly believe how much Arnie, a little guy, was able to put away. He stood up ready to make his way back to the buffet.

Jan hadn't finished what was still on her plate and was already reaching satiety. "No, you go ahead. I'm still working on this. Have you ever considered lining your jacket pockets with plastic baggies? That way you can take some wonton soup home with you."

Arnie didn't know when he was being teased. He considered the feasibility of Jan's idea and said "Hmm, maybe." Jan had just made a favorable impression on him.

When he returned to the table after reloading a plate Jan asked him, "Any other advice?"

"Yeah, there's no need to tip."

"I mean, about the Sentinel-Herald."

"Get on the good side of the IT people. If your computer dies you'll need them."

Finally, Arnie had said something that made sense to Jan.

"Can I ask you something?" Jan asked. "During your interview did Jack Tweedy ask you who your favorite Beatle was?"

Arnie laughed. "No, he asked me who I thought was the better magician – David Copperfield or Doug Henning. Honestly, I never heard of either of them."

"What did you say?"

"I said 'Copperfield, definitely Copperfield'."

"Looks like that was the right answer."

On their walk back to the paper Jan mentioned that she'd been invited to a luncheon welcoming the new MacNaughton interns to be held in the board room the following week. Jan asked Arnie what she could expect.

"Chicken," said Arnie.

"I see," said Jan. It looked like she'd just have to find out for herself. She thanked Arnie for being her buffet companion and said that she hoped they could have lunch together again before he went back to school.

Back at the Sentinel-Herald Jan reported to Pell Newcomb. He smiled and said, "Your first assignment: go the public library and do a story on the summer reading program, okay? Get a camera from Bernice Maxwell over in the Graphic Arts Department, okay?"

Pell gave Jan a data sheet and wished her good luck.

Using a GPS device provided by the newspaper, Jan drove Joseph the Car to the Main Library, a large neoclassical building of limestone and brick. Outside the building there were banners and lawn signs advertising "Summer Reading Program: Leap into Reading." The image on the signs was a kangaroo with a joey in her pouch. The joey, naturally, wore glasses and was reading a book. Once Jan was in the rotunda she was greeted by the head of Children's Services, a bubbly, stocky woman named Mary Dunham. Mary had short black hair and wore fabulous old red and black bakelite earrings.

"Hello, you're Jan Pancake," she said.

Jan was surprised. How did this woman know her?

"I saw your picture in the paper about a week ago," Ms. Dunham explained.

"Oh?"

"You're the new intern at the S-H, right? I'm Mary Dunham, Head of Children's Services. Call me Mary."

They shook hands, and then Ms. Dunham led Jan to the children's room talking a mile a minute about the City's Summer Reading Program. Jan had to ask her to hold off the recitation until Jan had a chance to get her tablet out so she could take notes. Once they were in the room and seated on really small furniture Ms. Dunham went on about "summer slide" which is the catchy term educators use for the measurable drop in academic performance children experience while they're out of school for the summer.

"...which the Summer Reading Program combats," Ms. Dunham said proudly. "And we have the statistics to prove it." She went on to prove it while Jan furiously took notes.

"Now I'll show you our Maker Space. We're focusing on STEM: science, technology, engineering, math."

She led Jan into a room full of kids who were sawing, soldering, using glue guns on pieces of plastic, wiring, metal and wood.

"This year the kids are making drones and racing them. It's very exciting. Drones are the future."

Did Jan hear right? Could Arnie Stavis know what he's talking about, she wondered. A guy who'd seriously consider pouring hot soup into his pocket?

A young man who was serving as ringmaster, teacher, and shrink for all the kids in the room came over to say hello. Mary Dunham introduced Jan to Edgar Trzeciak, her assistant.

Jan took a lot of pictures of smiling kids and their projects and library staff. Jan thanked them and was heading out of the building when Mary Dunham called her back.

"Do you have a library card?" Dunham asked,

Jan confessed that she didn't. She explained that she was new in town and hadn't even gotten new license plates or her driver's license from the State. Ms. Dunham said that she had it within her power to overlook Jan's lack of acceptable identification. Jan was issued a library card.

Jan thanked Mary and Edgar once again and drove back to the newspaper. Pell Newcomb indicated that because the summer reading program wasn't exactly a hot story there was only a soft deadline; something like "in the next few days" was the way he put it.

Still, Jan's enthusiasm couldn't be dampened. She was covering a story for a mid-sized city newspaper, how about that!

She asked Newcomb whether her picture had been in the newspaper.

"Sure," he said, and used his hands to describe the borders of an air newspaper and read the air headline: 'Sentinel-Herald Welcomes New Interns.' It was in the paper about a week and a half ago. I figured you knew. I'll get you a copy."

"I already have a fair idea of what I look like," Jan said. She didn't want to make it seem important. But then she remembered that her parents would like to see it. She'd send a copy.

"Thanks, that'd be great."

Newcomb outlined the steps Jan would have to take to get her article in the paper. She would start the process by organizing her notes, writing the article, and uploading the photos she'd taken. Next stop: the copyediting desk. After that, to press, thence to porches and breakfast tables all across Greater Akron.

Jan's article about the Library's summer reading program didn't need much editing. Jan had written tons of articles like this for her high school and college newspapers, The only mistake she made – and it really wasn't a mistake – was composing a headline for that article. Claire Hahn, the copy editor, called Jan over and explained that at the Sentinel-Herald it was the copy editor's job to add headlines to news articles.

As the weeks went on, and Jan was assigned to cover local events and meetings she got adept at organizing her stories in a variety of constructive ways. In school, teachers had drummed the inverted pyramid format for stories into her head. Now she was learning to avoid formulaic writing, to experiment with more novel treatments for stories. She received encouragement from Pell Newcomb and Claire Hahn. She got valuable instruction from Jack Tweedy, who emphasized the importance of crafting concise, clear leads and then building on them.

One day Newcomb called Jan over to his desk. He had an article on the previous day's City Council meeting in his hand. It was written by Jan. "Look, Jan, writing can be taught, but you learn it through trial and error."

Jan began tentatively, "I think maybe I could've written this differently, but…"

Newcomb sensed her apprehension. He interrupted her. "I think you're doing great. That's what I wanted to tell you." He smiled. "In a few weeks I'd like you to try your hand at some obituaries. That's in addition to helping cover the local news beat. Okay?"

At first glance that may not have sounded like much of a promotion, but it was. Writing a good obituary calls for particular writing skills, especially a keen eye for details and a sensitive interviewing style. Jan took his offer as a compliment.

"Okay," said Jan.

"There's another intern starting today, Nick Taylor. He'll have that desk that Arnie used. Show him the ropes, okay?"

Jan nodded.

"Everything else okay?" Newcomb asked. "Is Tweedy helping you?"

"He's great," said Jan.

CHAPTER 20

Jan absolutely loved working at the Sentinel-Herald. She was proud to be a member of the working press. She loved knowing that at breakfast tables all over the region her words and sometimes even her byline were being read. She was learning a great deal about newspapering because the people she worked with were generous in sharing their knowledge. She felt that she was part of the newspaper fraternity. She loved knowing the special language shared by its members: knowing the difference between a hammerhead headline, a kicker and a wicket; knowing about mainbars and sidebars; and knowing that a bulldog edition wasn't a special newspaper made just for canines or that a dog watch wasn't another crazy product some Americans waste money on to indulge their pooches. She admired the people she worked with, people who were able to put out a product every day of the week, week in and week out – a product that was accurate and informative. It always amazed her. Their expertise seemed to be taken for granted by the average reader. She wished the public at large appreciated the importance of what these people did.

Jan went to introduce herself to the new intern. Nick seemed nice enough. Jan was able to give him a tip she thought might prove useful: how to tell the print edition people apart from the people who worked on the digital version. It was pretty easy: the print edition people were older, wore a sort of uniform of rumpled gray suit, wrinkled white shirt, dark tie and sometimes a fedora for old times' sake. Their hair was cut by barbers using electric clippers. The exception to this was Jack Tweedy: on those occasions when Jan saw him he was invariably wearing a well-fitting suit, sweater vest, and immaculate shirt and beautiful tie. The digital staff was younger and wore trendier clothing – jeans, mostly, and tee-shirts – and hipper glasses. Their hair was cut by stylists using scissors. In fact, the digital people paid a great deal more attention to their hair, possibly because they generally had more of it. The women who worked on the digital edition often had hair in colors not generally seen in nature except in parts of the Brazilian rain forest or by special order. Jan had no idea where they got their glasses frames.

"Both groups work here on the same floor, but culturally they're from different planets. It's amazing how well they work together," said Jan.

Nick dressed more like a digital person than a print person. He asked a number of questions about the computers, the programs and databases used at the newspaper. He thought it was funny that Jan lived at a place called Dobbins Doggy Lodge. He had found a place near the University to live. Jan wanted to be friendly to the guy but remembered the first few weeks of freshman year at Philander. She had hung around a couple of other freshmen who she soon discovered she had nothing in common with. The friendships withered after a while and for the next few years she'd run into those girls and feel uncomfortable. Jan wondered whether this Nick viewed her as competition.

"So, are you working on Lifestyle?" he asked.

Jan bristled. Lifestyle used to be called the Women's Section. "No, Local and Metro. Are you asking me that because of my gender?"

Nick stuck out his palms out traffic cop style. "Uh, no. sorry, I just wondered. No offense."

It was Jan's turn to apologize. She did by offering to show him some interesting places in the old building. She took him to the bottom floor where the presses were. It was a huge room filled with gigantic, extremely loud machinery and gigantic rolls of newsprint. The floor vibrated. Men in blue work clothes wearing hats folded out of newsprint attended to the machines. As Jan showed Nick around the pressmen would smile or touch their caps to them. By now they knew Jan.

"I think this is amazing," said Jan. "Look at how fast those rolls of paper move! And how the papers move on that conveyor belt! I come down here a lot just to watch."

Nick nodded, but clearly wasn't as transfixed by the spectacle as Jan.

"The next place I'm going to show you is spooky," Jan said. She led him to a door off a hallway that didn't see much traffic. Opening the door Jan flicked on the lights which were older fluorescent fixtures. The room was crammed with old machines, some pewter colored, some a wrinkly dark green.

"These are all the pre-computer machines the paper used to use," explained Jan. Huge linotype machines were lined up in a row and old AP and UPI newswire teletype consoles were crammed against the wall. In another area old photographic enlargers and developing tanks and paraphernalia were piled up. The place was practically an archive of old newspaper technology. The stuff looked as sturdy and solid as an old steam locomotive.

They walked around touching and peering at the complex machinery.

"Amazing, isn't it?" said Jan.

"It's progress. We've advanced," said Nick.

"Maybe, but at what cost?" asked Jan. "The people who operated these machines were skilled workers. They knew the machines inside and out and took pride in knowing that. There was value that was lost when these machines were replaced by computers."

"They should've seen what was coming and gotten retrained. If they didn't then they lost out on a lot of good paying IT jobs."

Jan didn't say anything.

"Look, that's progress," Nick said.

"I think you're missing my point," Jan said. She gave a patronizing sigh.

CHAPTER 21

That evening Myrt called just to chat. School was about to begin the fall semester. Myrt went on about classes, teachers and students. She yakked about student romances and whether the food in the dining hall might be better this year. Though she laughed and commented at the right places, Jan felt a vague sense that she was beyond all that, that it was all past and she was now participating in the real world while Myrt was living on a magic mountain.

Am I being smug, she wondered.

Jan talked about her encounter with Nick.

"Is he cute?" asked Myrt.

"That's really beside the point, Myrt," Jan said. "I acted, I don't know, sort of like a smart aleck, like I was back in high school."

"It wasn't all that long ago that you were in high school."

Jan said, "Seems like a long time ago."

"You felt threatened," remarked Myrt.

"No, well, maybe," she admitted.

"Anyway, thanks for the subscription. I look for your byline. Your articles are good."

"I'll bet they assign him to sports," Jan said. "Because he's a man."

"You don't know that."

"We'll see."

"Do you want to work on sports?" Myrt asked. A reasonable enough question, but Jan found it exasperating.

"That's not the point!"

"But do you? You didn't even go to that big Soap Box Derby thing, did you?"

"Well, no. Everyone else was covering it and someone had to stay at the paper in case something important came in."

"Like, maybe, an emergency puppet show had to be covered," Myrt said.

Jan could have gotten defensive at this point at Myrt's snide remark. Or testy. But it wasn't in Jan's nature. So, Jan said, "Yes, maybe," and laughed. "And I would have been there to cover it."

Myrt said, "So, how about if I come up next weekend and we do a little decorating? Your place looks adorable."

Jan had emailed some pictures some weeks before. She was now referring to the little house at Dobbins Doggie Lodge as "Little San Simeon".

The original San Simeon, now a California State Monument, is a castle built by William Randolph Hearst, the newspaper baron. The main house has 56 bedrooms and 61 bathrooms. Jan's cottage had one of each. San Simeon bears the same resemblance to Jan's rented house that Chopsticks resembles Rachmaninoff's piano concerto No.2.

"Great! I can't wait for you to come," said Jan. She really meant it. She missed Myrt.

CHAPTER 22

It was Friday late afternoon when, as usual, Jan pulled up to the front of her cottage at Dobbins Doggy Lodge. Apparently, Mr. Dobbins had been looking out for her arrival. He hustled over from his house and hailed Jan as she was climbing out of Joseph the Car.

"Miss Pancake, Jan, I have something to ask you," he called out.

Uh, oh, what had she done? She got out of the car.

He got within a social distance of Jan and said, "I know you've said you like dogs."

Jan nodded.

"And I've noticed that you don't seem to go out too often on weekends."

Drat, he noticed. That's embarrassing.

Dobbins sensed her embarrassment. "I mean, things around your house seem nice and quiet on weekends, so I'm wondering if you'd consider being the weekend caretaker at the kennel. I'll lower your rent, say, four hundred dollars a month?"

Jan thought about it and shook her head. "I go to church Sundays."

Mr. Dobbins frowned. "Oh." Then, "Let me think on it. I'll get back to you if I come up with something."

Jan nodded, turned back to her car to fetch a bag of groceries and went into her cottage.

The fact is, Jan hadn't been to church in a couple of months. The first chance she could after moving to Akron she had visited two churches, both bigger than Pastor Linger's, and hadn't found them friendly. She sat in the back and had not been approached by anyone. She hadn't gotten the feeling of family she had always felt at First Calvary. The sermons were dull and left her empty. When she called home her parents advised her to give them a chance. It was unreasonable to expect her to feel as warm in a new church as in the church she'd grown up in. They were right, of course, but she didn't much like being thought of as unreasonable. It made her wonder what it was she expected from a church. Inspiration? Friendship. Clarity? Entertainment? What should she expect?

As she put away the groceries she thought about how an extra four hundred dollars could come in very handy.

CHAPTER 23

When Myrt visited Jan a few weeks later she didn't settle for bringing a scented candle as a housewarming present. Not Myrtle Wright. Myrt brought a carload of housewarming gifts. Some of them were very practical, such as a fine set of knives. Others were perfect for making the cottage comfy, such as colorful throw pillows, scatter rugs, and, yes, scented candles. But the gift that Jan liked the most was a beat-up grey fedora that Myrt picked up at a used clothing store in Lexington.

"You know, that hat suits you; it really does," Myrt said.

Jan had hardly taken the hat off since Myrt gave it to her and demonstrated its versatility.

Myrt snatched it from Jan's head and positioned it at a rakish angle on her own. The angle concealed one eye and left the other available to cast a cynical eye at the world. "Look, I'm Jean Gabin," she said with a French accent.

Jan, of course, didn't know who Jean Gabin was but surmised from Myrt's pantomime that he must have been a gangster. Then Myrt gave the hat back and showed Jan a few Bob Fosse moves. Jan wasn't the most adept dancer, but got the jazz hands down pat. She and Myrt laughed until they collapsed on the floor.

"It's a great hat, Myrt."

"Yeah, too bad it probably has bugs," said Myrt.

"What?" said Jan, sitting up straight.

"Just kidding," said Myrt, "but I did buy it at Thelma's Attic. That was the place that gave me those bugs a couple of years ago."

"Oh," said Jan. She took the hat off.

"Jan, I had it cleaned and blocked."

"What's blocked?" asked Jan.

"Don't know. It's what they do to hats."

Jan put the hat back on. Myrt said, "Come on, we've got to get these curtains up."

They got serious and began installing curtain rods as Myrt did her impersonation of Ethel Merman singing "Curtain up. Light the lights. We've got nothing to hit but the heights." She would've flung her arms out for the finale of "Everything's Coming Up Roses" but she was holding up a curtain rod that Jan was screwing into the window frame.

Myrt asked, "Have you heard from Tim?"

"He's called a few times," replied Jan. "He sent me some hilarious shots from Williamsburg." Jan put down her screwdriver and retrieved her smartphone. She began scrolling through her stored pictures. They began pointing and laughing.

"Look at him!" squealed Myrt. "He looks like something out of a John Constable painting," referring to the work of the eighteenth century British painter.

It was true. Dressed up in costume as a colonial era farmer Tim really looked the part. Colonial Williamsburg was a stickler for historical accuracy.

"He said he's gotten some muscles – which is good – and sunburned – which is bad. He'd rather have been a blacksmith interpreter."

Myrt looked good. A summer on Little Saint Simon's Island will do that for you. She'd had a summer romance with a boy from Swarthmore that didn't amount to much.

"My parents liked him, though," said Myrt, raising her eyebrows. She picked up the hammer again.

"Don't you think calling this place Little San Simeon is a little…what?" Myrt was searching for the right word.

"Pretentious?"

"I was thinking ridiculous and slightly vulgar."

Jan laughed. "Where's your irony, woman? And anyway, William Randolph Hearst was a newspaper man and I'm a newspaper woman."

"He's dead, and from most of what I read so are newspapers."

Jan looked sternly at her friend. "Many newspapers are closing – true. But there will always be newspapers in one form or another as long as there are curious people, knowledge seekers with a desire to find things out. So, I don't want to hear about newspapers dying."

"You're right. Sorry. I'll never say it again.

Monday morning Jan gave Myrt a tour of the Sentinel-Herald. Myrt was impressed that everyone seemed to know Jan. She thought that Nick, the other intern, was a dweeb. Jan asked Pell Newcomb if she could bring Myrt to the morning daily news meeting.

"It'll give her an idea of how a daily newspaper operates."

Newcomb thought it was inappropriate. Myrt said she'd hang around and wait until the meeting was over. At the meeting Jan was assigned to cover a meeting of the Akron Chamber of Commerce and the Public Library where an award was being given to a nine-year old girl for reading one thousand books. The award ceremony was scheduled for "around ten o'clock." Jan asked Pell if Myrt could tag along with her. Pell couldn't see a reason why not.

"You can wear your new hat," said Myrt.

"I don't think so," said Jan.

Pell Newcomb asked, "New hat?"

Myrt proudly explained that she had bought Jan a vintage gray fedora. "It has a band where she can insert her press pass."

Myrt was embarrassing Jan. Jan rolled her eyes at Newcomb.

"Old friend," she said, figuring that that explained a lot. On their way to the parking lot Jan griped.

"Did you want to make me look silly?"

"Moi?" Myrt said innocently.

They took Joseph the Car to the Library and found their way to the children's room. The librarians, Mary Dunham and Edgar Trzeciak, were pleased to see Jan again and happy to meet her friend. Trzeciak, a slight figure with sandy hair, a goatee, and large black-framed glasses, smiled at Myrt a lot while Ms. Dunham was off trying to scare up the nine-year old girl. Trzeciak introduced a nicely dressed, white-haired woman who was President of the Friends of the Akron Public Library group. Jan typed the woman's name down in her tablet. Nearby, an older woman, probably the young voracious reader's grandmother, and a woman who most likely was her mother, were seated in small chairs thumbing through picture books. A table full of cupcakes and juice boxes lay near them. Some little kids curious to see what was going on were hanging around waiting for the refreshments to open for business. Trzeciak asked Myrt a number of questions about life at Philander. Eventually, Dunham returned with the little girl, Candy Eccles. Dunham introduced the member of the Third Estate to Candy.

"Candy, why do you read so much?" Jan asked, tablet at the ready.

Candy gave a straightforward thoughtful reply. "Because I like to."

Jan typed the answer and posed her next question: "How do you keep track of the books you read?"

Candy gave her a look that let her know that that was a dumb question. "On my tablet, of course." She had been well raised, so she didn't add "duh" to her answer. There was no need to embarrass an adult unnecessarily.

"Do you have a favorite book?"

Without hesitating, Candy responded, "Johnny Tremain. I think it's the best book that was ever written."

"Why?" asked Jan and Myrt at the same time.

"Because his hand never gets better. That's real life," said Candy, "not like the movie version."

Myrt and Jan looked at one another. Such a curious response from such a little girl. Dunham and Trzeciak stood there chuckling.

Then it was time for presentation of the certificate. Ms. Dunham produced the document, handed it to the President of the Friends of the Library Association, who made a few remarks and handed it to Ms. Eccles. The President shook hands with Candy and everyone clapped. Experience had taught all the little kids that now was the time to head for the cupcake table. Candy Eccles' mother and grandmother served as hosts. Jan took pictures of Candy surrounded by her family, the Library staff and the President of the Friends group.

When they returned to Joseph the Car Jan gave Myrt a choice: either go to the Chamber of Commerce meeting with her and get bored to death or get dropped off at Little San Simeon and take a nap or whatever. Myrt chose not to get bored to death so Jan dropped her off and went back to the newspaper. Instead of napping Myrt took her car into the city and poked around shops. She drove to the Stan Hywet Hall and Gardens but the museum was closed because it was never open on Mondays.

That evening Jan and Myrt made dinner. They decided on chicken fricassee. It took no time at all to find a recipe on the internet. It took much longer to make the dish. That gave them plenty of time to catch up on things. Myrt asked about Stan Hywet Hall. Jan had never been there. She looked up the name on the internet and shared what she learned: Stan Hywet was an Old English word for 'stone quarry'.

Myrt said, "It's funny. When a house gets big enough it gets its own name, like Kykuit, the Rockefeller mansion, or The Breakers, the Vanderbilt's so-called cottage, or…"

"Or San Simeon. Don't forget Little San Simeon,"

"And what about The White House?"

Jan shook her head. "No, that's fine. It's white and it's not even called a mansion or a palace; it's called a house. That's humble."

They were discussing the name 'Monticello' when Jan's phone rang. The caller identified himself as Edgar Trzeciak, the Assistant Manager of Youth Services at the Akron Public Library. Jan raised her shoulders and made a face that asked, *What's coming next?*

"You remember: black glasses, blue sweater, goatee?"

Jan said she remembered him. He sounded nervous as he explained that he enjoyed seeing Jan and Myrt that morning. He said he'd enjoyed talking to Myrt and thought there was a "rapport" between the two of them.

Jan didn't say much but she motioned Myrt over to her side of the table to eavesdrop on the conversation.

Trzeciak said that it was difficult to meet women when one worked in the children's room of a public library.

"I can see that," Jan said.

"And it's so rare to find people one can warm up to…"

"Uh huh," Jan agreed.

Myrt stifled a giggle.

Trzeciak finally got to his point. "I'm wondering if perhaps you might furnish me with sufficient information that would allow me to contact Myrtle with the purpose of seeing her again."

He sounded like he was reading from notes.

"Perhaps I could speak to her?" Trzeciak asked.

Myrt violently shook her head and silently and in an exaggerated manner mouthed 'no'.

"Well, I can take your number and give it to her when I see her," said Jan, trying not to giggle. Jan made sure not to say something untruthful, for Jan made a practice of never lying. Trzeciak sounded a little disappointed and a little relieved but agreed to the arrangement.

Jan found a pen in her handbag and took dictation on a napkin.

After a recitation of Trzeciak's telephone number, the spelling of his last name and an exchange of "okays" and "rights" and "goodbyes" and a "see you" or two, Jan clicked off. Myrt returned to her side of the table.

"Well," said Jan, "here's his name and telephone number." She slid the napkin across the table.

"Well," said Myrt.

They burst out laughing.

"Now what?" said Jan.

They laid out the ground rules for the discussion to follow: "Let's not talk this thing to death," they agreed.

"Go out with him? I can't pronounce his name. What is this?" she said, pointing to the napkin.

"I think it's Polish or Ukranian or Slovenian or Samoan or something." She gave Myrt the best approximation of the pronunciation she could manage.

They talked about the mysterious Mr. Trzeciak. Myrt didn't express a whole lot of interest. Jan said that if Myrt wasn't interested in him she should simply not call him and leave it at that. Myrt asked Jan how he'd gotten her phone number in the first place. Jan sat back in her chair and began wondering the same thing. She didn't think the people at the newspaper would give it out. Suddenly she snapped her finger.

"I know how," she said just the way a certain TV detective reveals the solution to the case. "I got a library card when I first started work. He looked it up on the Library's patron database."

"Wouldn't that be illegal?"

"Absolutely. A violation of the confidentiality of records laws. We studied that in my Journalism and the Law class. He could get in real trouble…"

"…if you blew the whistle. Are you a whistle blower? He could be a stalker."

"I think he's just a lonely, sad guy. This could be the first and only time he's done this sort of thing."

"You're not the one being stalked," Myrt pointed out.

"It's flattering in a way, don't you think?"

"To be stalked? I don't think so," replied Myrt. "It's creepy."

Jan said that she didn't think this situation could be called 'stalking'.

"I think you should report him," said Myrt. "Why wait until he strikes again."

"Myrt, he hasn't struck the first time. It could hurt his career, his family. I think a little Christian charity is called for here. He's just a lonely, nerdy guy."

Myrt reluctantly admitted that maybe she was overreacting a bit and that Christian charity was a good idea.

"What do I tell him the next time I see him?" asked Jan.

"He probably won't say anything, but if he does just tell him I have a boyfriend."

"Do you have a boyfriend I don't know about?" asked Jan.

"Maybe, baby," said Myrt with a smirk.

Jan asked whether Myrt liked the fricassee.

"A little disappointing," was her answer. "Next time let's make chicken paprikash. I like the sound of that – paprikash."

"Me too."

CHAPTER 24

Myrt had to leave Akron without seeing Stan Hywet Hall and Gardens, the American Toy Marble Museum and Dr. Bob's Home, this last the residence of the late co-founder of Alcoholics Anonymous. Myrt's first class was in two days so it was time for her to get settled back at Philander. She vowed to return to visit Jan and see the notable sights of Akron the next time. She had enjoyed her visit and would call as soon as she got back to school. She surprised Jan by giving her a quilt she had made. The pattern was known as "Sebastian's Great Circle." Jan was delighted.

"You're becoming a real Appalachian," she told Myrt.

"I worry about that."

Myrt left while Jan was at work so Jan didn't miss her until she returned to Little San Simeon that evening. She smiled when she thought about the experience with Edgar Trzeciak but it made her wonder: why did Trzeciak find Myrt attractive enough to date but not Jan? It was true, Jan acknowledged, that Myrt had a curvier figure, bright red hair, and was more energetic and bubbly; Jan was more reserved. Was it bad to be reserved? Jan decided to work on becoming bubblier; then she decided that if she wasn't a bubbly person then so be it. Being a reserved type of person wasn't a bad thing. And if this meant she would end up as what a previous generation called "a career girl" then that was okay, too. To paraphrase her mother, it would be mankind's loss. She loved her job. And maybe that Trzeciak guy really was a stalker.

What about Tim? It seemed a little harsh, but Jan was beginning to think of Tim as "unfinished business." He would call occasionally. She enjoyed the calls but didn't immediately miss him after the call was over the way she thought she should if she really cared about him.

Pell Newcomb had talked about Jan possibly taking on some of the local obituaries. Jan decided to immerse herself in what some newspaper people called "the dead beat." She learned that obituaries are one of the most popular features of newspapers, as popular as sports and often the first section many readers turn to. She went to the newspaper morgue and went through a few years' worth of obituaries to get the hang of it. She learned that the most interesting obituaries are a hybrid of a feature story and the traditional obituary. She decided that she would make an effort not to follow the timeworn formulas that obituary writers often rely on.

She determined that it was important to somehow go beyond the facts of the deceased's life to what made that individual unique and special. She approached Pell Newcomb and told him that she thought she was ready to "cover the dead beat." He invited her to sit down on a chair next to his desk. He seemed happy that Jan had taken the initiative to approach him.

"Okay, first of all you've got to pronounce the word correctly," Pell said. "It's 'obit-uary', not 'obitch-uary', understand?"

Pell explained that obituary writing was not 'gruesome', that the obituary writer in many cases ended up part of the grieving and healing process for the bereaved.

"It calls for a great deal of sensitivity. The great thing is that you get to talk to a lot of interesting people. You won't be writing about world famous people; the news people write those obits. You'll be writing about the local people, the unsung person. But you'll get to uncover the extraordinary in ordinary people. You'll be in a position to let the community know how extraordinary they were. If you succeed you'll have a compelling narrative."

The way Newcomb explained it made it seem important. He went on to explain that the small basic obituaries are those little free ones submitted by the funeral directors. Then there are the obituaries written by the paper which are paid for by the family or friends. There are others that are news features.

"You'll write local feature obituaries and you'll write future obituaries of well-known Akronites. That will mean talking to some important local people."

That seemed a little creepy to Jan.

"Not at all," Pell said. "We have to have obituaries prepared for those people and they have to be well-written.

"Look, I'm sure you've heard the cliché that newspapers are the first draft of history. Well, obituaries are contemporary history. It's important to get it right."

CHAPTER 25

"You're going to write obituaries?" Tim said incredulously when Jan spoke to him that week. He began giggling. She could imagine him on the other end of the phone. The sight was not endearing.

"Why can't you cover sports? Or the comic strips?"

"Tim, my boss wants me to try obituaries. They're the most popular part of the newspaper. I might get to do sports, too. Obituaries aren't a full-time assignment."

Jan was beginning to regret answering the phone. She thought it best to change the subject. "So, you're going to be taking the LSATs, right?"

"Right. Will you be going to funerals and things?"

"I don't know, Tim. Maybe."

Jan tried to steer the conversation back to topics non-necrological but it was like turning an oil tanker – it took a while and in the meantime…

"You won't even know the people and you're supposed to write nice things about them? What if they weren't nice? What if they're zombies?"

Jan was getting exasperated. She said, "Tim, I want to talk about something else, okay?"

They talked about folk dancing, the new Dean of Students, and other Philander-centered topics before ending the conversation.

After she clicked off Jan sat at the kitchen table and said out loud, "Zombies? Cover the comic pages? He really is from a strange planet."

CHAPTER 26

The subject of the first obituary Jan was assigned to write wasn't a zombie or an unlikable person. He was Mr. Forrest Zook, who died at the age of eighty-one from pancreatic cancer. He was a prominent farmer whose apple orchard, Sunset Farm, was famous for the quality of its apples. Jan telephoned and spoke to his widow, Alice, got the vital information about next of kin, etc., and learned a great deal about farmer Zook. From what his widow told her Mr. Zook was a kind and gentle man. It turned out that many of the apple trees on his property came from seeds distributed by John Chapman, known as Johnny Appleseed.

"Forrest was proud of his apples," said the Widow Zook. "Have you ever had any of his apples?"

Jan confessed she hadn't. Mrs. Zook urged Jan to visit Sunset Farm. Jan said she would drive over to pick up a photograph of her husband. Mrs. Zook gave her the address. Then Mrs. Zook said something that surprised Jan.

"You know, you're the first person I've talked to about Forrest since he died where I haven't ended up crying. Thank you."

Jan was moved almost to tears by these words. She thanked Mrs. Zook. She was surprised when she looked at the clock and discovered that she'd been on the telephone nearly an hour. Before she made the call she had expected that the conversation would be difficult. She intended to be very controlled, very composed. But it turned out to be effortless.

Jan drove out to Sunset Farm. Alice Zook emerged from her house and embraced Jan. She invited her in for some tea and apple cake. Jan didn't get the sense that Mrs. Zook was lonely. Their conversation revealed that, on the contrary, Alice had lots of good friends and family. She was always happy to add to her circle of friends. After an hour or so of conversation Jan collected a photograph of Forrest Zook, shared a hug and took home a large basket of apples. Jan had made a friend.

The next day she spent an hour writing the obituary and turned it in to Pell Newcomb. He marked it up a little and called Jan back to his desk.

"Good job, but I think you're capable of digging down deeper," was all he said.

CHAPTER 27

"Haven't seen you in a coon's age," said Mary Karnes when she ran into Jan on the street outside the Sentinel-Herald building. How're you doing?" asked Mary Karnes.

Jan responded, "Tolerable," which in West Virginian means "pretty well, thanks."

Having established their Appalachian bona fides and ready to move the conversation forward Mary said, "Say, how about you come over tonight? D.J.'d love to see you."

Jan agreed and went to the Karnes' house for dinner that evening. It was a nippy fall evening and Jan wore a red wool duffel coat she'd bought with some of the money she had saved by being the weekend caretaker at Dobbins Doggy Lodge.

Jan felt right at home with the Karneses. In fact, it was practically an order:

"Make yourself at home," Mary demanded.

At dinner Mary told Jan that she'd been hearing good things about her work performance. "A West Virginian girl making good," Mary said. She approved. "Look, I don't want to get in your business or nothing, but what's your social life like?"

"Mary, that's none of your business." D.J. admonished Mary from across the dining room table; but he wanted to know the answer, too.

"Hush," Mary replied to D.J. Turning to Jan she put her on the hot seat. "Well?"

Jan really wasn't all that comfortable talking about it, but she was a dinner guest - it was only good manners to say something if the host wanted her to. "Well, there's Tim back at school. I told you about him. Other than that…nothing." She looked down at her plate of chicken and dumplings. She pushed a dumpling around with her fork. It was easier than facing Mary.

Mary shook her head. "Well, we're going to fix that," she said. "You come for dinner Saturday, Miss. And dress up. I'll have a nice boy for you here."

"How're you going to cook him?" asked D.J.

"Hush, D.J. We'll have barbeque," said Mary.

Jan was a bit apprehensive, but really, what did she have to lose? She worried that if she were to meet her maker right then and there the last meal she'd have shared with a guy would have been the Chinese buffet with Arnie Stavis. She wondered, *Is this the way obituary writers start to think?*

"Sure," said Jan, "I mean, thanks."

CHAPTER 28

Saturday morning Jan made a cobbler from some of the Sunset Farm apples she still had left from the basket Mrs. Zook had given her. That night she took the cobbler to the Karnes' house. In the driveway, along with the Karnes' two cars, was a BMW. She rang the doorbell, was admitted by D.J. and was introduced to Ned Edwards. Can a guy be described as willowy? Ned was willowy. A bit under six feet tall he had a pale complexion, sandy brown hair the same color and as wavy as ramen (before cooking) that ended up on his forehead no matter how much he finger-combed it over to the side. He wore small rimless eyeglasses. His teeth were straight and white and composed one part of a pleasant smile.

After the customary period of idle chit-chat in the living room they repaired to the dining room and sat down at the dinner table. It was apparent that Mary had already briefed Ned that Jan worked as an intern for the Sentinel-Herald because he asked Jan what desk she worked.

Anticipating a derisive remark to follow her disclosure Jan said, "I work the dead beat." She intended to shock him or at least watch his response.

"You write obituaries," he stated. "I'll bet that's a challenge, and darned interesting."

Now she was embarrassed to have been so flippant. "Yes, I really like it. It's not the only thing I do at the paper. I'm a general assignment reporter, too."

Ned nodded.

Mary said, "Jan, you and Ned have the same title: he's an intern, too. At Mercy General Hospital."

Ned said, "You write about my failures."

They all found that funny. The ice broken, the dinner conversation flowed easily and comfortably. When Jan asked the Karneses how they knew Ned they explained that they knew him from church. Ned asked Jan where she attended church.

"I haven't found a church that makes me feel at home," she confessed.

"If you'd like I'd be happy to take you to church with me Wednesday evening."

She accepted the invitation. That led to an exchange of telephone numbers stored in the others' phone. D.J. and Mary exchanged sly smiles.

After a delicious barbeque dinner they shared coffee and apple cobbler in the living room. Naturally, the Karneses and Ned made a big fuss over how delicious the cobbler was. Mary put some cobbler in a plastic dish, covered it with wax paper and offered it to Ned to take home.

"If it's all right with Jan. After all, it's her cobbler."

Assured that Jan would be flattered if he'd take it Ned gladly accepted. After a while Jan and Ned thanked Mary and D.J. and left. Out on the driveway they told each other how much they enjoyed meeting one another and meant it. They confirmed their date for Wednesday night.

When Jan got back to Little San Simeon it wasn't too late to call Myrt. She flipped the light switch, flung her coat on the couch, kicked off her shoes and dialed.

"Myrt I met a really nice guy." Jan expanded from there on the details.

"You lucky stiff," said Myrt. She had begun calling Jan 'a lucky stiff' soon after Jan let her know about her obituary duty. "You'll see him again, right?"

Jan told her about their upcoming church date.

"Cats!" Myrt exclaimed. "This sounds good."

"You're pre-med. What sort of intern-y things should I talk to him about?"

"Talk to him about shingles. That sort of talk always turns me on. Or intestinal parasites."

"Thanks, Myrt."

They ended their phone call the way they always ended their phone calls. It had started out as a parody of West Virginians but over time had become an expression of their connection.

"Luv ya!" Myrt said in a high pitched yelp.

"Luv ya!" replied Jan, also in a high pitched yelp.

CHAPTER 29

Monday brought a three-alarm fire that completely engulfed a two-story apartment building on the corner of Floyd and Bud Streets. While no residents were hurt, two firefighters were injured, one from smoke inhalation, the other suffering an injury to his shoulder caused when a door frame he was passing through collapsed. The building was a total loss. Jan was part of the team that covered the fire; she submitted an article on the history of injuries to firefighters in that older district of the city that was made up of mostly wooden multistory housing. The article was used as a sidebar to the article that was front page news.

Jan was also assigned to write an obituary for a bus driver who sang opera. She interviewed Tony Bello's widow, Sophia, a couple of fellow drivers, and some longtime bus passenger who always looked forward to hearing Tony sing as he drove his route around Akron. Tony had been an Akron bus driver for twenty-seven years. He was proud of his excellent record for safe driving and even prouder of the record he cut during the early nineties of opera excerpts which is still available for sale at a record store on Trainor Avenue. Tony's rich tenor voice could be heard around town on summer days when he drove with the bus's windows open. "Like an angel he sang," according to Pat Mulroney, a passenger who made a point of taking Tony's bus when he could. "I think of Tony as an opera singer who happened to drive a bus," said his supervisor, Edward Snowden. For many years Tony lent his voice to the All-Saints Church choir. Now, according to Jan's obituary, Tony had joined Jesus' choir of angels.

When Jan turned this obituary over to Pell Newcomb his comment was "Clever, a bit self-indulgent, and I'd hope you would have dug deeper. You didn't get down to what made him tick. You show that he was a special character but you don't show what made him tick, do you see what I mean? Next time, find out what made that person's life meaningful, okay? I think you can do it."

Jan nodded but wondered whether she really could do it. Maybe she didn't have the ability to write with the kind of flair

Newcomb demanded. Not everyone did. It took a special gift and Jan despaired that she might not have it.

Maybe that's as good as I can do? she asked herself.

Jan was still down when Wednesday evening rolled around. Ned showed up at Little San Simeon somewhat early so Jan walked him over to see the kennels. Since Jan had started to be the weekend attendant she had gotten to know a couple of the dogs, including the Dobbins' two collies, pretty well. Being the attendant was easy, she explained. Make sure there was fresh water, administer medications, and give the dogs their food as specified on a chart that required tracking. It was all well-organized.

"And I'm supposed to play with them," Jan explained, as she patted Lucy, an old blind sheltie. Had she not been wearing 'go to church' clothes Jan might have been tempted to get on the kennel floor and roll around with Max, a spirited westie who barked more than was entirely necessary.

"Oh, yeah, and I have to clean up after them."

Ned nodded. He didn't talk much. Jan searched for something interesting to say.

"You know what's interesting?" Jan said, "Mr. Dobbins is a jazz fanatic. He plays the clarinet. I can hear jazz playing in his house for hours at a time. Do you play an instrument?"

Ned nodded. "I play the piano."

CHAPTER 30

In the car on the way to church Jan asked Ned about his piano playing then followed the topic up with questions about being an intern. "Are the hours as brutal as I've read about?"

He shook his head. "They're not as bad as people make them out to be."

"Here we are," Ned said as he pulled over to park in front of a small brick church in a residential neighborhood. Ned got out of the BMW and walked around to open the door on the passenger side. "I really think you'll like it here," he said as he took Jan's hand to help her out of the car.

Inside the church they headed for some seats, acknowledging smiles and greetings from various parishioners as they made their way along the aisle. Ned smiled and said "hello" back.

The service was illuminating, involving the congregation in more singing than Jan was used to. Pastor Burns was a charismatic, middle-aged man given to significant pauses and frequent flashes of wit as he preached.

After the services there were light refreshments served in the foyer. Jan stayed close to Ned, which didn't seem to bother him at all. A few church members came over to say hello to Ned and to meet Jan. She recognized a couple of people from Chamber of Commerce and City Council and Rotary meetings she'd covered. They asked her polite questions about how she was adjusting to life in Akron and her job. They hoped she was happy. While she may have been the object of their attention Jan never felt they were judging her. They urged her to consider joining their congregation.

When they'd had enough they made their way back to Ned's car. Once the car was running and the seat belts were fastened Ned asked a bit timidly, "Well?"

Jan played coy. "Well, what?"

"Well, did you like it?"

Jan laughed. "Yes, I did. I like your church and I like you and I want to go to church again with you. Okay?"

There was something about this guy that made Jan uncharacteristically bold.

Ned smiled. "It's still early. Want to go for coffee?"

"Of course."

At the coffee shop they talked about so many things: great pressing world issues and whether the coupons in the free circulars distributed at the supermarket were better than the coupons in the Sentinel-Herald and many topics in between. Ned asked Jan if she'd like to go to a Mercy General Hospital mixer for interns, residents and staff to be held a few weeks hence. She said she thought it sounded like fun.

CHAPTER 31

At the daily morning assignment meeting Jan was assigned an obituary for a man named Dickie Yount. The only thing she was told about the man was that he had been active in the Great Soap Box Derby races decades ago. Jan went to the morgue to find out about him. It turned out there was an abundance of information on Dickie Yount in the archives from the 1940s until the mid 1970s. Dickie was a local boy, son of Fred Yount owner of Yount's Appliances, an appliance store that remained open until 1990. Fred Yount promoted himself as the 'appliance king'. Newspaper advertisements of the period showed photographs of Fred wearing a crown and a robe sitting on top of a washing machine. His royal shoes rested on a microwave oven.

Royal blood seemed to run in the family: Dickie became part of the Great Soap Box Derby royalty when he won the race in 1955. A cousin won eight years later. Fred was Official Marshal of the race in 1971. After working as advertising manager for Yount's Appliances, President of the Jaycees, and a member of a host of local social and fraternal organizations Dickie was named General Manager of the Great Soap Box Derby. In that role he visited Lions and Rotary and Kiwanis Clubs, Chambers of Commerce, PTAs and every other organization he could find across the country talking up the Great Soap Box Derby. He called himself "Mr. Derby."

There were literally hundreds of photographs of Dickie with Derby winners, celebrity participants, officials and sponsors. There were dozens of photographs of Yount participating in social and civic activities, with governors and mayors. He was usually shaking hands or holding a plaque. He seemed to insert himself into most every group photograph taken in Akron during the 1960s. He was a short guy with a big smile so you could generally find him in photographs on the second row end. Had he been taller he would have placed himself in the second row center. In the pictures of his wedding he's standing next to the bride.

During the 1970s Dickie wore tinted aviator-style glasses and clothes as bright as a disco ball. He favored suits that wouldn't have looked out of place in the Akron High School's 1968 production of Guys and Dolls.

Jan was surprised that the paper didn't have an advance obituary for someone of Yount's local prominence. She organized the clippings and on her tablet opened a new file and created a timeline. She created a list of the some of the people who would have known Yount, then returned to her desk to use the news databases to try to locate those who were still alive. The first name she telephoned was Yount's widow whose name and telephone number were provided by the funeral home.

Jan didn't get nervous making calls like this anymore. The phone rang three times then a woman's voice said, "Hello?" Jan identified herself, expressed her condolences and asked Mrs. Yount a question designed to elicit a quotable response.

The first words that Estelle Yount spoke were not quotable. Following a few choice swear words she said, "You're calling me now, now that Dickie's dead? You ***s, where were you the last thirty years? You wouldn't give Dickie the time of day. And now you call!" A loud click followed.

What was that all about? Jan waited until Pell Newcomb was no longer conferencing. She went over to his desk and asked him whether she could talk to him. He agreed and she described her conversation with Estelle Yount. Newcomb drew his lower lip under his upper lip and slowly nodded.

"Maybe I shouldn't have given you this obit."

Jan asked, "If he was part of the Great Soap Box Derby shouldn't the sports desk write the obit?"

"Ordinarily, but this time they don't want to do it." He made the hand motions umpires make when the runner is safe while shaking his head. "Maybe I should assign it to someone else."

Jan knew there was something interesting here and like a good reporter she sensed a good story; she wanted in. "I'll do it, Pell, really." She turned around and walked away before Newcomb could countermand his decision. He didn't call her back.

Jan said to herself, *I've already got the best headline – 'From Soap Box to Pine Box' – I have to write this obituary!*

Jan wrote the obituary based entirely on the archive's clipping file. It was a paste-up job. The copy editor made a face when she read Jan's headline and spiked it.

"*That woman has no sense of humor,*" Jan grumbled to herself.

That Saturday she roped Ned into going to Dickie Yount's funeral by promising to bake him a pineapple upside-down cake. Besides, it was a lovely fall day. When they showed up at the church there were only around twenty people in attendance. Jan had decided that she wouldn't bother Yount's widow. There was a young man in his thirties who Jan figured was probably Dickie's son, and a young woman around the same age who was probably his daughter. The priest said a few things about Dickie being a good family man. He followed this with a recitation of the various social, civic and governmental groups Yount was involved with. The priest evidently had used Jan's obituary as reference material.

When the service had concluded and the pallbearers had carried the earthly remains of Dickie Yount from the church Ned asked Jan whether going to funerals was a necessary part of her job.

"No, I've already written this man's obituary. There are just things about this that I think are interesting. Let's see if there's anybody who'll talk to me."

Once they were outside the church, Jan didn't dare approach the family, which was moving in a protective huddle toward the limousine. Hanging back there was one older man dressed not in a suit and tie but in slacks, dark shirt and brown overcoat. Jan went up to him, identified herself as a reporter for the S-H, and asked if she might ask him a couple of questions. The man made an amused gesture that said "what the heck, what have I got to lose?" He identified himself as Morris Youman.

"Were you a friend of Dickie Yount?" Jan asked.

Mr. Youman laughed. "A friend? The guy hated me!"

Jan and Ned exchanged puzzled looks.

"Do you mind telling me why?" Jan asked.

Mr. Youman nodded then painstakingly sat down on the brick steps of the walkway that led down to the sidewalk. He stretched his legs out and turned his face to the sun to warm himself.

"You'll have to excuse me: bad pins." He pointed to his legs.

Jan and Ned followed suit and sat down, too, but failed to make similar 'oomph' sounds.

When he was ready to talk Mr. Youman said, "I'm the guy who used to fix the Great Soap Box Derby. At least, that's what I tell people 'cause it sounds good. That's why Dickie hated me. I may have fixed the Derby," - and here Morris Youman waved the index finger he favored in the air – "but I'm not the guy who ruined the Derby. That was Dickie." Youman spoke with a slight growl in his voice.

"Oh?" asked Jan.

"Well, to be fair, there was more than one guy who done that. But Dickie certainly had a big role."

Jan gave Mr. Youman an encouraging look. "Oh?"

"Look, the Derby was never completely on the up-and-up, except maybe at the beginning back in the 1930s. The racers are supposed to be built by the kids; that's what the rules say. That was to laugh. Come on, maybe the first few years, but after that the fathers were making them, and after that fathers were paying engineers to design those things. The kids who made their racers by theirselves never won. I mean, come on, these were kids."

"What was your role? What did you do?" Jan asked.

"Me, well, officially I worked security at the Derby for twelve years. That means I was supposed to make sure that after the cars had passed inspection they were all stored under the grandstand in an impound area behind chain link fencing every night. I was supposed to make sure that nobody tampered with them."

"And?"

"Well, I was supposed to, but sometimes you know how it is - things get in the way of what you're supposed to do, know what I mean?"

Youman winked to indicate that he knew Jan and Ned were wised up.

"Like?"

Youman seemed taken aback by the question, as though Jan were totally naïve and that he'd given her credit for being more wised up than she really was. "Like money, girlie. Guys'd slip me money so they could tamper with their racers. They'd slip me money; I'd turn my back.

Jan asked, "Kids or their parents?"

"Come on, girlie, what kids have got money? Parents, mostly fathers; even mothers. Capisce?"

Jan asked, "So, they'd tamper with racers to make them faster? Did they tamper with other people's racers to make them slower?"

Mr. Youman smiled. "Like I said, I turn my back. I see nothing; I know nothing. Look, don't kid yourself: the Derby was always about money. There was a lot of money riding on those little racers. A lot of gambling went on. You know why I can tell you this and not worry about seeing it in the paper?"

Jan shook her head.

Morris said the following as though he were talking to a kindergartener: "Because your newspaper has always been one of the sponsors of the Derby. Your paper didn't want to make the Derby look bad."

Jan ignored this remark. "So Dickie Yount hated you because you were corrupt?"

"Corrupt? That's kind of a hard word. I wasn't any worse than others. I made a little extra money making book Derby week. It's no different from those people who live near a football stadium who charge people $15 to park on their front lawn on game days, ten bucks less than the parking lots."

"Opportunism," said Jan.

"Right," said Youman.

Jan asked, "Was Mr. Yount corrupt?"

Youman shook his head. "Naw, he wasn't crooked. He didn't have to be. What he was was stupid."

Jan asked, "If Dickie Yount hated you why are you here? Why would you go to his funeral?"

Youman gave a wry smile and raised his hands, palms up. "Nostalgia, I guess. Dickie may have hated me. I didn't hate him. May he rest in peace."

Jan couldn't think of any more questions. She asked Mr. Youman whether she might talk to him again if she had other questions.

"Yeah, okay, if one of you'll help me up." He gave her his telephone number.

Jan and Ned helped Morris Youman back up onto his pins. Youman slowly and arthritically walked to his car.

Ned and Jan headed for Ned's car.

"That was interesting," said Ned. "He's some character."

Jan asked, "Ned, do you want to go to the Great Soap Box Derby Museum tomorrow? It's the only day of the week that it's open."

"If I say 'no' will you take the pineapple upside-down cake away?"

"No, but I'll turn it rightside up. You wouldn't like that," she growled in mock menace, trying to imitate the way Morris Youman spoke.

"Whatever you say, girlie."

CHAPTER 32

That evening Jan and Ned were at Jan's kitchen table eating pineapple upside-down cake when Jan's phone rang. Jan licked her fingers and answered. It was Tim just calling to say 'hi'.

"Tim, I've got company so I really can't talk long."

Tim edited his topics down to a few bullet points. The last was that folk dancing was great last week. They were learning Appalachian clogging.

That interested Jan. "Who's teaching it?"

"Your brother drove up with another guy."

"What! Josiah?"

"Uh huh."

"Whose idea was that?"

"Myrt's," said Tim.

That threw Jan for a loop.

"Jan, can I ask you a question and you won't get overly sensitive and yell at me?" asked Tim.

"Sure, but I you know I don't yell at you."

"Right", said Tim. "Okay, why is it your family frowns on dancing, but Appalachian clogging is okay? Clogging is dancing, isn't it?"

"Good question. I guess because it's Appalachian. Look, Tim, I really can't talk now. I've got a guest."

She said goodbye, clicked off the phone and sat a little stunned for a minute.

Ned was concerned. "What?"

Jan told him that his brother Josiah had gone to Philander to teach a clogging class.

"Does he know how to clog?"

"Sure, he's good."

Ned was satisfied with that answer which, as far as he knew, explained everything that needed to be known. He pointed to a crumb that was sticking to Jan's cheek.

"What?" she asked.

"Crumb," he said, pointing to her cheek.

Swiping at the crumb with the back of her hand, Jan said, "Do you mind if I call my brother?"

Ned didn't object. He cut himself another piece of cake.

Jan punched the numbers. When Josiah answered she said, "Josiah, did you go to Philander?"

Jan hit the speaker button so Ned could hear.

"Yes," Josiah answered. "Me and C.J. went. C.J.'s a better clogger than me."

"Whose idea was it?" Jan asked.

"Myrt's."

"So you've been in touch with Myrt?"

"Yuh."

Jan maintained her composure and asked, "Are you seeing Myrt?"

"Yuh. Is that a bad thing? I like her. She's smart."

"What about Lally?"

"Oh, yeah, well…" Josiah's voice drifted off.

Jan could see that this conversation wasn't going much farther so she asked how the rest of the family was. Josiah said they were all fine.

"Well, then, see you later," was all Jan could say.

"Right, see you later."

Jan clicked off and sat at the table. Ned could tell that Jan was upset.

"Jan, you just found out that your brother is seeing your best friend. Why is that a bad thing?"

"I don't understand it myself. I feel betrayed but I shouldn't. I mean, nobody went behind my back or anything, right?"

"Right."

"I don't know why, it just seems sneaky. The college is my thing. The farm is Josiah's thing."

Ned looked at her askance.

Jan realized how silly that sounded.

"I mean, I know they didn't have to ask my permission. They're both adults."

"Right."

It dawned on Jan that Ned was being intentionally noncommittal. "You're going to agree with me no matter what I say, aren't you?" Jan said smiling.

"That's right." Ned smiled back.

"You're awfully smart. That could be why I like you a lot."

Jan got up from her chair, went over to Ned and kissed him. It was then she noticed that his brown eyes had flecks of gold.

CHAPTER 33

Mr. Dobbins relieved Jan of her caretaker duties at one o'clock Sunday as agreed. Ned picked her up and they drove to the Derby Museum which was located downtown on Washington Boulevard. The museum occupied a set of rooms on the ground floor of a seven-story building. The sign posted on the side of the front door said that the museum was open daily in July and August, Sundays from one o'clock until five from September through June. Still, Jan and Ned weren't sure that the place was open as they approached because there were no lights on inside. Ned tried the door and found it unlocked, so they entered.

"Hello?" Jan called out.

They heard the sound of light switches and the buzzing of fluorescent bulbs flickering to life, at least the ones that were working. They heard the sound of feet shuffling and from a back area a man slowly coming out to greet them.

"Hold yer horses," was the greeting. As he approached them he added, "Yeah?"

Ned said that they wanted to visit the museum. The man thought that over for a bit then brightened and smiled. "Good," he said. "Don't get many visitors this time of year."

Ned asked, "What time of year do you get a lot of visitors?"

"No time of year," the man replied and began laughing. "Ever been here before?"

Jan and Ned shook their heads.

"Okay, then, want a tour? No charge, but if you want to make a donation to the museum that'd be most appreciated." He pointed to a transparent plastic box resting on an oak table.

Ned began to fish in his pocket.

"Wait 'til the tour's over," the man warned. "you might want to give more." He paused. "Then, again, you might want to give less. My name is Bill Barnes."

"You're the curator?" Ned asked.

"I don't know that I rate a fancy title like that at all," Barnes chuckled, "but I run this here museum. Come along."

Barnes stopped in front of a wall that had large letters painted at the top that read "What is the Great Soap Box Derby?"

"Okay, the first thing you should know is that it is a gravity powered race. The little racers are gravity powered – that means no motors." He muttered to himself, *Gravity's a great thing.*

He shepherded his tour group to an exhibit entitled "The Early Years".

Barnes asked, "You folks come from far?"

They told him they were locals and identified themselves by names and by professions.

"Well, a doctor and a newspaper gal. You're two smart people. So you won't need me to explain things like gravity for you. Would you prefer to show yourselves around rather than have some old nitwit tell you things you can read for yourself?"

Ned and Jan didn't want to hurt Mr. Barnes' feelings. They shrugged their shoulders.

Mr. Barnes got the message. "Well, if you've got questions I'll be in that little office back there." He pointed towards the rear of the room and headed in that direction.

Ned was the type of person who read all those labels on exhibits at museums. The thing is, he remembered what he read. Jan liked to go to museums and get a feel for things, an overall sense of their flow and continuity – their gestalt. Then she could look at the artifacts or works of art and appreciate them individually.

Jan captured a sense of the Soap Box Derby racers: "They look like Twinkies," she said.

There were little racers all over the place.

Jan was delighted. "Look, Ned, little racers on the walls and on the ceilings!"

"I had an apartment like that once," joked Ned. "Had to hire an exterminator."

Ned conceded that some of the Soap Box Derby racers did look like Twinkies, especially the yellow ones.

"Some look like jelly beans," he said.

In one exhibit there was a batch of the tiny racers hanging from the walls.

Ned said, "They remind me of the way some ski lodges in Vermont have sleds hanging from the walls. You know," he said, leaning into Jan as though sharing a great nugget of wisdom in confidence: "sledding is a lot like the Great Soap Box Derby."

"How so, Professor?" Jan asked whimsically.

"It harnesses the power of gravity," was the response.

Jan nodded. "Ah, yes, gravity. It always comes down to gravity, doesn't it?"

They broke out laughing then shushed themselves. They didn't want to disturb Bill Barnes and cause him to return. They preferred being alone together.

The exhibits were interesting. The main exhibits were chronological; blown up photo murals covered lots of wall space. As you walked along you went from black and white photos of the nineteen thirties and forties to color photos of the nineteen fifties up to the recent past. Photos of the grandstands likewise changed: the stands were full for the 1930s through the sixties, then thinned out from the seventies on. Some of the pictures had been taken from a Goodyear blimp.

There were helmets and jackets and trophies and photographs of mothers hugging their winning sons. Photos from recent years showed parents hugging winning daughters, too. Lots of endearing goofy smiles. There were the shovels that broke ground for Derby Downs back in the thirties. Jan and Ned learned that the raceway was a WPA project that gave Akronites needed jobs during the Great Depression.

Jan took Ned's hand as they stood in front of the exhibits.

"This event was huge. The crowds were enormous," marveled Jan.

"Says here there were over a hundred thousand people some years," said Ned who was reading all the little placards.

The photographs of the early days of the Derby, back when kids made the racers out of soap boxes, old baby buggies and anything else they could find looked like stills from old Our Gang movie shorts.

"Look at that little peanut! He couldn't be more than seven," Jan said, pointing to a black and white photograph of a little boy standing next to his racer. She squealed with delight at the picture.

There were photographs of the huge awards banquets which were held every year at the Mayflower Hotel. Crowds everywhere. And parades on downtown streets with marching bands from across the country, motorcycle brigades, boy scouts and girl scouts, drum majors and majorettes.

There was a display of entry tickets from every year. The tickets always billed the Derby as the "Greatest Amateur Racing Event in the World."

"That's something," said Jan.

"Kind of a Lilliputian Le Mans," quipped Ned.

"Hey, that's pretty good," remarked Jan.

There were cases full of shiny trophies.

There was a wall of photographs of the celebrities who participated in the Derby over the years. In the nineteen forties there were actors and other celebrities. Jan and Ned could identify Abbott and Costello, Bill "Hopalong Cassidy" Boyd, Burns and Allen, Jimmy Durante, Jack Dempsey, thanks to the placards labeling the photographs.

Jan pointed to a couple of gentlemen in a group photo of celebrities. They were dressed in what we've come to think of as explorers' outfits – pith helmets, jodhpurs and puttees, and hunting jackets. "Who were they?"

Ned couldn't recognize the faces either.

"I'll ask," he said and began walking to where Bill Barnes' had pointed earlier.

"It's not important," Jan said.

But Ned wanted to know. He found Barnes eating Pringles in the little curatorial office and escorted him back to the wall of celebrity photographs. Barnes squinted at the wall. He pointed at one man, then the other.

"That's Clyde Beatty, the lion tamer, and that's Frank "Bring 'em Back Alive" Buck. He'd go all over the world collecting animals for circuses."

They thanked Barnes who returned to his curatorial office and his Pringles.

Jan said, "I wish Myrt were here. She's addicted to old television shows and movies. She'd know who a lot of these people were."

Some of the people Myrt might've been able to recognize were Jimmy Stewart, Ronald Reagan, Emmett Kelly the clown, Roy Rogers and Dale Evans.

There was one celebrity Jan had no trouble recognizing. "Yoicks, there's Vice-President Richard Nixon."

When it came to the nineteen sixties, seventies and eighties the number of celebrities Myrt would've been able to identify dropped significantly. Celebrities who attended were now less than big-time stars, mostly second tier character actors from old television series and soap operas. Remember Judy Carne from Laugh In? Larry Storch from F Troop? How about Linda Hayes from Room 222? Linda who? Room what?

Ned remarked, "It's just the reverse of what you'd think: You'd expect to be able to recognize the recent celebrities and not be able to recognize the older ones."

"Who's that?" Jan asked pointing to the photograph of an attractive woman cheering from the celebrity section of the grandstand.

Ned looked at the label accompanying the photograph. "It says it's the actress who played Mannix's secretary on the Mannix television series in 1975."

That one left Jan and Ned scratching their heads.

There was a chart that showed the winning times from 1933 until 2007. The times didn't change much from year to year: it seemed as though twenty-eight seconds was about average.

"It's hard to believe thousands of people would come to watch races that took twenty-eight seconds," Jan said.

Ned said, "I think I'd prefer it to going to the Indy 500 and sitting for hours watching cars go round in a circle. It's all relative."

"I see what you mean. It's easy to endure a twenty-eight second race," said Jan. She pointed to a mock-up of a young person sitting in a racer. "He's wearing a helmet and he's scrunched down so you can't see his face. It would be hard to root for someone you can't even see."

Jan looked around the room they were in and said, "This is all very interesting." She looked hard to find any photographs with Dickie Yount but failed. She took Ned by the hand and walked over to the curatorial office.

"Excuse me, Mr. Barnes, I can't help but notice that there're no photographs of Dickie Yount in the museum. He was General Manager of the race for a few years, wasn't he?"

Mr. Barnes reacted as though he'd just bitten down on a rancid Pringle. "Yount? The Board didn't want to include pictures of that hambone. He was general manager when Chevy dropped its sponsorship of the Derby. Over a million dollars lost right there. He was G.M. when the cheating scandal happened. Don't talk to me about Dickie Yount."

Jan asked, "What was he like?"

"Yount? You know those annoying insects that buzz around your face that you try to swat and just keep missing? The ones that go for your ears? That was Yount."

"You know he died last week?" said Jan.

Barnes lowered his head. "I know. I read the obituary."

Jan whispered to Ned, "I wouldn't have been able to use that annoying insect quote in my obituary anyway."

Ned agreed.

Mr. Barnes crooked his finger in the direction of an exhibit and said, "Let me show you something." He put down his Pringles stood up and led Jan to an exhibit that was off to the side in the second room. The sign read "The Magnetic Nose".

"The magnetic nose? It sounds like a 1950s horror film, doesn't it? The Magnetic Nose of Doctor Domesticus," said Jan. She made scary 'whoo, whoo' noises.

Barnes ignored her. "1973 Timmy Nolen cheated. Won the race, got the trophy, got the silk jacket. Two days later they discovered a magnet in the nose of his racer. Stripped him of his title. He refused to give the jacket back and he destroyed the trophy."

Barnes swept his hand toward the racer. On one side of the vehicle was the legend "Sponsored by the Golden, Colorado Jaycees."

Bill Barnes pointed to a framed x-ray on the wall behind the racer.

"See? There's the magnet."

Ned asked, "How would a magnet help?"

Barnes crooked his finger again, motioning them to follow him. He led them to a display of a starting gate that was used from 1965 until 1971. "You see: metal. Timmy's racer had a button in the headrest. Moving his head back triggered a button that activated the electromagnet in the nose. The magnet was drawn to the starting gate. It gave him maybe a half second advantage. Probably would've won anyway. Fast racer. Probably the same one that won the year before." Anyway, all of these monkeyshines happened on Dickie Yount's watch. He was so busy having his picture taken. A new laundromat couldn't open without Dickie Yount there to get his face in the picture. Any other questions?"

They both answered, "No, thanks Mr. Barnes."

"Call me Bill."

Bill turned in the direction of his office.

"Wait, Bill, can I ask you a question?" said Jan.

"Ask me anything."

"What is it you like about the Great Soap Box Derby?"

Mr. Barnes looked thoughtful and scratched the back of his neck before he answered. "Well, in its day it was wonderful. It was exciting and the kids couldn't have had more fun. They came to Akron and people paid attention to them and then they went home and remembered it their whole lives. I think that's wonderful, don't you?"

Jan and Ned nodded in agreement.

"They made friends here and their families had a great time."

Jan asked, "What did you do at the Derby? Did you race?"

Bill Barnes smiled. "No, never raced. Let me show you." He led them to the exhibit labeled "Derby Camp."

The Camp was a WPA project. There were old tee shirts and caps like the ones Spanky McFarland and The Dead End Kids wore. There were programs and songbooks and photographs of kids on benches eating dinner and sitting around campfires toasting marshmallows. Barnes pointed to a photo of identically outfitted counselors. "Here I am." He grinned and joked, "I'm the one in the white tee shirt that says 'Camp Derby Counselor'. Derby Camp was great for the kids. Every night there was entertainment, storytelling, and lots of celebrities showed up. See?" Barnes pointed to a photograph of a tubby guy talking to a bunch of kids. "Andy Devine. He was a terrific guy. Came year after year."

After thanking Bill Barnes Jan and Ned tossed a couple of bills into the donation box and left the museum. Walking toward the car Ned smiled. "That was a good one about the magnetic nose. I don't think he appreciated it."

"Thanks."

"I think the Danish astronomer Tycho Brahe had a metal nose," Ned recollected.

"Was it magnetic?"

"I don't know."

Jan giggled. "He'd be able to do that spoon trick no sweat."

Ned didn't know anything about the spoon trick.

"Tweedy showed me. I'll show you at dinner."

When they got into the car Ned said, "Too bad the museum doesn't have a simulator that lets you feel what it's like to race one of those little cars."

"Twenty-eight seconds. It would be a short ride."

"Good point. You know, Ned, if we have a future together I don't want our relationship to be like a Soap Box Derby race."

"Explain."

"Short and boring."

"You'd prefer long and boring?"

Jan laughed. "No, silly."

"Then long and exciting it shall be."

"Well, I'm glad we settled that," said Jan.

CHAPTER 34

The following week Jan wrote an obituary that she enjoyed writing. Florence (Flo) McCauley, 84, passed away on October 13. Mrs. McCauley was a mother and homemaker for most of her life. Her claim to greatness – though Mrs. McCauley was too modest a person to claim greatness – was her magical ability to remove any household stain. Neighbors and friends of neighbors would make pilgrimages to 84 Waldo Avenue, ruined raiment in hand, appealing to Mrs. McCauley to remove stains they found impossible to eradicate themselves. Mrs. McCauley invariably brought the vestments back to life. "It was like a miracle what she could do," according to Jackie Salada, a neighbor. She was able to accomplish her stain removal activities without benefit of any advanced laboratory equipment. She never charged for her labors. "However she did it, she's taking the secret to the grave," said Paula Stevens, a longtime neighbor. Mrs. McCauley had a loving family. No one ever said a word against her and she was never known to utter an unkind word. Her life was without stain.

Pell Newcomb approved this obituary without changing a word.

"This is very good, Jan," he said.

Jan beamed.

Mrs. McCauley's daughter dropped off a photograph of the late Mrs. McCauley at the front desk at the S-H. According to the receptionist she was immaculately dressed and her manners were impeccable.

Jan went up to the fourth floor to pay a call on Mary Karnes. She wanted to ask her what she knew about Dickie Yount. Mary was seated at her desk working, but she welcomed Jan in and invited her to sit down.

"How are things going?" she asked. She obviously meant 'with Ned'.

Jan told her that things were going great. She didn't get to see him as often as they'd like. Did Mary know that interns sometimes work sixteen hour shifts?

Jan asked about the Derby.

"You can talk to someone over at the University but I can tell you what I know without the academic gobbledygook."

She launched into a lecture free of gobbledygook.

"Back in the Depression there was no money and nothing to do to entertain yourself with for free except watching flagpole sitters and that's boring, so people came out to the Derby. It had started with a few local kids making little carts out of soap boxes they'd gotten from the back of the A&P and racing them around. Well, a newspaper photographer took a photograph and it got in the paper and the newspapers were smart and saw that it was a great way to sell newspapers, and the city saw that it was a great way to promote the city, and the businesses saw it was a great way to make money. They figured newspapers and companies all over the country would sponsor local races and the thing would grow and it did. There was a lot of money involved in promoting the Derby. Movie stars saw it as a way to promote their careers. Chevrolet saw it as a way to advertise and sell cars. How good a job of promoting it did they do? So good that kids dreamed of coming to Akron the way the prettiest girl in school dreamed of going to Hollywood. Can you believe it? Akron, for pity's sake! What they couldn't figure out was how to make it not boring."

Jan said, "But it's not boring for the kids racing."

"But it is for a spectator who doesn't know a kid who's racing."

Jan reluctantly nodded. "But the races take only around twenty-eight seconds."

"That's twenty-eight seconds too long. And you know how Little League got ruined because fathers got involved and it wasn't fun anymore? Well, that's what happened to the Derby. Then came television and the late sixties and seventies, what with the hippies and rock festivals, the war in Vietnam and Nixon and the politics. That whole change in attitude? Well, the Derby became an artifact from a time past, like dinosaurs, except kids get excited about dinosaurs. The Derby had always been promoted as a symbol of American youth and good clean fun, but American youth were rejecting the old values and it really wasn't fun compared to all the things kids could do once the Depression was over and people had more money. Interest waned. Then there was the double whammy: Chevrolet dropped sponsoring it and the following year was the cheating scandal, so the Derby was on its last legs. They've tried to promote it as a family activity but family activities these days are the kids playing videogames in their bedrooms and the parents wasting time on Facebook in the living room. Any questions so far, class? Otherwise, next week's lecture will be the causes of the French and Indian Wars in under seven minutes."

Jan said, "I read that back when Chevrolet sponsored the Derby they gave a scholarship to the first place winner and a new car to the second place winner. Why would you give a car to a kid who's maybe thirteen years old? I can understand the scholarship, but a car?"

Mary answered, "General Motors owns Chevrolet so it was cheap for them to give away a car. It promoted the brand. Back then GM owned Frigidaire, too, but they must have decided that a thirteen-year-old would rather get a car than a refrigerator. If you wanted a refrigerator your mother would go on Queen for a Day, but you wouldn't know about that."

"Tell me about the cheating scandal."

Mary shook her head. "I'm not the expert on that. I wasn't here then; I was still in Flyspeck, West Virginia. It seems like it was all kind of mysterious. Jack Tweedy's the guy who knows all about that, but it's something he won't talk about. People don't ask him."

Jan dramatically threw back her shoulders, raised her chin and said, "Jan Pancake, girl reporter, will ask."

But maybe not right away. First, she decided she should go to the morgue and spend some time reading up on the scandal.

CHAPTER 35

"Myrt, you're seeing my brother?" Jan asked. Was this the kind of open ended question reporters are supposed to ask? Jan had put off calling Myrt for a few days but felt compelled to confront her some time, so why not now as long as she was on a school bus on her way to an away high school football game? Some of the boosters were blowing toy horns. Some were shouting. Others were shouting and blowing horns, which is harder than it looks.

"Yes, I'm seeing your brother. What's all that noise?"

"I'm on a bus full of high school football boosters. Don't change the subject," yelled Jan.

"Don't yell."

"I have to yell. Otherwise you won't hear me."

"I'll tell Josiah you were yelling at me. Are we still best friends?"

"What? I can't hear you."

"Jan, I'll call you later. Think happy thoughts. Luv ya." Myrt hung up.

Jan was subbing for one of the regular sports reporters. She'd only gotten the request from the sports desk the day before so she had to bone up on the rules of football, learn what she could about the various strategies employed and the reasons behind them. The sports desk had its own stylebook containing lists of which clichés were 'in' and which were not.

"We keep the cliché list current," the sports editor explained. "A cliché on the avoid list that hasn't been used for a year will be placed on the active list. Understand?"

Jan said she understood, but she didn't, not really.

The sports editor sensed her confusion. "I'd explain it by telling you that 'tides shift'," said the sports editor, "but that's on the inactive cliché list right now."

Jan found the whole thing mysterious. Why was it okay to call a basketball player a 'hoopster' but not okay to call him a 'cager'? She didn't know. A baseball could be a 'horsehide' but not a 'white pellet' or 'the old apple'? Why not? For that matter, what was wrong with calling wrestlers 'grapplers' since grappling was what they did. What was wrong with saying that an athlete 'came to play' when, in fact, he showed up at the arena, suited up and gave every indication that he was willing to participate? Jan didn't know. But she enjoyed the bus ride, had fun sitting in the press box eating hot dogs and liked interviewing the student athletes after the game.

She watched the girls and boys sitting next to one another on bleachers and could easily tell which ones were couples. For the moment they were happy.

So what was wrong with Myrt seeing Josiah? Nothing, she decided.

CHAPTER 36

Jan spent hours reading clippings in the morgue. The newspaper no longer could afford an archivist. Jan had learned that Bernice Maxwell, the Graphic Arts Editor, could answer most of her questions whenever she was stumped. The task of looking up articles on the Great Soap Box Derby was made somewhat easier because the majority of articles were written from July until October, a few weeks before the Derby took place and a few weeks after the event. Still, Jan knew there would probably be relevant articles throughout the year.

It was Bernice who told her that the Akron Public Library had started digitizing and indexing articles from the Sentinel and the Herald starting with 1930. Bernice told her that the project advanced by fits and starts because of chronic Library funding cuts. Bernice believed that the indexing had progressed up to around 1975 before it stalled most recently. The index was not yet online so Jan would have to go to the Library to access it.

Jan used her lunch hour to visit the Library. Naturally, the first person she ran into in the rotunda was Edgar Trzeciak. When Trzeciak ask about Myrt Jan told him that she was now in a serious relationship.

"In fact, it's with my brother, Josiah," Jan boasted.

Edgar seemed put out. "She should post that on her Facebook page."

Jan saw no point in disagreeing with him and asked him where she could find the Sentinel-Herald database. Edgar said he'd take her to the local history room where the dedicated computer was located. As they headed in that direction, their heels clicking loudly on the terrazzo floor, Edgar asked, "What about you?"

Jan asked, "What about me?"

"Are you seeing anyone?" Edgar asked.

Jan smiled and told him she was seeing an intern at Mercy Hospital. "I'm not on Facebook."

"Well, if you two break up give me a call, okay?"

Jan didn't respond to this request but she smiled and thanked Edgar for taking her to the newspaper index. She was so glad there was a Ned. She wished he were there so she could give him a hug.

She spent that lunch time and three more lunch times reading about the Great Soap Box Derby Scandal of 1973 and making notes. Mary was right: the Derby races themselves really were boring. But the shenanigans surrounding the races were fascinating. Greed, competition, marketing and the exploitation of American youth created a toxic stew that inevitably led to disaster. And if there's one thing newspaper people are good at covering it's disasters, Jan figured. She decided she'd see if there was really a story in an event that rocked the nation more than forty-five years ago.

One thing she noticed was Jack Tweedy's byline on lots of articles. Mary had warned her that it was something Tweedy was reluctant to talk about. But Jan remembered an old family story that involved her grandfather, Rufus Jobe, and the farm. There was a man who lived somewhere in Logan County who owned an outstanding bull that was the envy of farmers near and far. Many people had made offers to buy it but the farmer always refused. Rufus went to see the farmer and talked to him. The farmer sold him the bull. Why? The price Rufus offered wasn't any better than anyone else's. Naturally, the family wanted to know the reason. "I think he took a liking to me," was her grandfather's only response. Jan hoped Tweedy might take a liking to her.

When she had turned in her assignments one day she went to Tweedy's tiny office and asked whether he had the time to talk to her.

"Remind me, what is your name?" Tweedy asked. She told him. "Oh, of course." He invited her to sit. He swiveled from his desk to face her, placed his hands on his knees and said "Yes."

Jan sat up straight in the chair with her hands folded in her lap. "Mr. Tweedy, for my honors thesis at school I'm thinking of writing about the Soap Box Derby cheating scandal of 1973. I'll do it on my own time. I've done a lot of reading and I'd like to interview you as a source."

A sorrowful look came over Tweedy's face that made Jan wish she hadn't asked. But she didn't say anything. A minute passed before Tweedy said, "You write the local feature obituaries, don't you?

"Uh huh."

"You're doing a fine job." He paused. "I'll let you know tomorrow."

But Tweedy didn't go to the newspaper office the next day. And when he showed up the following day he looked unhappy and avoided Jan. When it appeared that their paths were going to intersect at the elevator Tweedy ducked into the staircase. Jan didn't dare approach him. Eventually, though, late in the day he shuffled over to her desk and said, "Okay, tomorrow," turned around and shuffled back to his little office. Some of the other reporters in the room watched this short exchange. A few seemed curious – concerned even - but none said anything. Good newspaper people pride themselves on respecting the privacy of others; at least those they respect. There was respect for Tweedy in that room. Jan was aware of this.

Jan had found out over the months she'd been working at the paper that the newspaper fraternity was made up of some pretty fine people. They were helpful to her and they were helpful to each other. She sensed that any competitiveness within the ranks was of the salutary kind.

"It's not a cutthroat business," one reporter explained to her. "It used to be back when every city had lots of papers. Lots more throats. Lots more cutting. Not anymore. We're mostly all just doing the best we can because we know that now we're involved in a fight for survival. The cutting that goes on these days are jobs."

CHAPTER 37

Ned's birthday was the second week in November and Jan wanted to get him something special. She had spent time in stores looking for something distinctly Akronian that wasn't a cheap souvenir. She didn't imagine he'd get too excited by a "Welcome to Akron" snow globe in the shape of a tire. Then it occurred to her to get him something distinctly Appalachian. She called Josiah and asked him to buy and send her a piece of art glass from West Virginia. A sweater could get moth eaten or shrink, but Ned could appreciate a piece of art glass forever...unless it broke. Josiah agreed to find a piece.

"Sure, that's a good idea. So, when do we get to meet this guy?"

"Thanksgiving. Are you inviting Myrt?"

Josiah hesitated before answering. "I don't know. What do you think? Things are a little awkward between you, aren't they?"

"No, things are good. At first I wondered whether she was being sneaky, but she really wasn't, was she? I mean, she just wants to love and be loved like everybody else."

"Okay then." Josiah sounded relieved. "And I'll send you a really nice piece of Blenko for Ned."

Jan thanked him.

When it was Ned's birthday Jan made a special dinner and a right-side-up cake. After dinner she gave him his gift which she had wrapped herself. As soon as he opened it he said he loved it. It was a beautiful vase, clear but for some delicate blue swirls.

"But I'm saving the best surprise for last," Jan said.

"Better than this?" asked Ned.

Jan explained that they would have to wait a while. She had gotten some movies on DVD from the Library. One was called An Affair to Remember. It had been recommended by Myrt. She had called it "a perfect weepie" and she was correct: it was sentimental and romantic and corny and implausible. In short, it was perfect. Jan and Ned sat on Jan's couch, snacked on popcorn, and watched movies until two-thirty in the morning. Then Jan told Ned to get in the car.

"Jan, it's the middle of the night."

"Hush," Jan replied. She started Joseph and refused to tell Ned where they were going. At this hour all was quiet, even the streets of downtown Akron. Jan pulled up to the Sentinel-Herald and said, "Here we are."

They climbed out of the car and entered the building. The building was very quiet. Jan got the two of them cleared by the security guard. She led Ned to the door towards the back of the building. The security guard at his desk pressed the button which unlocked the door where the giant presses were. They entered and found that the production staff was waiting for Jan. She had made arrangements for this days beforehand.

"Ned, you get to start the presses."

Ned broke into a great smile. One of the pressmen led him up some metal grate steps to a gigantic machine and pointed to a large green button. Ned looked down at Jan, his face glowing with childlike glee. With a little flourish of his hand he pressed the button. The gigantic presses rumbled to life. As the machine picked up speed the vibrations increased as did the steady roar. One of the pressmen ripped a sheet off the line and fashioned a paper hat which he placed upon Ned's head.

"You're now a pressman," said Leo the pressman.

"You mean because I pressed a button?" asked Ned.

The production people smiled and joked and congratulated Ned on his birthday. Some applauded; others slapped him on his back.

"That was unbelievably great," Ned said as he climbed down the steps and hugged Jan. He had to raise his voice to be heard above the thrumming of the presses.

Jan thanked the production staff. They smiled and went back to work.

Back in the car on the way back to Little San Simeon Ned could not get over his birthday present. It was after four o'clock in the morning but Ned was still overwhelmed and not a bit tired. Neither was Jan, so they went to a diner for pie and coffee.

"I'd have to say that that was the best birthday I've ever had. How did you know?"

"What used to be your best birthday; I mean, the one that just got bumped down to number two?"

Without hesitating Ned said, "When I was five my mother was out shopping and ran into the mother of one of my neighborhood friends. The woman showed my mother a shirt that was in her basket and asked my mother whether it would fit me and whether I'd like it. My mother said, 'it would probably fit, but why are you buying Ned a shirt?' The woman seemed surprised. 'It's for his birthday present.' That's when my mother learned that my older brother had biked all over the neighborhood inviting kids to my birthday party. So, my mother had to scramble and put together a kids' birthday party."

Jan laughed. "So how many kids showed up?"

"Dozens! It was a great party."

"You wouldn't have had a party if not for your brother."

Ned looked wistful. "It's the only thing I've ever been grateful to him for." Then he burst out laughing.

CHAPTER 38

When Jan took the three steps up to Jack Tweedy's little office she found Ryan Mitchell in there with Tweedy. Mitchell was one of the older editors responsible for the Sunday edition. She heard him say "Jack, you don't have to do this" before he noticed she was there. He immediately stopped speaking and looked at Jan with an expression that gave away the fact that she was the subject of the discussion. He gave her the briefest half smile, excused himself and awkwardly left in what seemed like a hurry. Tweedy stood up briefly in courtesy to his new guest. Jan apologized for interrupting his conversation.

Tweedy shook his head dismissing her concern. "Please have a seat. You wanted to talk about the Derby scandal."

"Yes, sir. It seems from what I've read and been told that it was a watershed moment in the nation's history or at least an apt metaphor."

Tweedy smiled. "Allow me to appropriate a title from a Pete Seeger song, 'Wasn't That a Time'. But you probably don't know who Pete Seeger was."

"I certainly do. I grew up singing some of the songs about unions and coal miners that he used to sing."

Tweedy bowed his head in apology. "That's right. You're from Kentucky."

Jan corrected him. "West Virginia."

"Ah, a beautiful state," Tweedy said. "A lot of those Derby winners came from Charleston. It's a lot like Akron in many ways. Charleston used to have some great rib joints. Do they still have that one rib joint, gosh, I don't remember the name of it? I can picture it – a big red sign that said 'So good you won't need your teeth'."

He closed his eyes and tried to conjure the name.

Jan had a feeling that keeping Tweedy on subject might prove challenging.

"I'm sorry, I don't really know Charleston all that well. Timmy Nolen, did you know him? That was the name of the boy who cheated in 1973."

Tweedy seemed to stare off in the distance. Quietly, almost whispering, he said, "Very well." He blinked a few times like someone coming out of a dream state and his voice became stronger. "You have to go back a year before that or even years before that. There had always been cheating. It was unrealistic to expect children to make those racers by themselves. Some kids made them all by themselves, some got help from a parent when they needed it, but some kids never even worked on their cars. That was Timothy Nolen. His uncle, Roger Dunphy, turned the idea of the kid-made car upside down. He hired an engineering professor at Georgia Tech to design a racer and then had it manufactured by a company that had contract work with NASA. And to make doubly sure he'd win he installed that electromagnet device. When I say 'he'd win' I mean it – it had nothing to do with his own son or his nephew. It was all about him pulling one over on everyone else; showing how smart he was."

"His own son won the year before."

Tweedy said, "Right. Same racer, different year. After Roger Jr. won in 1973 Roger Sr. had the car shipped back to Colorado before anyone had a chance to really look at it. With a new paint job and a new driver Dunphy won the next year."

"Who was this Dunphy?"

"A rich, arrogant engineer who made a fortune coming up with the first plastic ski boots."

Jan asked Tweedy his impressions of the scandal.

"To me it was about an unhappy boy. I was a twenty-six-year-old reporter, so I may have been twice as old as Timothy but I still wasn't all that much older."

Jan asked, "Could you tell he was cheating, I mean, without looking inside the racer?"

"Certainly. Way back then when the Derby was a big event the Sentinel put every available reporter and stringer on it. The women who wrote the Living Section wrote articles about the kids' racing uniforms and about the food served at Camp Derby. I remember writing a sidebar story about one kid who sprained his ankle horsing around at Derby camp. I interviewed the kid and interviewed the Derby doctor and wrote about sprained ankles. I asked the doctor whether he could offer a long-range prognosis. I was being facetious, mind you, and the doctor said, 'He won't race this year, but I'm confident he should be able to race a year from now.' I reported this news with the same seriousness I might've used reporting the outbreak of World War III. It was madness. A sprain!" Tweedy laughed.

Jan steered him back to her question.

"But that's my point," Tweedy said, "there we were all of these talented reporters rooting around for any story. We watched what was taking place and listened to rumors. We knew there was a lot of grumbling in the crowd and among the other racers and their parents about Timothy Nolen's racer. His times in the heats got slower instead of faster. Tires get hotter the more times they get used and the hotter a tire is the more air is in it and the easier it rolls. Timothy's times should have gotten better, instead they got worse."

"Meaning?"

"Meaning he had to be using an electromagnet that was draining power with each run."

"I've read that the magnet gave him an advantage at the starting gate."

Tweedy affirmed this. "We could see it, the way the racer nudged up against the metal starting gate. When the gate lowered the racer was already in motion."

Jan said, "I'm not sure I visualize is properly. Mr. Tweedy, would you go with me to Derby Downs and show me the starting gate so I can see how it was?" She knew this was asking a lot; but she couldn't know just how much. Tweedy sat silently in his chair, biting his lower lip.

Jan sensed his reluctance. "I'm sorry, I shouldn't have asked."

Tweedy responded, "No, no, perfectly all right. Let's go. Unless you've got an assignment."

Jan said, "I'll ask Pell, but I don't think so." Jan stood up, excused herself and walked over to Pell Newcomb's desk. They consulted briefly. Jan returned.

"I'm good," she said. "Just let me get my bag. How about if I meet you in the parking lot. My car is the old Ford Taurus. It's beige…and blue…and off-blue…and sort of greenish. We call it Joseph."

"I had a Great Uncle Joseph. Went down on the Lusitania."

"Be just a minute." Jan went to gather her coat and bag.

It was a cold mid-fall day. When Tweedy emerged from the Sentinel-Herald building he wasn't wearing a coat. Jan had been waiting for him by her car. When she saw him coatless she went over to him and scolded him. "You need a coat, really."

Tweedy shook his head.

"Look," Jan said, "you need a coat. Get inside the car; I'll get your coat. It's in your office, right?"

Tweedy nodded and followed her instructions. She returned with his coat and placed it on his lap.

"You know where Derby Downs is?" Tweedy asked.

"I think so."

Jan left the lot and drove to Derby Downs, a ride of about twenty minutes. She parked in the lot next to the University of Akron's football stadium adjacent to the famous Goodyear Air Dock where generations of Goodyear blimps were built and hangared. They walked up the inclined track of Derby Downs. Tweedy pointed out the level part of the course near the starting gate. The entire raceway was only sixteen-hundred feet long and only wide enough for three of the little racers.

"You see, ordinarily a racer just sits at the top of the hill. Timothy's racer sort of crept up to the metal starting plate and then lurched forward when the starting gate dropped. You see here" – Tweedy leaned over and pointed the spot out to Jan – "this is where the plate folds down when the race starts.".

"In one of my articles I wrote..." and here Tweedy used his hands to draw air sentences... "Timmy Nolen's racer 'kissed' that plate but it was an unchaste kiss which led, like so many kisses of its nature, to cheating."

"Hey, that was good writing" said Jan smiling.

"That was darned good," Tweedy said proudly. "Let's walk down past the grandstands and the administration building. Tweedy walked slowly pointing out the administration building built during the Depression as a Works Progress Administration project. It was made of cement with the architectural detailing typical of 1930s era post offices. By the time they reached the bottom of the hill Tweedy was winded. He asked Jan if she'd mind if he sat down for a spell. He sat on a bench near the grandstands. The clouds above were darkening. Jan joined him on the bench.

"Over there in that pedestrian tunnel under the grandstand was where I found Timothy after they announced that he was being stripped of the title. He was staying at the Mayflower Hotel then, because Camp Derby had closed and all the kids had already left. He was in his aunt and uncle's suite at the hotel and the news was on television. Walter Cronkite announced, 'Well, ladies and gentlemen, there's one little boy in America unhappier than Richard Nixon this evening and it's little Timmy Nolen who cheated in the Soap Box Derby.'"

"Nixon was stonewalling the Watergate hearings at the time."

"Right. Timothy left the hotel and came here. It was empty, real quiet, still hadn't been cleaned up from the Derby. Timothy had taken off that gold jacket, balled it up and had thrown it in that trash bin." He pointed at a trash receptacle.

Jan asked, "Why were you here?"

"No reason. I had come here just to walk around, clear my head and try to figure out the meaning of life. I used to walk here in the evenings because it was usually empty. Anyway, I heard sobbing echoing from that tunnel. At first I thought maybe it was an injured animal. The tunnel was dark, so I was a little afraid to go in. When I did I could make out Timothy huddled in the corner. I knew who he was. I'd seen him at the races, at the Awards Banquet, and on television. I hadn't interviewed him - the sports guys did that. I was general assignment at the time, remember, but for the Derby it was all hands on deck. Even copy boys covered the Derby."

"I went up to the boy and said, "Timmy, I'm Jack Tweedy. I'm with the Sentinel. Are you all right? Can I help you?"

"No," Timmy sobbed

"Well, you can't stay here," I said. "I took off my jacket, lay it down on the cement floor and sat on it with my back against the tunnel wall next to the boy."

"Why not? Is it your tunnel?"

"No, if it were mine I'd jazz it up a little. Some paint, maybe put up an Escher poster."

Lame humor didn't work. Timmy continued to sob and repeat "Leave me alone."

"What was I to do?"

Tweedy couldn't just leave the kid there. After pacing around in the tunnel about ten minutes or so Tweedy offered to take the kid to his apartment. "We'll have dinner and you can figure out what you want to do."

"You won't tell my uncle?"

"No," said Tweedy.

"Swear?"

After Tweedy swore, Timmy agreed to go. Tweedy pulled the boy up to his feet and they walked to Tweedy's car. Tweedy knew the biographical facts about Timmy's life: his father was dead and his mother was hospitalized with a serious illness at the Mayo Clinic. Timmy was living with his Aunt Vivie and her husband Roger Dunphy in Aspen. Their son, Roger Jr., had been the winner of the Derby the previous year. Roger Junior hadn't been interested in making the trip to Akron.

"Do regular people live in Aspen?" asked Tweedy, just to make conversation as they walked to his car.

"Regular rich people," said Timmy.

They got to Tweedy's car and motored to his apartment, a duplex in a slightly seedy part of town. It needed painting. There were a lot of similar wooden two-story houses built in the early part of the century. Tweedy parked on the side of the house and led Timmy up the worn wooden steps into his apartment which was sloppy since Tweedy hadn't expected company.

"Make yourself comfortable," he said, motioning to some worn out furniture. Timmy flopped down on a divan.

"This place is pretty crummy," said Timmy.

Tweedy turned on the television. He figured the sound of the television would mask the telephone call he intended to make from his bedroom.

He dialed the Sentinel and asked for Tom Higgins, the managing editor. He was told Higgins had left but would probably be returning later. Tweedy thought for a minute and asked whether Sam Gibbons, the local news editor was still there. He was. Tweedy explained the situation.

"He says he won't go back to his aunt and uncle. They're staying at the Mayflower. Any ideas?"

"They're his legal guardians, I think. We'll have to talk to them. Where's he now?"

"In the living room watching TV."

"That might not be such a good idea. Roger Dunphy decided to hold a press conference. Tom Higgins and Ryan Mitchell are covering it. It's called for 7:30."

Tweedy looked at his watch – 7:35 pm.

"Look, as soon as I can I'll talk to Tom," Gibbons said. "We'll talk to the Dunphys and figure something out. In the meantime, keep the kid entertained and fed."

"Right."

Tweedy hung down the phone and entered the living room. The press conference was taking place. Timmy was rapt. Tweedy walked toward the television intending to turn it off but stopped near the television and watched. In the same room where the awards ceremony had been held two days earlier Roger Dunphy was standing at a lectern placed on a table facing a couple dozen reporters and as many photographers. He was wearing a powder blue leisure suit with contrasting stitching and – for the benefit of ladies everywhere – an open wide-collared shirt allowing full display of the gold medallion around his neck and his manly chest. Because the lectern hid his feet it was hard to tell whether he was wearing what used to be called 'The Full Cleveland'; that is, white patent leather belt and white patent leather shoes. (Incidentally, in Cleveland that ensemble was known as 'The Full Akron'.)

"Timmy, the only appropriate place for men to display gold medals around their neck is the victory stand at the Olympics," said Tweedy.

Before the microphones were turned on one member of the press turned to another. "This Dunphy reminds me of that young guy on the Lawrence Welk Show. You know, the one with the big head and all those teeth who dances."

"Dancing teeth? Oh, right, I know who you're thinking of: the one who was a Mouseketeer. I think his name is Bobby," reported the other.

So much for in-depth reporting from members of the third estate.

The hotel had added twenty additional phone lines for the legion of reporters from all over the country covering this event. Apart from the reporters there were about two dozen people in the audience that Tweedy could recognize - some local officials and many Derby folk. Tweedy noticed that Dunphy's wife was not in the room.

Dunphy tapped a microphone to make sure it was working then said as part of his prepared statement, "The device was built for the car by Timmy, but entirely at my suggestion." This statement triggered an immediate explosive response within the room. Cameras and flashes went off and the reporters began yelling questions. Most of them were "You're blaming Timmy for putting the magnet in the racer?"

Tweedy had always enjoyed the sounds a salvo of clicking cameras made and the whine strobe flashes made, but not now. He remained standing transfixed by the spectacle of a man fixing blame on a thirteen-year-old boy.

Dunphy went on to say that he hadn't originated the idea of a magnetic nose, that it had been used plenty of times in the past. "I wouldn't have used it, but I thought it was important for Timmy to win. He lost his father and his mother is gravely ill. This is something he needed. And, look, cheating has been going on since the beginning. Cheating is as American as apple pie."

This statement caused a furor. Suddenly, a small man standing in back in a group of Derby people rushed forward screaming "Liar!", made his way around the table, tripped over some microphone cables, and grabbed Dunphy by the big wide lapels. He fell, pulling Dunphy down with him. It was Dickie Yount, the man who called himself 'Mr. Derby'. Yount wrestled with Dunphy until the security staff for the Mayflower pulled him off Dunphy and hustled him out of the room. Yount continued to scream, "Liar!" as he was dragged out attended by a lot of head shaking from the press. Yount's official Derby shirt had been torn in the encounter and he was limping as he was forced out of the room.

The members of the local media recognized Dickie Yount, but reporters from outside Akron had to wonder who was being dragged out of the ballroom.

"Any idea who that nut is?" a national reporter asked a local.

"That's Mr. Derby," replied a local. He grinned.

Dunphy smoothed his hair and straightened his shoulders. He regained some of his smug composure, but the sound equipment was all askew and the members of the press had heard about as much as they needed to write their stories. The television cameras had recorded as much tape as they needed for the eleven o'clock news.

"Obviously some kind of a nut," said Dunphy, trying to put his own twist on the grappling match. He said this to the backs of the attendees leaving the room.

Tweedy, still standing in front of the television, turned to Timmy. He didn't know what to say.

The Chief of Police of Akron stood watching the televised press conference in the City Attorney's office. The City Attorney, usually jovial, was frowning.

"That man is a disgrace. We've got to get him on some charge or other."

The Chief of Police, usually dour, smiled. "Yes, we do. Dickie is making Akron look ridiculous."

"I'm talking about Dunphy," the City Attorney responded.

"Oh, yeah, him, too."

It had gotten dark at Derby Downs.

"Mr. Tweedy? I think it's time we got back, don't you think?" said Jan.

Tweedy smiled at Jan and agreed. They could pick up the story later. They made their way back to Jan's car and drove to the Sentinel-Herald building. Jan thanked Tweedy and stayed in the parking lot until Tweedy was safely in his car and on the road.

CHAPTER 39

"God Is My Assignment Editor." read the sign that Jan posted on the bulletin board at her desk. It was the credo of Richard Pearson, the late dean of the Washington Post obituary writers. Jan liked it – it made her feel privileged to be a writer of obituaries, a writer of peoples' lives. At that moment she was working on the obituary of a man named Richard Whittaker, a remarkable man and a barber by trade. One day in the 1980s Mr. Whittaker was in his barber shop listening to the news on the radio when he learned about the alarming percentage of Black men with dangerously high blood pressure. One of the problems, the reporter said, was that Black men fail to get their blood pressure taken. A simple enough, painless procedure, so how to explain this delinquency? The reporter chalked it up to simple stubbornness on men's part. Mr. Whittaker thought to himself, *Is there possibly a less stressful environment than a barbershop? No. What if there were someone at the barbershop ready to check anyone's blood pressure?* So, he contacted the Red Cross which agreed to send a nurse out twice a week. The Red Cross nurse found that men were more comfortable getting their blood pressure checked for free at the barbershop than anywhere else in the community. Men who proved to have high blood pressure received health information and referrals if requested. Word got out and other barbershops in Akron wanted to offer the same service. The Red Cross was happy to avail and began training barbers to measure blood pressure. And so with his little idea Mr. Whittaker probably saved dozens of lives from unnecessarily early deaths.

Jan had just gotten a couple of good quotes about Mr. Whittaker from his friends when Pell Newcomb came to her desk to chat. He claimed he was happy with the progress she was making and had an idea.

"Jan, I'd like you to write your own obituary. Call it your fauxbituary, if you'd like."

Jan resisted frowning. "Write my own obituary? That's a little – I don't know – gruesome?" she said. "Do you know something my doctor isn't telling me?"

Pell laughed. "No, I just think it's a good exercise."

"Well, I know exercise is good for you. Okay, is there a deadline, so to speak?"

Pell shook his head. "No, no deadline." He paused. "There's something else. You've been talking to Jack Tweedy about the Derby cheating scandal."

"Yes."

"I want you to know — that was a difficult time for Jack."

"He's been great. Very helpful."

"Yes, but…" Newcomb wasn't sure Jan was getting the point. "Look, just be careful. Jerry Murphy asked me to tell you not to push Tweedy to talk about things he might not want to talk about, okay?"

Jan vowed to be respectful of Tweedy's feelings.

Newcomb smiled. "I look forward to reading your obituary." As he walked away from Jan's desk he turned his head back and said, "I don't get to say that often enough."

CHAPTER 40

That evening Ned drove to Little San Simeon to pick Jan up for the hospital mixer. Jan was a little nervous. She had never met any of the people Ned worked with, though he had told her plenty of stories about them. When she came out of her bedroom she asked him if her dress was all right. He smiled. "Of course it is."

She thought, *Good, because I went through every dress in my closet before I picked this one.*

As Ned drove Jan told him about the practice assignment Pell had handed her.

Ned was thoughtful. "It would probably be a good idea for all of us to write our own obituaries a number of different ways: we'd write one the way we hope people will think of us, and the second the way we see ourselves. And then one that describes us the way we really are."

"Only God sees us as we really are. And he's the one whose judgment matters."

"If we let Him into our hearts He'll set us in the proper direction," Ned added simply.

When they reached the Hospital Ned parked the car, opened the door for Jan and held her hand as he escorted her into the building. Mercy General Hospital was a maze of buildings in different architectural styles. The original building was easy to identify. It was brick and limestone with large white columns centered at the front entrance. Ned steered Jan into that building, through hallways, up an elevator and across an enclosed bridge into another building towards a large function room from which emanated the sound of a crowd and music. Entering and making their way in the room, Ned conducted a quick surveillance of the room. A lot of people were wearing white lab coats, though none were wearing stethoscopes around their necks the way they do in television commercials. That probably meant that they were real doctors stealing time from their duties to come grab some food. There was a jazz quartet playing and a couple of tables with food, drink and floral arrangements which were leftovers from the first-floor gift shop's flower refrigerator. Ned spotted some friendly colleagues waving to him so he led Jan to their table. He introduced her.

"Jan Pancake, this is Skiggs and Nina Brooks and Elliott Entis, and Arnold Lentini and his wife Mildred, and Tony Bachelder and Barry Thomas. They're all doing residencies or internships."

They exchanged greetings. Ned asked whether he and Jan could sit at their table. Once permission had been granted Ned and Jan took their coats off and wrapped them around the backs of the two chairs they had claimed.

"I'm hungry. How's the food?" asked Ned.

Pretty good was the consensus, so Ned and Jan went to fill up. When they returned to the table they plunged into the conversation.

Skiggs asked Jan, "Did Ned say your name is Jan Pancake?"

Jan steeled herself for some stupid remark about her last name. Didn't they know that Pancake was not an uncommon name in West Virginia? "Yes," she answered.

Skiggs was excited. "You wrote the obituary for my aunt, Flo McCauley. Gosh, that was a good obituary. It made everyone in the family feel so good. Thank you."

Jan was gratified. "She must've been a wonderful lady."

"Yes, and it's true: she could remove any stain each and every time. It was amazing. Even blood."

Brooks said she had read it, too, and thought it was great.

Skiggs said, "It's funny. You made us feel better than the minister did. Reading your obituary was almost cathartic. That must be very gratifying for you."

"It is." Jan was eating it up. She was a celebrity!

The conversation and eating continued, then Elliott Entis asked Jan if she wanted to dance. There were a few couples dancing. Jan turned to Ned as though asking for his permission. Ned smiled and gave a palm up. She and Entis danced then returned to the table. Jan took a swig from her soft drink and asked where everyone came from.

Brooks was from Arizona. Skiggs was local. Arnold and Mildred were from Virginia Beach. Elliott was from Upstate New York.

"How did you end up working in a hospital in Akron?" Jan asked them all.

Skiggs raised one eyebrow and smiled. "Julia."

"Ah, yes, Julia," said Bachelder. "What about you Elliott?"

Elliott pretended not to immediately remember this Julia person but slowly the memory came back. "Oh, yes, now I remember – Julia. Was that her name?" He explained to Jan, "She was the woman who escorted me around when I came for my interviews."

Jan asked, "Who is Julia?"

Skiggs, Bachelder, Thomas and Elliott looked back and forth at one another. Elliott grinned and answered, "You know, she picked me up at the airport, got me settled at the hotel…"

Skiggs snickered.

"…had meals with me when I didn't have appointments to eat with staff, that sort of thing. She was, umm, very nice."

Elliott volunteered, "After I decided on Mercy Hospital and moved here I went to administration to look her up. They said she wasn't here any longer."

Barry Thomas offered, "I had her." His face reddened as he realized how that sounded. He added, "I mean, as my escort. Very nice gal."

Entis turned to Jan. "How about another dance, Jan?"

Jan was interested in the conversation that was taking place but she smiled and went to dance with Elliott Entis. Elliott thought of himself as a dashing figure, a real ladies' man. He was not an especially good dancer.

While they were dancing, Jan asked "This Julia person. I get the sense that …Let me just ask: were you intimate with her?"

Brooks laughed, "Women find me irresistible."

"I take that as a 'yes'. What about the other guys?"

"You'd have to ask them."

When the dance was over they returned to the table.

Ned had some news it pained him to share with Jan. "Jan, I'm so sorry, Skiggs just told me that the rotations have been posted. I'm pulling the days around Thanksgiving. I can't go to your folks for Thanksgiving. What about the week after that?"

Jan was crestfallen. I don't want to go back home by myself. I'll stay here for Thanksgiving with you."

Ned said, "No, you should go."

Jan said that they could talk about it later. She was quiet for a moment then asked Arnold Lentini whether Julia had been his escort when he came to Mercy for his interview.

"No, they assigned someone from Pediatrics, a fellow named Sterns. Nice guy."

"Same here," said Nina Brooks.

Jan nodded. "Hmm," she said.

On their way back to Jan's house Jan was dispirited. Ned sensed her unease and opened a conversation saying, "About Thanksgiving – our church has a big community Thanksgiving dinner. I helped out last year. It's for anyone who doesn't have another place to go. Mostly homeless. The church members do everything. I know it's not like going home for Thanksgiving, but…"

Jan broke in, "That sounds nice. I'm sorry if I'm being grumpy. It's this Julia business." She turned to face Ned. "Ned, you didn't say whether Julia was your escort, too?"

Not turning his eyes from the road, Ned answered, "Yes."

Hesitantly, Jan asked, "Were you intimate with her?"

"Ned smiled and turned his head to face her. "No, I wasn't."

Jan closed her eyes and exhaled audibly.

Ned explained. "I had the feeling she was available, she gave me lots of hints, but I think she got the idea I wasn't interested."

"Were you?"

"No." He smiled. "Christian values or something."

They arrived at Little San Simeon. It was late and both of them had to be at work early the next day. Jan kissed Ned goodnight and said, "This was a very interesting evening."

She opened the car door and climbed out. Ned drove away.

CHAPTER 41

"Cut down in the prime of her tragically short life, Janice Pancake was one of America's most promising young journalists."

Naw, thought Jan, *I can do better than that.*

"Life was a little murky for the Sentinel-Herald intern, but things had recently taken a very positive turn as young Jan Pancake recently found a wonderful boyfriend. But in the end it was too much ambition that was the undoing of Jan Pancake."

Naw, that's nobody's business but mine. Darn, writing your own obituary is hard. When you're young you've got fewer stories to pick from.

Naw, that's just an excuse.

Composing her obituary would have to wait. She had arranged to meet with Mr. Tweedy in a few minutes. As she walked across the newsroom Jan wished she had baked something for Tweedy. Blueberry muffins would be simple. That might me him happy, or at least happier.

In Tweedy's office they picked up their conversation.

"Where were we?" asked Tweedy.

"Timmy didn't want to go back to his aunt and uncle." Jan said.

"Right. Back to the story. Tom Higgins, the Managing Editor and Sam Gibbons, the Local News Editor, had talked with Dunphy and his wife. The one thing that was clear was that Timothy didn't want to be with them. Every time I'd ask him what he wanted he gave me the same answer:

'I want to be with my mother.'

"Eventually I got a telephone call from Higgins."

"'Jack, do you remember the movie It Happened One Night, with Clark Gable and Claudette Colbert?'"

"Yes," I answered.

"'Clark Gable happens upon Colbert who, naturally, is an heiress. She's run away from home and doesn't want to be discovered. Gable, wouldn't you know it, is a newsman and recognizes her. And, of course, the world wants to know her whereabouts and why she ran away. So Gable sticks with her for the sake of the scoop and naturally they fall in love during the course of the road trip.'"

Tweedy had never chit-chatted with Higgins about movies before; he was wary.

"We were thinking, Sam and I, that you could take the kid to the Mayo Clinic to be with his mom and you could file stories about the trip as you go."

"Take him, like on an airplane?" Tweedy asked. He really hoped the answer was 'yes'.

"No, by car; by Sentinel van to be specific."

Tweedy said, "That's the movies, Mr. Higgins. Not real life."

Higgins was undeterred. "Okay, another example. How about Roman Holiday, with Audrey Hepburn and Gregory Peck? Same story. There's got to be something to it if I can name two movies with that plot right off the top of my head."

Tweedy said, "I've read that there are only seven distinct plots in Hollywood. So it's only natural..."

Higgins interrupted. "Look, let the kid stay at your place tonight. Come to the office tomorrow. We'll go over the details." Higgins hung up the phone.

Tweedy hung down his end of the line and paused to think of the situation he was in. *This isn't the fish out of water plot, so which one is it?* he asked himself. *Why can't it be the one where I'm in Rome with Audrey Hepburn?*

Cause that's the movies, silly.

Entering the living room, he explained the situation to Timmy and told him that he'd have to spend the night Chez Tweedy. Since the apartment had one bedroom Tweedy moved his bedding into the living room and made up the bed in the bedroom with semi-fresh sheets for Timmy. Then he gave Timmy a choice: macaroni and cheese or cheese and macaroni.

Just like in It Happened One Night Tweedy mumbled to himself as he spooned out the macaroni and cheese. *Only instead of a beautiful heiress I'm stuck with a depressed kid who picks at his fingers.*

After dinner they settled down to a little television. The first item on the local television news that evening was about the fight that occurred at a hotel restaurant/lounge caused by a couple of patrons who recognized Roger Dunphy sitting at the bar. Dunphy sustained some minor bruises and a cut over the eye. The assailants fled. Police could not find any patrons able to identify the two.

Timmy sat forward on the couch with his elbows on his knee, his hands cupping his chin.

Tweedy could only wonder what Timmy's thoughts were that evening.

The next morning Tweedy and Timmy made their appointment with Higgins, the Managing Editor, and Gibbons, the Local News Editor. Timmy drew stares and whispers as he and Tweedy made their way across a newsroom that was noisy with the sound of keyboards and shouts of "Copy!" In the Managing Editor's conference room Higgins and Gibbons sat them down and outlined their plan. Tweedy would drive Timmy to see his mother in Rochester, Minnesota and look after him. After a few days he would put him on a plane to Delaware to be with his Aunt Sarah and Uncle Bill.

Gibbons turned to Timmy. "We've spoken to both of your aunts and uncles. What do you think about this?"

Timmy sat and said quietly, "Okay."

Tweedy spoke up. "Sir, I don't think it will look right – I mean, an adult male and a pubescent teen driving practically across the country. Isn't there something called the Mann Act? Or maybe it's the Man and Boy Act. I don't know. Do you see what I'm talking about?"

When Tweedy was flustered he resorted to gibbering.

Higgins had an answer. "Of course we've thought of that, so we have a chaperone picked out to go with you. One who can take photographs to accompany the articles you file. You know Click Gunderson."

Tweedy indeed knew Marjorie "Click" Gunderson; had a crush on her, in fact. A year ago he'd asked her out and been rejected.

He recalled her saying, "Jack, you're a nice guy, but I'm not going to date a guy with a gambling problem. A gambling problem is a sure marker for other problems."

Tweedy wasn't sure whether Click was being ironic when she used the gambler's term 'marker' in her observation and wasn't about to ask. He never asked her out again but he maintained the crush.

Tweedy brought up another issue. "How will Click get the pictures back to here from wherever we are?"

Gibbons had an answer. "Easy. You'll stop at local newspapers along the way that have those new United Press machines. We just got one. It takes eight or nine minutes to send a photograph over a telephone line. I'm sure Click knows how to use it."

"Model 16S," said Higgins so that everyone would know he was up on the latest technology.

"I put in for vacation for next week," Tweedy complained.

Higgins and Gibbons glared at Tweedy.

Do you like newspapering, Tweedy?" asked Gibbons?

"Well, yes, sir, I do. What does Click think?"

Higgins fielded this question. "She's excited to do this."

"It means a bump in pay for you," Higgins said. He didn't appear to be all that thrilled to make this offer.

Tweedy puffed up his cheeks and blew out. "Okay."

"It's settled. And, believe me, this is going to sell newspapers. The kid's a celebrity."

Tweedy asked Jan whether she'd seen any photos of the news van they used on the trip. Jan hadn't, so they took the stairs to the mezzanine to the morgue. Tweedy knew the dates so he located the drawer and withdrew the right folders. He laid the pages on the table and pointed to a couple of photos from 1973 that showed a young Tweedy, Click Gunderson and Timmy Nolen in front of a large van with the Sentinel's logo painted on the side. (sidebar: The Sentinel didn't merge with the Akron Herald until 1997.) They stood at the table and examined the photos.

Without thinking Jan exclaimed, "Look how young you were!" Her face flushed and she quickly apologized. "I'm sorry."

Tweedy said, "Nothing to apologize for. You don't hear me apologizing for once having been young, do you?"

Tweedy looked so youthful in the photos. He had extremely long sideburns. Click wore a pantsuit and clunky shoes.

Jan pointed to the young woman in the photo. She was tall and had her blond curly hair pulled back in a ponytail. "This is Click? She was pretty."

Tweedy nodded.

"And Timmy. He was a nice looking boy."

In one of the archive folders in the clipping file was the official Derby program for 1973 which was printed by the Sentinel. According to the Derby biography "Thirteen-year-old Timmy, who is called 'Big Tim' by his friends, is 4-feet, 11-inches tall and weighs 68 pounds. He has blond hair." At the time the photo was taken Tim had braces on his teeth.

Tweedy said, "The Derby biography said Timothy's nickname was 'Big Tim'. Roger Dunphy called him 'Ellie Mae' because he liked being around critters – dogs, cats, rabbits, any kind of animal. You know, the Beverly Hillbillies? Timothy probably liked being around animals more than he liked being around people."

"That's sad," said Jan

Pointing to the photo of the van Tweedy said, "It had seats for six and a darkroom set up in the back."

Jan asked, "I still don't see why the Dunphys would agree to this. They were Timmy's legal guardians. Why wouldn't they take Timmy to see his mother? She was dying, correct?"

"After that press conference Timmy refused to have anything to do with Roger Dunphy. And Roger Dunphy kept his distance from Timothy. Timothy didn't feel the same way about Vivie Dunphy. He liked her.

"Higgins and Gibbons decided that we'd leave for Rochester two days later, Thursday. I took Wednesday off, went home and packed. The Dunphys sent Timothy's stuff over from the hotel. Wednesday night we had pizza delivered. Higgins had told us to show up at six a.m. Thursday. He was really afraid that news might leak out that we had Timothy. The Herald would've sent over reporters and a cameraman. You see, there was such hoopla over the missing boy cheater. The Herald was the rival paper then; it had a banner headline "Where is Timmy?" The Dunphys weren't talking and the Sentinel news staff was sworn to secrecy. It was a nutty time what with Watergate and that Arab oil embargo. There were all sorts of cults – Moonies, Scientologists and Hare Krishnas, you name it. There was a popular radio talk show host named Meader Braun who speculated that Timmy had been abducted by one of the cults."

Jan asked, "Cults? Really?"

"Oh, yeah. You couldn't go to the airport without running into Hare Krishnas with shaved heads and orange robes chanting and begging for money. Then there was the Baader-Meinhof Gang blowing things up in Europe. The Anarchists' Cookbook, which taught readers how to manufacture bombs, was a bestseller. But here in Akron the talk was all about the big cheating scandal and 'Where Is Timmy?' The Herald ran a poll – turned out Roger Dunphy was the most hated man in America, followed by Richard Nixon." Tweedy shook his head and chuckled. "Attorney General John Mitchell was a distant third. Crazy times."

Tweedy looked at Jan.

"You know something? My long-term memory must be better than I thought. Not too many people remember John and Martha Mitchell." He paused. "It's this short-term memory that's proving so difficult. I lose my keys so often I have a locksmith on speed dial." Then he returned to his story.

"I remember Thursday was a warm day — it was August, remember — and sunny. Click was in the side lot waiting along with Higgins and Gibbons and Clark Russell, a reporter. She'd already loaded her equipment and things in the van. Timothy and I pulled in. I introduced Timothy to Click.

"Hi," Timmy said.

"Hi," said Click.

"*This could be a long trip*, I thought. We piled our own stuff in the van. The van had plenty of room. Then we posed for photos — these photos." Tweedy pointed to the old newspaper. "Higgins gave me a company credit card and cash, which I had to sign for. I learned later that the paper's lawyers had drawn up some insurance papers that Dunphy signed. They gave us a whole bunch of Triple A maps. Clark Russell was there to cover the event. We gave him a few good quotes. At the time I thought to myself, *Well, I'm now part of an event.* And so we drove off."

Jan said, "Just like that. Who drove?"

"I drove the first leg. I remember calling out through the window 'Next stop, Havana.' I thought that was cute. At the time lots of planes were being skyjacked and diverted to Cuba."

Tweedy seemed to find this a natural point to pause his narrative. Jan said, "I'll put these folders away." Tweedy turned away from the table and began to walk towards the door. While gathering the folders, Jan had an idea.

"Mr. Tweedy, my boyfriend Ned and I are going to be helping out at the community Thanksgiving dinner at our church. If you aren't doing anything Thanksgiving we'd really love to have you."

Tweedy smiled. "I usually spent Thanksgiving at Jerry Murphy's, but maybe... How about if I let you know tomorrow?"

"That would be great. It's Calvary Baptist Church on Maple. Do you know it?"

"Very well," said Tweedy.

When Jan got home she called Myrt. The call went to voicemail. Jan left a message.

"Myrt, if you're not going home for Thanksgiving you are welcome to stay with me. Ned and I and maybe Jack Tweedy are going to work at our church — that is, Ned and I; I don't know about Mr. Tweedy. He seems so lonely. Anyway, there's going to be a community Thanksgiving and we're going to help. You'll help, too, if you come. And invite my brother. He's big and strong and he can probably lift turkeys in both hands. So, come. Let me know, okay?"

The next day Myrt called and said she'd come with Josiah. And Jack Tweedy said he'd come.

Jan called Ned. "Ned, I am so smart! I'm having Jack Tweedy and Myrt and my brother here for Thanksgiving and I'm not going to have to do any cooking!"

Or so she thought.

CHAPTER 42

Jan wiped the back of her hand across her sweaty forehead. Even using an electric mixer it was hard work making massive amounts of mashed potato. Her muscles ached from lifting and moving around the large stainless steel pans. But she couldn't complain. Ned, Myrt and Josiah were working just as hard. Tweedy was doing his part, too, setting the tables and fetching things for the cooks. The doors to the fellowship hall would open to the community at four o'clock. It was two-thirty now and there was a sizeable crowd already milling around outside. When Josiah went outside to take a break he eavesdropped on the conversation of a number of the millers. A lot of them had very strong feelings on current political events and the domestic policies of the current administration. Given that many of them appeared to be street people Josiah was surprised that they were so well informed on current events. Tweedy was able to provide an explanation for this: the homeless are big users of the resources of the public library, especially the bathrooms and the computers. They're always on the internet."

Jan said, "Being homeless only means you're experiencing homelessness. It doesn't mean you're not socially aware and involved and a good citizen. Right, Mr. Tweedy?"

Tweedy gave a noncommittal bob of the head.

Josiah asked, "Can homeless people vote if they don't have a home address?"

Jan didn't know. Neither did Myrt or Ned. Tweedy did: "The homeless absolutely have the right to vote, but there are obstacles that don't make it easy, take my word for it."

Jan said, "Maybe I should do a story for the paper on that."

Tweedy thought that was a good idea

"Are you okay, Mr. Tweedy?"

Tweedy nodded and smiled. "I'm fine, dear girl, thank you."

"I'm glad you were able to come."

Tweedy said, "I used to come here regularly many years ago. In fact, this very room."

"Oh?" said Jan.

"The odd AA meeting. And Gamblers Anonymous."

Tweedy relieved her of the need to say anything by turning back to his task of filling pitchers full of water.

There were a good number of church members pitching in for this Thanksgiving dinner. Turkeys had been dropped off by members for weeks before. It was one of the church's major outreach programs and had been staged yearly, so the planners made sure the dinner went off without a hitch.

"If only our lives were as well organized as this dinner," said Myrt.

Jan asked, "Are you referring to something personal, Myrt?"

Myrt smiled and shook her head.

"Oh, I don't know. I'm a little conflicted, yes."

"Would this be about Josiah, and if so, is it something you think it wise to discuss with his sister?" It occurred to Jan that her interviewing skills had been sharpened by months of working for the paper.

"Maybe we can talk about it…soon," said Myrt. "I hope you don't still think we went behind your back."

Jan smiled and shook her head.

"Good," said Myrt. "I want you to know something. I'm crazy about him."

Crazy about my brother, Josiah? What do you know! thought Jan. *That's nuts!*

"We're four bars working on five," said Myrt.

"Meaning what?" asked Jan.

"Meaning our signal is getting stronger," Myrt replied with a twinkle in her eye.

When four o'clock came around and it was time to open the doors everything was ready. Pastor Burns thanked all the volunteers, told them they were amazing and opened the doors. In an orderly fashion the crowd poured in. It may have been a dinner for the entire community but the crowd seemed to be mostly the homeless community. When they were all seated Pastor Burns thanked everyone for coming. He asked everyone to hold hands. Standing in front of the kitchen Myrt took hold of Josiah's hand, who took the hand of Jan, who took the hand of Ned, who took the hand of Jack Tweedy. Pastor Burns lowered his head and offered a blessing.

"Bless this Thanksgiving meal and all those who are here to share it with us in Jesus' name, Amen." It was a short blessing. He knew people were hungry.

The diners waited patiently as they were called up by table to be served. Jan, Josiah, Myrt and Tweedy stood behind the serving tables dishing out traditional Thanksgiving food. Some of the diners were a little too insistent that they be given large portions.

"Come on, Mike," Tweedy scolded one diner. "If you're still hungry after everyone's been served you can come back for seconds if there's still food left. You know that."

Mike grumbled but accepted Tweedy's ruling. Once everyone was served the serving and cooking staff helped themselves and sat down for dinner. They were exhausted and they felt great. The best part was that the cleanup crew, the church's youth group, was already hard at work.

CHAPTER 43

To a hammer everything looks like a nail. To a reporter everything looks like a story. There was something about what she heard at the Mercy Hospital mixer that struck Jan as odd and worth looking into.

Ned lived in a hospital dormitory and ate most of his meals at the hospital cafeteria. Jan felt sorry when Ned's schedule left him no time to eat anywhere else but the hospital so when she had the chance she would bring a basket lunch or dinner and they would eat in the cafeteria. The Hospital staff eating there would cast jealous looks toward them. Jan had prepared spaghetti and meatballs and salad for this evening's repast.

"Ned, about the way the Hospital recruits interns…"

"Yes?"

"At the table where we sat at the mixer…"

"Yes?" Ned could tell that Jan was leading up to something.

"All the single guys at the table were turned over to this Julia person to escort them while they were in Akron. The married man and the single female had that pediatrician."

"Mike Sterns."

"Right. Doesn't that strike you as fishy?"

Ned chewed on some salad and thought. "What are you thinking?"

"Describe this Julia."

"Well, this Julia, as you refer to her, was very pretty and charming."

Ned had hardly finished his sentence when Jan made her point. "And she made it obvious that she was available for, well, whatever."

Ned tilted his head a bit. "So?"

"So I think maybe the hospital enlisted Julia to make a favorable impression on medical school graduates who have to decide what hospital to select for their internship. By itself that sounds innocent. My question is: why wasn't this Julia enlisted to escort the married man or the woman around?"

Ned sat up a little straighter in his chair and put down his fork. "You're suggesting that the Residency and Internship Program Director hired her to...what?

"To give the guys — let's call it a memorable time. And when it came time to consider hospitals, well, there'd be at least one extremely friendly face they'd remember at Mercy Hospital. That would certainly influence a good number of med students. And give Mercy a bigger pool of candidates to choose from."

"You think Julia was a paid escort? I mean, an escort like on those websites?"

Jan looked across the laminate table at Ned. "It would be easy enough to find out. Someone from the Sentinel-Herald could snoop around."

"Ned put up his traffic cop hand. "Whoa, I don't know about that."

"If you're worried about getting in trouble, they won't have to know that you even know me."

Ned smiled wryly. "Jan, remember that tall guy with the shaved head and the prominent Adam's apple that I introduced you to?"

"Yes."

"That was Phil Abrams, the Residency and Internship Program Director."

"Oh." Jan sat at the table and didn't say anything for a minute. Then she smiled and said, "I'll have to use one of my disguises."

"Jan, no disguises."

"Oh, well, I made bread pudding for dessert. Come on, we'll share it. Grab a spoon."

CHAPTER 44

"I can't believe it! Tim is going with Anna Pavlova?"

Jan was on the telephone a week after Thanksgiving and catching up on campus goings on.

Myrt said, "Can you believe it? He says he gets a kick out of her...literally." Myrt snorted.

Jan said, "Tim is the sort of guy who needs to be with someone. He doesn't do well by himself."

"And get this: she sold the NFT of her dance for two hundred thousand dollars! They're thinking of leaving school and moving to France together."

Myrt now had a single dorm room. Jan could visualize Myrt listening to her eclectic music, sharing her bed with piles of books and a laptop and a bag of potato chips. Ah, good old college days. Did Jan miss them? Not for a second. Well...yes...sometimes.

They talked about Thanksgiving. Myrt and Josiah had enjoyed themselves. While Jan was at work they had spent a day exploring Akron.

"Jan, Josiah really likes Akron. He's talking about moving there."

"How ya gonna keep 'em down on the farm after they've seen Akron?" cracked Jan. "Tish, tosh, it's just talk, I'm sure. He loves farming and he loves West Virginia. Still, after you've finished med school you can get an internship at Mercy Hospital."

"Whoa there, girl, that's a long time from now. Josiah's great but God only knows what the future will bring."

True enough.

Jan went on to tell Myrt about her suspicions about the hospital's internship recruitment program.

"I'm going to interview some other interns. And I spoke to the Local News Editor, Pell Newcomb. He said we can look at the hospital's accounting books without stirring anything up. The Hospital is non-profit so its financials are available online."

"What will you look for?"

"1099s for independent contractor work charged to the Residency and Internship Department. That'll give me Julia's information. Then I can talk to her and then interview the Program Director."

Myrt was impressed. "It's amazing. I'm dealing with all this rinky dink stuff up here on the magic mountain and you're out there in the dirty, corrupt working world doing important things. I am so jealous."

"There's just one thing, Myrt. I'd love to get a scoop and all, but I don't want it to be at the expense of Mercy Hospital."

"First, do no harm," Myrt quoted Hippocrates. "I see your point. Just see where it leads then decide what you want to do."

Myrt could be very wise at times.

They ended the call in their traditional manner, crying out "Luv ya!" in unison.

CHAPTER 45

"Before we pick up where we left off, could I ask you a question, Mr. Tweedy?" Jan was seated in Tweedy's tiny office with a cup of coffee in hand and her tablet on her lap.

"Of course, and I don't see why you don't call me 'Jack' After all, we've shared Thanksgiving dinner together. I thanked you for that, didn't I?"

Jan nodded. "You did, but I'm sorry, I wouldn't feel comfortable calling you anything but Mr. Tweedy."

Tweedy shrugged. The gesture meant *suit yourself.*

Jan got down to business. "As newspaper people we're supposed to report the news, not be the news, right? But this whole thing – taking Timmy to his mother…" She didn't have to complete the sentence.

Tweedy smiled. "I know what you're thinking: We were involving ourselves in the news, participating in it instead of observing and reporting it. To paraphrase the style manual: 'The only time a newspaper uses the first person is on the editorial page, and then it's the first person plural.' Well, you're right. But it was 1973 and the journalism world was turned upside down by what they called 'the new journalism' or 'literary journalism.' Gay Talese, Tom Wolfe, Hunter S. Thompson, Truman Capote – they were all turning journalistic conventions upside down and inserting themselves into the stories. They were exploring and pushing the boundaries of reporting. Some of the rest of us were riding their coattails. And some of us may have been losing our way. By the way, do you need a copy of the AP Style Manual?"

Jan shook her head.

She had learned about the New Journalism in her Reporting Affairs class. She had studied the writing of Gay Talese and others, and admired their work, though she was often shocked by their frequent use of profane language.

"Maybe in the case of Timmy Nolen we were carrying it a bit too far, and as you'll see we suffered the consequences." Tweedy's features sank.

Jan was alarmed. "Mr. Tweedy, are you all right?" She got up from her chair and moved close to where Tweedy had slumped a bit in his chair.

After a minute Tweedy straightened himself in the chair and affected a smile.

"I'm fine," he said.

"Maybe we should try this another day?" asked Jan.

Tweedy shook his head. "No, no." He waited a minute until his head had cleared and resumed his story. As he became immersed in the story his voice gained strength.

"We hit the road and made it as far as Fort Wayne that first day. I drove and Click Gunderson sat on the passenger's side and Timothy had the back bench. The van had an eight-track tape deck and I thought we'd buy some tapes when we found a store. I asked Timothy what kind of music he liked.

"New York Dolls, Bob Marley and the Wailers, The Fugs."

"I'd never heard of those groups. Until we found tapes of groups Timothy liked we'd have to listen to the radio. That was mostly The Carpenters, Led Zeppelin, The Rolling Stones and the Beatles.

"Timmy, we'll camp here in Fort Wayne tonight and tomorrow we're going to my family's farm in Michigan. You'll enjoy that. There'll be a bunch of my relatives your age for you to play with."

"Okay."

"Timothy was the most dispirited kid I'd ever met. I'd planned to go to the family farm that week for my vacation – I went every year, it was a tradition – so it seemed like a good idea. Click could get some shots of Timothy having fun; that is, if we could get him to have fun.

"I found a pay phone and called the Sentinel and spoke to Tom Higgins. He told me that the edition that broke the story that we were taking Timothy home to his mother sold like hotcakes. The photo of the three of us in front of the van made the front page.

"How are you and Click getting along?" Higgins asked.

"Okay. She took a picture of Timmy in front of the Welcome to Fort Wayne sign. We'll wire it to you as soon as I've finished my story."

Higgins said, "Try to get Click in a photo or two if you can. She's photogenic. And stay in touch."

"Yes, sir," I said and hung up. The pay phone was in a W.T. Grants Five and Dime. Timothy was picking out tapes he liked. Click was waiting nearby for me to finish so she could use the phone. To call a boyfriend? Parents? So far, I didn't know much of anything about her.

But she sure was cute. She had a mop of blond hair done up in corkscrews, big brown eyes and a really cute mouth. She was pretty tall and had a nice figure. Yes, indeed, a lovely girl."

Tweedy had closed his eyes as he talked about Click. He gazed over at Jan. "I'm sorry; was talking about Click's figure out of line? You never know these days."

Jan assured him that she wasn't offended.

Tweedy continued. "She usually had a camera slung around her neck on a wide leather strap and wore one of those vests with all the pockets. For film and lenses and such things.

"I watched her chatting on the telephone and tried to figure out who she might be talking to. I could see her laugh a couple of times but I couldn't glean anything from that. I was being silly and I knew it.

"We checked into a Holiday Inn. Each of us got his own room. After dinner at Howard Johnson's, we returned to the motel and made sure Timothy was secure for the night. The Sentinel's foreign correspondent – that was me - wrote his dispatch from the front – Fort Wayne being the front. Click developed her photos in the van."

The van had blackout curtains on every window enabling the entire vehicle to be a darkroom. A red light on the side of the van near the door was not illuminated, indicating that it was safe to enter. Tweedy knocked on the van door. "Do you mind if I come in?"

Click told him it was okay.

He climbed in and watched Click at work. She was wearing baggy pants and a sleeveless army green tee shirt. Her hair was up in a ponytail.

Tweedy read parts of the article he was writing to her and talked about the trip ahead.

"You know, I don't really gamble. They're just dollar bets."

Click nodded. "If you say so."

"Everyone at the paper gambles. It's an occupational hazard."

Click didn't stop working.

"I guess I'll turn in." said Tweedy. "Good night."

Click said, "Uh, huh."

CHAPTER 46

Tweedy shifted in his chair. "In your research have you come across anything about the kidnapping?"

Jan shook her head. "Kidnapping? No."

"There's a reason for that and it's all part of the story, so before we go on you should try to talk to a couple of people: Vivie Dunphy and Roger Dunphy Jr."

"They're both still alive then?" asked Jan.

Tweedy gave her an amused look. "I'm not suggesting you communicate with the dead. You may write obituaries but that would be taking things a little too far. Yes, they're alive and living in the Denver area. Her name is now Bassett."

Jan was embarrassed. Ordinarily at this point she would have asked if Tweedy had their telephone numbers, but after that gaffe she didn't want to appear any more incapable than she just had. She'd use the newspaper's online databases to get that information. Then if she failed she'd ask Tweedy for help.

Jan stood up and stretched. "Well, I've got to get back to work. Story about the opening of a new animal shelter. Thanks, Mr. Tweedy."

Jan returned to the newsroom floor. Later, after she'd finished her work for the day she dug into the databases and found the telephone number for Vivie Bassett. She picked up the phone and called. It was three o'clock Mountain Time.

"Ms. Bassett? This is Jan Pancake. I'm a reporter with the Akron Sentinel-Herald." She felt the need to clarify. "I'm actually an intern at the S-H and working on my honors thesis. My topic is the Soap Box Derby cheating scandal."

Jan was seated at her desk at the newspaper. On the other end of the telephone line came a sound like a cross between a groan and a large sigh.

"Ms. Bassett?" Jan asked.

"Yuck, that old thing."

"Would it be okay if we talk about it briefly? It would be a great help to me to be able to report things correctly. Is this a good time to talk?"

Ms. Bassett sighed. "How old are you, what did you say your name is?"

Jan told her.

"Good God," Ms. Bassett said. "That poor little boy. He's been gone for such a long time. Okay, what do you want to know?"

Jan told her. Bassett unfolded an amazing story.

"Roger was an unforgettable character. But not a nice unforgettable character like in the Readers Digest. He could be just plain awful. These days they'd say he was a bigger than life character. I don't know what that means, do you? Sounds like he had a glandular condition or something."

Vivie guffawed at her own joke.

"Anyway, Roger was a dreamer, an engineering genius who started the ski boot company and made it big. When we were married he looked a lot like that dancer on the Lawrence Welk show, the one with the big smile and all the teeth. That's what everyone said. When he smiled Roger looked like he had as many teeth as a barracuda. In many ways he was a lot like a barracuda; yeah, a cross between a barracuda and Vince Lombardi."

Jan didn't know who Lawrence Welk was or Vince Lombardi, but she wasn't about to interrupt. She could look them up later.

"He had big ideas. He thought of himself as the best and brightest, and he saw us as a Rocky Mountain version of the Kennedys. Even called where we lived the Compound. He insisted that we all live a vigorous life, which meant playing sports. He belittled Timmy because he didn't like sports. Roger had big plans just like the Kennedys. He used to say, 'Vivie, Dunphys are winners.' Roger had an itch to get into politics and figured he could go all the way. He'd already held a few local offices and served on a number of boards. Then the cheating thing happened and that kidnapping foolishness and that was the end of that. Instead of a member of the Kennedy family he ended up looking more like one of the Corleones."

Jan sat in her chair and listened as Ms. Bassett spun out her story. When Ms. Bassett ran out of story Jan asked her about herself.

"After I divorced Roger I met a very nice man. Lou Bassett was a real estate developer in Golden. We were married for thirty-two years until his death."

Jan used her obituary writing skills to pry some information about Lou from Ms. Bassett. The information was not of use for the cheating scandal story, but it helped Jan cement a bond with Ms. Bassett. Ms. Bassett insisted that Jan call her Vivie and asked if Jan wanted to exchange photographs of one another. Jan agreed to email her a picture. At the end of the conversation Ms. Bassett offered to talk to Jan again if she wanted.

"And I'll tell Roger Jr. that you might call. He's got an interesting slant on things, too."

CHAPTER 47

Ned had been reluctant to accede to Jan's request to introduce her to other interns.

"I think you're invading their privacy," he said when she called him at work. He was clearly uncomfortable saying this.

Jan disagreed. "I'm being straightforward about it, Ned. I'm telling them who I am and why I'm asking. I'm a reporter. I'm not looking into this for any prurient purpose and it's up to them whether they respond to me or not."

"It will make it seem like there was something, well, sleazy about their internships. Illegitimate." His voice rose as he said, "That includes my internship."

Jan said, "This could be my first scoop. Shouldn't you be encouraging me."

Couldn't he see how important this was to her?

Ned was curt. "Please don't tell me what I should be doing."

A minute of uncomfortable silence passed between them before Ned said, "I regret taking you to that mixer." He sounded petulant.

"And do you regret meeting me?" Jan asked.

"I have to get back to work." Ned clicked off.

Jan held her cellphone to her ear for another minute. She was shaken by the call. She had trouble focusing on her work that day and had trouble sleeping that night. She hoped Ned would call. Terminating their conversation as abruptly as that, she decided, was immature. She called Myrt and described how uncooperative Ned was being. Myrt would see her point.

"You're being a jerk" was what Myrt said. "You're as stubborn as a rusty zipper."

"Stop talking like a hick, Myrt," commanded Jan. "Besides, I thought the cliché was 'stubborn as a mule'."

Myrt said, "Can't help it. Somethin' about the mountains of West Virginia have got a holt of me."

Jan ignored the remark. "Look, it's my responsibility as a reporter to expose wrongdoing if that's what it proves to be. I'm going to interview the Director of the Residency and Internship Program and try to get to the bottom of it."

"It's a hospital, Jan. Hospitals help people. How will that help people?"

Is everyone against me? Jan thought it best to change the subject. "How's Josiah?"

"He's good."

The conversation was awkward so Jan cut it short by saying 'goodbye'. No high pitched 'Love ya'. She wished she hadn't called Myrt.

Then and there she made up her mind: she would seek out the interns she hadn't already met and she'd do it without any help from Ned. He shouldn't tell her what she should and shouldn't do.

The hospital directory provided her with names and email addresses. She composed an email identifying herself and explaining that she was investigating some of the practices of the hospital. She asked them to talk about their experience when they interviewed for their internships. She asked how the interviewing process could have been improved. She requested that responses be as detailed as possible and added that all responses would be kept confidential.

Jan showed the email to Pell Newcomb before sending it out.

"You don't mention anything about the escort services they received."

Jan said, "Pell, I couldn't bring myself to ask. You think I have to?"

Newcomb shrugged his shoulders. "It's your story."

She returned to her computer and clicked 'send'.

Encouraged by Pell Newcomb, Jan examined the IRS filings for Mercy General Hospital. The account for the internship program showed a 1099 for Julia Butler, 1050 Beaton St., Chicago. That showed that she was a non-salaried casual contractee. A quick check with Reference USA provided a telephone number for Julia Butler at that address.

Here goes, thought Jan.

"Julia Butler?"

"Yes?"

"I'm Jan Pancake at the Akron Sentinel-Herald. I'm investigating the internship program at Mercy Hospital here and…"

Click.

Maybe I shouldn't have used the word 'investigating', Jan wondered.

Or perhaps there was something wrong with the telephone line. *I'll call again just to be sure.*

"Ms. Butler?"

"If you want to talk to me you'll have to do it through a lawyer." Click.

She reported her conversation with Julia Butler to Pell who thought for a minute before saying, "That's interesting, very interesting. What's your next step?"

"To make an appointment to see the Residency and Internship Program Director.

After a couple of nights of lost sleep Jan texted Ned asking whether he'd like to meet. He texted back that he had a heavy work schedule and wouldn't be available for a while.

But wasn't he the one who said interns' hours 'were not so bad'? Suddenly he didn't have time for her.

But Ned did have time to call Josiah and ask him to discourage his sister from looking into the hospital internship program; "that is, if you're talking to Jan and the subject happens to come up."

After a long day of dealing with farm issues this wasn't the sort of telephone call Josiah welcomed. He liked Ned all right but didn't want to interfere in his sister's relationship. "Sorry. You understand, right?"

Ned said he did and apologized. After he hung up Ned regretted making the call.

Josiah didn't mention it to anyone.

CHAPTER 48

Timmy, Tweedy and Click breakfasted at a pancake house next to the Holiday Inn. Tweedy asked Timmy if he'd slept well. Timmy shook his head. Tweedy and Click glanced at each other. Timmy looked as though he hadn't had a good night's sleep in days. He hadn't eaten the way a thirteen-year-old boy usually does either. Click encouraged him to eat his pancakes. Did he want something else, then?

Yes, he wanted to see his mother.

Click hoped a little distraction might jolly Timmy up. Magic is all about distraction so she offered to show him a trick.

"I can balance this spoon on my nose. Watch," she said.

Click balanced the spoon. Tweedy was impressed not only by the trick but by Click's well shaped nose. Unfortunately, Timmy didn't show any interest in her magic or her nose.

At least, Tweedy thought, they'd be going to his family's farm in Michigan for a couple of days. Maybe Timmy could play and make friends. There'd be plenty of Tweedy family members who would make a fuss over him. Tweedy thought it would be just what he needed.

While Click and Timmy were cleaning up and packing Tweedy drove to the Fort Wayne Tribune and had his article and the photos that Click had taken and developed the previous night wired to the Sentinel. The procedure took about ten minutes so Tweedy looked around at the newspaper's setup and introduced himself to a couple of reporters. They struck Tweedy as a pretty nice bunch of newsmen. They were aware of the Derby cheating scandal but dismissed it as just last week's news...which it was. Most of them just shook their heads and made clucking noises that indicated that the world was in a sorry state and what can you do? The conversation provided Tweedy with a little perspective on what the Akron community thought of as a Very Big Event.

He returned to the Holiday Inn where Click and Timmy were waiting. They loaded the van with their luggage, drove to a filling station to wait in line to have the gas tank topped off, and headed toward Michigan.

Tweedy asked Jan whether she'd had a chance to talk to Vivie Bassett. Jan said she had so Tweedy said, "Yes? Well then, you know what was going on back in Akron. So, you fill me in." He sat back to listen.

Jan began. "The big news in Akron was that the District Attorney was trying to figure out what charges he could bring against Roger Dunphy. 'Contributing to the delinquency of a minor' seemed the most promising. The problem was one of jurisdiction. Dunphy's home was Colorado. Could the D.A. bring charges in Summit County, Ohio? Until he figured out this knotty problem the D.A. ordered Roger to stay in Ohio.

"Incidentally, that D.A. was the officer of the court who years later prosecuted the famous case of Larry Turley, the Ohio Eyeball Slasher. Did you know that?"

Tweedy nodded. He knew about Mr. Turley. In fact, he had gone to summer camp with one of Turley's victims. They hadn't been in the same bunk.

Jan continued. "Roger was stuck. If he strayed from his suite of rooms at the Mayflower Hotel he'd end up in a fight with some local hothead or another. His dreams of higher office were vanishing. He sat in the living room of the hotel suite and stewed about the situation he was in — *Really, I haven't done anything that lots of others haven't done for years, only that stupid fairy nephew got caught'* — and drank. He couldn't relax and have a drink at the Mayflower cocktail lounge. Ordinarily he drank with Boyd, and Boyd handled the drunks. Roger sat in the living room and had an idea. After all, wasn't he one of the best and brightest? He called his company in Denver and spoke to his assistant, Boyd.

"Boyd, get to Akron as fast as you can. And you know those ski masks?"

"You mean the ones we're considering carrying this winter?"

"Yeah, bring a couple of those."

"Okay, boss."

This Boyd character had worked for Dunphy for around ten years. Before that he'd bounced around, spent some time in jail for minor offenses that would be overlooked today, did two tours of duty in Vietnam, then had a sort of conversion - to skiing. He went from being an ordinary bum to being a ski bum, which sounds so much more glamorous. He'd take any work that would help him support his skiing fixation. Roger Dunphy was building a ski empire and Boyd began working for him. Even though he wasn't one of the best and brightest, Boyd became indispensable because he became Roger's fixer. He'd do what Roger Dunphy told him to do, no questions asked. He was Roger's pit bull. As the years went on he did less and less skiing and more and more drinking. Vivie had no use for the guy and let Roger know it.

"Roger, the man is a thug," was her complaint.

"Yes, but he's my thug," was Roger's response.

Boyd packed his bags and flew into Akron Fulton International Airport. He rented an Impala and drove to the Mayflower. Roger hadn't told Vivie that Boyd was coming so it came as a shock to her when she responded to a knock on the door of the suite to find Boyd there. Boyd stood in the doorway not saying a thing. Dunphy got up from the couch, didn't explain why Boyd was there, and said, "I'm going out."

He walked out, closed the door behind him and asked Boyd, "Did you check in?"

"No."

"Good."

Dunphy opened the door and called out to his wife, "Boyd and I are going on a sales call. Can't tell you when I'll be back." With that, he closed the door and walked to the elevator, followed by Boyd.

The rental car was outside. Boyd and Dunphy climbed in.

"Just drive, I don't know, anywhere."

So Boyd drove. "Boss, you haven't been getting very good publicity. Do you think it's going to affect sales?"

"Of course it's going to affect sales, you moron," said Roger.

They drove some more in silence.

"Boyd, I've got a plan. The way I see it what I've got is just a public relations problem. Which can be fixed. Look at Nixon. Right now it doesn't look too good for him. But the man is a public relations genius. Remember the Checkers speech? It looked like Ike was going to dump him then Nixon goes on TV and gives that speech? A work of genius. He'll pull off another move like that and come out of this Watergate business A-okay, just you wait and see. And I'm going to emerge from this stupid Derby business looking better than ever. Did you ever see the photograph of me and Nixon that's behind my desk?"

Boyd nodded. The photo was hard to miss, having been blown up to near life size.

Roger laid out his plan.

"We're going to kidnap Timmy."

"You mean like Patty Hearst?"

Dunphy gave a big toothy smile.

Boyd said, "But the SLA demanded a food giveaway What are you going to demand: a ski boot giveaway?"

Roger Dunphy had no sense of humor. He scowled.

"Sorry, boss," Boyd apologized. "So kidnapping, that's the plan."

"Right, that's the plan. And I will rescue him. I'll end up looking like a hero and the country will fall in love with Timmy, the plucky little near-orphan. And no one will remember that slight irregularity."

"You mean the cheating."

Boyd looked a little dubious. It hadn't been all that long ago, Boyd remembered, that Patty Hearst's kidnappers, the Symbionese Liberation Army went down in a hail of bullets. But he knew enough not to ask the boss any more questions other than whether they could stop somewhere, maybe have a drink. Dunphy said, sure, you find a place. Boyd drove until he found a tavern, a brick and glass brick establishment with a neon sign out front that read "Molloys". It looked quiet. Inside it was dark and smelled of stale beer, pickled pigs' feet and cigarettes. The strange thing was the tavern didn't sell pickled pigs' feet. It was the perfect spot to plot a federal offense. Dunphy sat at a table in the corner. There was no one in that part of the room.

"I'll get us a couple of beers, boss," said Boyd. He went to the bar and asked the bartender for a couple of drafts.

The bartender looked across the room at Dunphy. "Isn't that the guy what cheated in the Derby?"

Boyd didn't say anything. The bartender spat out of the corner of his mouth and drew a couple of beers.

"Finish this round and then you're out, okay?" said the bartender, shaking his head in disgust. "I don't want no trouble." His left hand slowly made a move toward the Louisville Slugger concealed under the bar.

Boyd returned to the table without saying a thing other than, "Real friendly town, this Akron."

"Boyd, there's a newspaper box outside. Get a copy. Need a coin?"

Boyd found a quarter in his pocket and left. He returned with a copy of the Sentinel which he handed to Dunphy. Dunphy grimaced and showed Boyd the front page photo of Timmy, Click and Tweedy smiling in front of the van.

"This reporter, this Jack Tweedy, gives the itinerary. Yesterday, Fort Wayne, next stop a little town in Michigan called – he consulted Tweedy's article - Inverness. We go I-73 and we'll run into them. They'll be easy to spot." He pointed to the photo. "That's the van they're driving."

"We snatch him and…what?" asked Boyd.

Dunphy spoke impatiently. "The reporter and photographer get the ransom note and report to the newspaper that Timmy's been kidnapped. While you hold the kid I'll hold a press conference announcing that I'll pay the ransom, I'll pay anything, do anything to get Timmy back."

Jan said, "It just amazes me that such a smart guy would come up with such a dumb scheme."

"O what a tangled web we weave, when first we practice to deceive," Tweedy replied, quoting Walter Scott. "And remember, there were kidnappings going on all the time back then. Patty Hearst and John Paul Getty's grandson, to name just two. Did you have a chance to talk to Dickie Yount's widow?"

"Back when I wrote his obituary. She was very hostile. I don't know what that was all about."

Tweedy smiled. "Try again. If she'll talk to you she'll have a story for you."

Jan said, "This is becoming like Scheherazade."

Chapter 49

Jan stood at Pell Newcomb's desk. "I've got an appointment for two o'clock with the Hospital's Residency and Internship Director. Do you think you should come with me?" Jan was ambivalent: she was ambitious enough to not want to share a scoop, but feared she lacked the experience to conduct an important interview by herself. Covering library puppet shows, Rotary meetings, and the opening of a new animal shelter was one thing; but breaking a big story, well, that was a different kettle of fish.

Newcomb said, "I think this one you ought to try by yourself. I think you're ready. See what the man has to say. And be ready to listen to some real B-S."

Jan nodded and started to head out of the newsroom.

"Hey, and good luck," Newcomb called out.

At fifteen minutes to two Jan climbed the stairs of the main building at Mercy General Hospital. She was nervous. She was doing her first watchdog reporting. She was also worried about running into Ned. She was wearing a serious reporter's outfit: a blue pantsuit, low-heeled sensible shoes. Her hair was done up in a chignon. She carried a briefcase containing a tablet, a notebook and a digital recorder. She had her set of questions at the ready. The directory in the lobby showed Phil Abrams, Residency and Internship Program Director to be on the third floor. Rather than take the elevator she took the stairs. She found the office, knocked, entered and introduced herself.

Phil Abrams, the tall shaved headed man with the large Adam's apple was seated at a desk. He stood, smiled and invited her to sit down. Jan thanked him, sat, organized her paraphernalia and asked whether she could record their conversation. Dr. Abrams was agreeable so Jan started the machine.

"I'm concerned about…" *bad beginning, she decided, start again…*, "That is, I've learned that when medical students come to Mercy to interview for an internship they are provided with escorts who shows them around the hospital, takes them to lunch or dinner when there aren't hospital personnel to do that, show them the resident dorms, et cetera."

Abrams smiled. "Yes. This is a good hospital and Akron is a great place, but there are a lot of great cities with hospitals competing for the best medical school graduates. So we try to make their visit as productive and enjoyable as we can. It's only natural that every hospital looking for residents seeks to lure the best med school graduates."

Jan smiled. "But, Dr. Abrams, not every hospital hires professional escorts to show the male candidates a good time, and by good time I mean, up to and including sexual favors."

Abrams suddenly had that deer in the headlights look. He began sputtering. He lifted himself up from his leather chair before plopping back down. "Are you accusing Mercy Hospital of pimping, Ms. Pancake?"

"Your word, not mine, Dr. Abrams," Jan said, pulling some printouts of the 1099 form belonging to Julia Butler from her briefcase. She placed them on Dr. Abrams desk. She gave him a minute to scan it. While he did she got ready to unload a surprise.

"I called Ms. Butler but she refused to talk to me. Doesn't that strike you as odd, Doctor?"

"No," replied Dr. Abrams.

Uh, oh. Jan didn't expect that answer. Now what?

Jan thought *'quick, what would Professor Coleman do? Nothing. He'd let Abrams squirm.'*

Squirm he did.

Then Abrams said, "As I said, there are lots of things we do to recruit good candidates that other teaching hospitals, bigger hospitals don't have to do. We pay for their travel expenses. Do you think Mass General does that? Or Mount Sinai? We take them to the finest restaurant in Akron. Other hospitals don't go to that trouble and expense because, let's face it, they don't have to. We're a medium-sized non-profit hospital."

"All the more reason why it's important for you to be a good steward of the hospital's resources, don't you think? To hire escorts as an inducement..."Here she shook her head. "I'd expect that sort of conduct in professional sports, but not a respectable hospital."

Jan sounded disgusted and she worried that she was editorializing, but she meant it. She struggled to find the right description. Finally, she found the right word. "It's sinful," she declared raising her voice. "What do you have to say?"

"I never said we hired escorts."

Jan looked him in the eye. "Do you deny it?"

Dr. Abrams couldn't bring himself to return her gaze. He lowered his head and said "I'm not saying that that's what we did. What happens happens. Besides, it wasn't my idea. It's a bad idea. And as a practice it has been discontinued, if it ever happened. Do you understand?"

Jan asked, "?"So it's been discontinued. As of..?"

"As of now," Abrams vowed. Then he began entreating Jan not to publish anything about it. "It will harm a lot of good people and the Hospital. We've got a great staff here and great support. We're a non-profit hospital; we don't have a lot of money. It's always a struggle to make ends meet. If word of this got out…"

The man's groveling was embarrassing. It made Jan feel bad.

Jan sternly told him she would be talking with the Managing Editor.

Jan thanked Dr. Abrams, whose Adam's apple was bobbing up and down, shook his clammy hand goodbye, stowed her things back into her briefcase, swung the briefcase strap over her shoulder and walked out of the office offering a "Good afternoon" as she closed the door behind her.

Wow, the power of the press! And I'm just a twenty-one-year-old intern!

Jan scurried out of the hospital building before someone could yell, "Fraud! She's just a college student! Stop her!" and found Joseph the Car of Many Colors still waiting in the parking lot. Her world was back to normal. But it wasn't, not really; and she didn't drive back to the Sentinel-Herald, .at least not immediately She sat in the car and thought about the short interview that had just taken place. And she trembled a bit and then sobbed a bit. What troubled her?

I should feel exhilarated, she thought. *But I don't. I feel dirty. Is this what journalism is? Trying to get the goods on people? Ambushing them? Was that my intention?*

Jan had humiliated Dr Abrams. She did not have a good feeling about that.

If that's the kind of thing I have to do to succeed in journalism, I'm not sure I'm cut out for it.

Jan felt ashamed. It occurred to her that Romans 11 warns us not to be puffed up with pride. Was she ignoring this warning?

Eventually, she started the car and slowly drove back to the Sentinel-Herald. She described the interview to Pell Newcomb and Jerry Murphy. She played the tape. They were excited.

"You nailed it, Jan" said Murphy. Newcomb agreed.

"So, you'll write it up and we'll put it in the Sunday edition front."

Jan hesitated and asked whether she could think about it. They were floored.

"Think about what? You've got a great story here. What is there to think about?" Murphy asked. He really was mystified.

"I have to ask – if they're really not doing it any more what's the point of publishing an article? The result will be to make the hospital and the internship program look bad. It'll affect donations and the volunteer program will suffer, to say nothing of the reputation of the hospital. It's a hospital, it's not like they're manufacturing weapons of mass destruction. They're helping sick people."

Murphy said a little stiffly, "Well, it's your story. It's up to you. But stories like this don't come around that often, and certainly not to interns. It could make your reputation."

Jan nodded. She was aware of that.

She also knew that she could use some advice. That night she called Pastor Linger. Diane Linger answered and effusively greeted Jan.

"I'll let you speak to Jon." She covered the phone with her hand but Jan could hear a muffled, "Jon, it's Jan Pancake. She sounds worried about something."

A few seconds later Pastor Linger greeted Jan. "What's the problem?"

Jan described her quandary without mentioning the aspect that concerned Ned. She didn't want the ethical issues to be muddied by personal concerns.

"This is a thorny one, Jan," Linger said. "Revealing that information will harm the reputation of the hospital and the interns, some of whom weren't even involved." He paused a while. "Is this the kind of thing newspaper interns normally deal with?"

Jan had to laugh. "No, they usually cover library puppet shows. I keep asking myself, 'What would Bob Woodward do?'"

Pastor Linger said, "The better question is 'What would Jesus do?' I think Jesus would say 'It's better to hope for a scoop later than to hurt a lot of people now. If the Director of the Residency and

Internship Program was sincerely contrite then no greater good will result from revealing his error in judgment."

Jan sighed loudly. "We all make mistakes, I know that. 'Let he who is without sin, et cetera.' I figured you'd say something like that."

"I expect that's why you called. You didn't need me to tell you that." He paused and said, "Now what about that young man you're seeing? What's the problem there?"

"Who said there was a problem?" Jan asked.

"Your friend, Myrt."

"What! When did she talk to you?" Jan was mortified.

"Josiah and Myrt visited us last week." His voice dimmed as he swiveled his head from the telephone to direct a question to Diane. "Honey, when did Josiah come here?" There was a muffled consultation then Linger returned. "Last Tuesday. I hope that whatever you decide regarding your scoop is one that Ned can live with."

"Ned's being a big jerk," Jan said. Suddenly she regressed from making decisions affecting a metropolitan newspaper and its community back to high school. She was embarrassed. "Pastor, it's just that he's freezing me out over this internship issue."

"Jan, I'm sure you can understand why he's upset."

"Sure, but he should talk about it; not sulk and stop answering my phone calls."

"I think you'll work it out before Christmas. Will we see you then?"

Jan said she hoped so. She thanked Pastor Linger.

Little San Simeon was nice and warm, but Jan felt like being in the cold, so she put on her coat and walked over to the kennel to play with Lucy, the blind sheltie that had been dropped off at the kennel and never picked up. Mr. and Mrs. Dobbins didn't mind taking care of the old dog and Lucy had made herself useful around the kennel by being a patient, likeable old dog. As Jan scratched Lucy under the chin, she reflected on her conversation with Pastor Linger. He was right, she decided, there would be other scoops. The next day Jan gave Jerry Murphy her reasons for spiking her first scoop.

"Publishing an article on that topic will not serve the public interest."

Murphy expressed some irritation but didn't argue with her. He didn't let on that he respected Jan for her decision.

Jan deleted all the emails sent by interns in response to her questionnaire without reading them.

CHAPTER 50

"'There are decades when nothing happens; and there are weeks when decades happen.' That's one of my favorite quotes," said Tweedy.

Jan tilted her head in thought. "Yes," she said and smiled. "I guess that's right. Who said that?"

"Fellow named Vladimir Ilyich Lenin. Just think about what was going on the season of the cheating scandal. The Vietnam War. The women's movement, Black people were demanding their rights. There was Watergate, and it turned out that the young woman on the Ivory Snow box had starred in pornographic movies. The country was in turmoil."

"And here in Akron there was a kidnapping that wasn't a kidnapping."

Tweedy asked, "Have you spoken to Dickie Yount's widow?"

"I have a date to meet her at her house after work."

Tweedy said, "Good. We'll talk again tomorrow."

It was a beautiful early winter's day, sunny but cold with occasional snow flurries when Jan went to speak to Estelle Yount, the widow of Dickie Yount. As she drove Jan reflected on her complex feelings toward Ned. It had been over two weeks since she had seen him. Her feelings vacillated between resentment and abject yearning. He must have figured by now that she wasn't going to publish anything about the internship scandal, right? True, he hadn't demanded that she withhold publication. But what right did he have to be so sanctimonious? And it hurt to know that he didn't trust her to make a decision that wouldn't harm either the interns or Mercy Hospital. She sighed when she thought about how much she missed him. What could she do to make things right again? She had been so looking forward to spending Christmas with him.

She reached Mrs. Yount's residence, a small, neat bungalow in the Larchmont neighborhood. Mrs. Yount was guarded but polite when she answered the door.

"I must be nuts to talk to you," she said as she ushered Jan into the house. "But what the heck. No harm now."

She invited Jan to sit at the kitchen table and put out coffee and Danish pastries. It made it easier for Jan to take notes and use her recorder while sitting at a table rather than juggle these items sitting in a living room chair. Jan had noticed as she walked through the living room to the kitchen the absence of any Great Soap Box Derby mementos anywhere in the living room.

The first thing Jan did was to extend her sympathy to Mrs. Yount on the recent death of Dickie. Mrs. Yount thanked her.

Jan expressed her surprise that she didn't see any Derby memorabilia.

Mrs. Yount first sighed, then smiled. "No, you won't. The Derby was everything to Dickie. You know, he was called 'Mr. Derby', don't you?"

Jan nodded.

"The Derby broke his heart, you know. The man lived and breathed Derby and then when things went sour they all blamed him. But that John Delorean he had a lot to do with it."

"Who was he?" Jan asked.

"General Manager of Chevrolet. You know, the Back to the Future car guy. It was his decision to pull the plug on Chevy sponsoring the Derby the year before the cheating scandal. That scandal wouldn't have happened if Chevy was still running things. Dickie was a victim. Without Chevy's money Dickie was understaffed. Made it hard to manage things."

Jan drank some coffee and made notes.

Mrs. Yount sighed. "Dickie wasn't perfect, God knows, but the real criminal in all of this was that Roger Dunphy. That man was no damn good."

Jan said, "I'm a little confused. According to what I read your husband took a job with Roger Dunphy's company shortly after the scandal."

Mrs. Yount put her coffee cup down and rested both elbows on the kitchen table as she leaned across to look Jan in the eye. "He should never have taken that job in Colorado. We should never have left Akron. We swore that we'd return when he retired. And we did, you know. And we were treated like we were traitors, scum of the earth. In the eyes of the people hereabouts maybe we were. But it wasn't Dickie who kidnapped that poor boy. That was your newspaper!"

Jan was stunned. This was the first time she had heard this version of the kidnapping. And so she listened as Estelle told her the story as she heard it from Dickie over forty-five years ago.

Estelle Yount concluded her version by asking Jan, "After all this time I still don't understand. What did the Sentinel get out of kidnapping Timmy? Can you explain it? It makes no sense to me." She was almost pleading for an explanation.

Jan shook her head slowly. Why would she think Timmy was kidnapped by the Sentinel? "I wish I could give you an answer," she said. "If I find out more I'll let you know, okay?"

Estelle Yount sat and quietly said, "When we moved back we were shunned and Dickie was blamed for things that happened so many years before. Such small-minded people. Dickie and I had moved on; why couldn't Akron?"

When Jan emerged from Mrs. Yount's bungalow she shook Estelle's hand and thanked her.

Mrs. Yount stood on the porch as Jan walked toward her car. "You tell the story right, okay?" Mrs. Yount said.

"I'll do my best," Jan responded.

CHAPTER 51

With the aid of maps supplied by the car rental company, Roger Dunphy and Boyd were on the trail of the Sentinel news van. They knew their quarry was somewhere between Fort Wayne and Michigan.

"I'm glad this car has air conditioning," were the first words Boyd had spoken in a couple of hours. This part of the country was flat, mostly agricultural and pretty boring unless maybe you were a farmer. There were few radio stations to choose from. Boyd's favorite song these days was Barry Sadler's Ballad of the Green Berets. Roger Dunphy, being a hipper guy than Boyd, favored the music of Donovan and The Strawberry Alarm Clock.

"Come on, Boyd, put on a little speed. I'd like to catch up with them some time before winter," Dunphy complained.

"But, Boss, speeding will draw the cops' attention," Boyd replied. "I don't think we want that."

Dunphy growled.

It is only appropriate that, were we announcing a Soap Box Derby race, we'd say "and bringing up the rear is Dickie Yount and Fletcher Crites." After the fiasco at Roger Dunphy's press conference Dickie Yount had kept a close watch on the activities of Roger Dunphy. He had staked out the Mayflower Hotel with his old friend Fletcher and when they spied Dunphy and Boyd leaving the hotel in a rented car they were determined to shadow them.

Estelle Yount had begged Dickie to let it go, to consider himself lucky that Dunphy hadn't filed assault charges against him. But Mr. Derby was a man obsessed. In Dickie's judgement Dunphy had brought disgrace to a hallowed American institution, - the Great Soap Box Derby, - and Yount wasn't about to let that offense go unanswered. He didn't know what he would do but he was set on doing something.

Dickie and Fletcher had met when Dickie was Head Counselor at Camp Indian Head, a summer camp in the Hocking Hills, and Fletcher was a counselor-in-training. Dickie loved being Head Counselor and had been popular among the campers. He told stupid dirty jokes, was bouncy and full of enthusiasm. These were just the traits that served him so well later when he took up the position of General Manager at the Derby. After a few years as Head Counselor, Dickie thought he could transfer these traits to his new job as Sales Manager at his father's appliance store. His enthusiasm served him well, as did the stupid dirty jokes; the bounciness not so much. When people are making big ticket purchases like stoves and refrigerators they want a salesperson who is serious and not so bouncy. So, it was just as well that the Derby position opened up, a position where bounciness was again welcome.

"Dickie, what if Dunphy is headed back to Denver? Are we going to follow him that far?" asked Fletcher.

"I don't know, Fletch. I don't know. I just know I have to do something."

"We're wearing shorts and tee shirts. Denver's in the Rockies where it's always cold and snowing."

"All right, Fletch, we won't go as far as the Rockies, okay?" Dickie said. Sometimes Fletch could be downright annoying. It may have been that trait that was responsible for his current unemployed status. Back when they were in high school Fletcher had gone through the same battery of vocational tests as the other students. His test results determined that he was a natural 'gofer'.

In the lead car of this Derby Jack Tweedy, Click Gunderson, and Timmy Nolen had finished a rousing chorus of the theme to "Cabaret" and were singing along with Ethel Merman in "There's No Business Like Show Business." The song was on one of the cassette tapes that Timmy had selected at W.T. Grants. The trio was getting along better than Tweedy had expected. Timmy was not as gloomy as he had been and Click was as charming as Tweedy thought she could be. What seemed to have broken the ice were silly riddles and jokes, the dumber the better. At one point they were firing riddles about places at one another.

"Why will Ireland never run out of money?" Timmy asked.

Neither Click nor Tweedy knew the answer.

"Because its capital is always Dublin." There was no response from the adults in the van. "Dublin? Doublin', get it?"

"I get it," Click said. "Okay, why will you never starve in the Gobi Desert?"

Silence.

"Because of the sand which is there!"

Both Tweedy and Timmy got it.

They also killed time exercising their imaginations by coming up with phony notable sites along the way.

"According to page 94 in the AAA tour book for the Midwest we'll be passing exit 15B that leads to the village of Gluterpuck where Chef Boyardee discovered his first meatball in 1931," said Tweedy, pulling this fake fact out of his imagination.

Further down the highway Click said, "We should visit the Town of Cellardoor, site of the third largest ball of dental floss in America. The American Dental Hygienists Association holds its annual convention in Cellardoor every September 12 unless the twelfth is a Tuesday; in which case the convention is held in May."

That tickled Timmy. To hear him giggle and laugh was gratifying to Tweedy.

When they drove by a new subdivision Timmy pointed to a ranch house under construction. "George Washington never slept there. And I'll bet he never will," he said solemnly.

"I'll take that bet," said Tweedy.

Click gave Tweedy a dirty look. Tweedy didn't seem to be able to convince Click that he didn't have a gambling problem.

Click drove while Tweedy took notes for his next article. Tweedy intended to call the Sentinel and talk to Tom Higgins at their next stop.

Timmy was looking forward to spending some time at the farm. Tweedy had promised that there were lots of wild animals in the woods there.

"We're low on gas. I think we should stop at the next station," Click said.

"Good idea. That'll give me a chance to call Higgins." He also intended to call the pressman who served as the newspaper's bookie. Just to say hello, of course.

The van, manufactured by the International Harvester Company, was a gas guzzler. This wasn't the best time to take long road trips in America. The Arab gas embargo was causing terrible shortages and long lines at filling stations across the country. Motorists were waiting for long periods, sometimes up to an hour, at gas pumps only to find that by the time they reached the front the station was out of fuel. Customers' patience was running low and fights frequently broke out. According to a poll reported in the Sentinel's Sunday edition, forty percent of Americans believed the gas shortage was a conspiracy created by a consortium of cable television operators designed to keep viewers home and in front of their TV screens.

As they approached the Sinclair filling station all three passengers groaned. The line of cars snaked out of the station lot onto the roadway.

Click said, "We have no choice. We don't know where the next station is. Besides, it's probably just as bad there." She added the van to the line.

"This is going to take a while," said Tweedy. "I'm going to find a phone and call Higgins." Tweedy climbed out of the van. "Can I get you anything?" he asked Click.

"No, I'm all right," she answered. Actually, she really did have to use a rest room but she was deathly afraid to use a filling station bathroom; in fact, she hadn't used one since she was seven. That was when her mother let her go unaccompanied to the women's room of a gas station on the New Jersey Turnpike. She had waited outside the room until a group of female gypsies from a travelling carnival departed the room. Whatever Click saw in that bathroom must've been so ghastly that she refused to ever talk about it, had nightmares about circus peanuts and chickens for a month, and never used a gas station bathroom again. She'd wait until they found a restaurant or the next cornfield, whichever came first.

Tweedy headed for the white and green building.

Timmy said, "As long as we're here, I'll go use the bathroom." This alarmed Click, but she didn't say anything. Timmy slid across the back seat and onto the pavement. He went inside the filling station and borrowed the men's room key.

Parked on the side of the roadway by the entrance to the Sinclair station was the nondescript rental car.

"I think this is our chance," said Roger Dunphy. "Pull up to the bathrooms."

Boyd slowly drove the car to a space adjacent to the front of the bathrooms. He left the motor running.

"Ski masks," ordered Dunphy.

They donned their ski masks. These were ski masks being considered for next year's catalog. Taking no chances, Dunphy was also wearing a fake mustache.

When Timmy emerged from the bathroom there was no one around. Boyd quickly got out of the car and approached Timmy. He grabbed him and said, "Come with me. Don't say a word or else." The men's room key clattered to the pavement.

Totally confused, Timmy allowed Boyd to push him toward the car. Dunphy opened the rear right door and Boyd shoved Timmy into the back seat. Boyd closed the door and climbed into the driver's seat. Dunphy quickly walked around to the front of the building. He offered a gas attendant an envelope, a twenty dollar bill and the men's room key. He was still wearing a ski mask and a fake mustache.

"Give this envelope to the driver of that Sentinel van over there. The twenty is for you, okay?" Dunphy said, pointing to the van that was still around ten cars from the front of the line.

The attendant took the envelope and the twenty dollars, said "you bet," and walked toward the van. He handed the envelope to Click.

Meanwhile, Dunphy scooted back to the rental, climbed in the back and ordered Boyd to drive. The entire operation took less than two minutes.

Observing this operation from his car parked about twenty yards away was Dickie Yount.

"Did you see that?" he asked Fletcher wide-eyed. "What's going on?"

Fletcher didn't know. "What do we do?" he asked.

"We'll follow them. You know he can't be up to any good."

Dickie put the car in gear and left the gas station hot on the trail of Roger Dunphy, Boyd and Timmy Nolen.

"Where to, Clutch?" asked Boyd.

Clutch was the name Roger Dunphy had given himself for the purposes of this kidnapping job.

"I told you: that motel we passed about twenty minutes ago," responded Clutch, affecting a gravelly basso profundo.

Timmy was in the back seat rubbing his elbow. "You didn't have to push me so hard, Boyd, you wrecked my elbow."

Clutch and Captain America (Boyd's self-appointed name) looked at one another in dismay.

"No point wearing this," Clutch said glumly, tearing off his fake mustache. He doffed his ski mask and turned in the seat to face Timmy.

"How'd you know?" he asked.

"Boyd wears that awful cologne, Hai Karate. I could tell it was him. I think he's the only one who still uses that stuff."

"Can I take my mask off?" Boyd asked. Dunphy ignored the question.

"Boss, you want I should shoot him?" Boyd (no-longer-Captain-America) asked.

Timmy shrank in his seat. Dunphy laughed.

"Timmy, he's kidding."

It was nice to know Dunphy could appreciate Boyd's sense of humor. But Boyd wasn't kidding.

Dunphy gave Timmy an explanation for the kidnapping.

"You see, the public will be sympathetic to you – a kidnap victim – and overlook the Derby cheating business."

"And Roger will look like a hero rescuing you by paying the ransom," Boyd contributed.

"How much is the ransom?" Timmy asked.

"Twenty thousand," Dunphy answered.

"That's all?" Timmy asked. "You're rich." He seemed disappointed.

"I didn't get where I am today by throwing away my money."

"Boyd, did you know that I once trained a jackdaw to talk?" asked Timmy.

"That's great, kid." Boyd said.

Dunphy muttered with disdain, "Ellie Mae."

Boyd said, "Boss, I don't think you want to sell those ski masks. They itch like crazy."

"They're for the winter," Roger said. "Don't you know your seasons?"

"They'll itch in the winter, too."

"Okay, Boyd, I'll take that under advisement."

CHAPTER 52

Seated at a red vinyl upholstered booth at The Imperial Golden Jade Dragon, Jan and Jack Tweedy were practicing many of the stratagems that Arnie Stavis had shared with her at the all-you-can-eat buffet.

"He was a pretty good intern," said Tweedy, "with an outstanding appetite. I'll mention that in any letter of recommendation he might ask for. I think he enjoyed his going away party, don't you?"

Jan thought for a moment. "He seemed to like the sheet cake a lot, but seemed disappointed by the going away present."

Jack seemed surprised. "I don't understand that. An <u>AP Style Manual</u> is a useful book to have."

Jan shrugged her shoulders. "Takes all kinds," she said drily.

Jack asked, "Say, have you ever seen the spoon trick, the one where you mysteriously make a spoon stick to your nose?"

Jan shook her head, so Tweedy showed her.

"Because I'm using a Chinese spoon it becomes the mysterious Chinese spoon trick. Watch."

Tweedy demonstrated. Jan was suitably impressed.

"Where did you learn that trick?" she asked.

"Old Shanghai by way of Old Fort Wayne."

They tucked into their meal.

"I've uncovered one discrepancy," Jan said between slurps of hot and sour soup. "Roger Dunphy Jr. told me that Timothy told him that it was a cologne called Jade East that gave Boyd away. Not Hai Karate."

Tweedy nodded. "Interesting."

"But the disguises were just for any onlookers at the gas station anyway, right?"

"If Roger Jr. said that's what Timmy told him, then we have to rely on that."

"Mr. Tweedy, kidnapping is a really serious offense. But it's a little hard to take this one seriously."

Tweedy said, "We didn't know at the time that it was a phony. We took it very seriously. Dunphy was a desperate man. All his dreams were going up in smoke and from his point of view it wasn't his fault."

"You were on the phone with Higgins when the snatch occurred."

"I was telling him how well everything was going."

The filling station attendant handed Click the envelope while she waited in the gas line. She opened it - a ransom note.

"Hark! This is an action communiqué from the soldiers of the People's Liberation Army. As part of our war on the fascistic parasitic insects which prey on the lives of the People we are demanding $20,000 for the return of Timmy Nolen. Do not contact the PIGS or he will be executed. The Sentinel will be contacted within the next two days with details. We also demand amnesty and free passage to a non-Imperialist country for our imprisoned brothers. Power to the People!"

The 'communique' was signed 'Avenger'

Click's face got hot and her hands shook so hard the letter fell in her lap.

Oh, no, it's the curse of the gypsies, was her first thought.

She was so flustered she began to scramble out of the van without putting it into 'park'. The van bumped the car in front. Click climbed back in, put the transmission in 'park', set the brake and slid out to the pavement. The driver of the car in front was already examining the rear of his Mercury Topaz. He determined there was no damage, gave Click a disgusted look and a dismissive wave of the back of his hand as though he were shooing a fly away. Click climbed back in and pulled out of line. She parked in front of the building, driving unsteadily, and looked around for Tweedy. Seeing him in the telephone booth she jumped out of the car and raced over to him. She waved the letter in Tweedy's face and yelled, "They've got Timmy!"

Tweedy was confused. "Who's got Timmy?"

"Tell Higgins you'll call him back."

He did. He took the letter and scanned it. "Have you looked for Timmy?" he asked.

Click shook her head.

"You go that way," ordered Tweedy, pointing to the corner of the station.

They headed in different directions around the building and met in the back where the restrooms were. They banged on the men's room. No answer.

"The key," said Tweedy.

They ran into the station and borrowed the men's room key then ran back to the restroom.

"I won't go in there," said a terrified Click.

Tweedy didn't argue. He opened the door and found it empty, filthy but empty.

He emerged safely and consulted with Click. They located the attendant who had given Click the envelope containing the communiqué and asked for a description.

"Tall, mustache, wearing a ski mask. Lots of teeth."

"Didn't you think it a little unusual for someone to be wearing a ski mask in August? Did you see the car he was driving?" asked Tweedy.

The answer to both questions was 'no'.

"Can you remember anything that struck you as unusual?"

"Oh, yeah," the attendant remembered, "he returned the men's room key."

To a filling station attendant that was memorable. He didn't mention the twenty-dollar payment.

Tweedy returned to the pay phone and called Higgins. He explained the situation and read the letter.

"A ransom note," said Higgins.

"No, a communiqué," said Tweedy.

"Get back to Akron as quickly as you can."

They did. First they had to fill up the van. They had lost their place in line, no cutting was allowed, so they returned to the end of the line. They had little to say to each other. Occasionally Click would sob. Occasionally Tweedy would hit the dashboard with his fist. They kept saying, "That poor kid." They both felt guilty, though they knew they had done nothing wrong.

They eventually got back to the Sentinel at two o'clock in the morning. Tom Higgins and Sam Gibbons were in Higgins' office and they didn't look happy.

At that hour there were just a couple of employees at work. As Click and Tweedy walked across the newsroom Tweedy noticed that the smack of his heels on the wooden floor didn't have the lively percussiveness it usually had.

I think I must be exhausted, he thought.

He was. He collapsed into a chair. Click kneeled down to see if Tweedy was okay.

"I'm okay, but I definitely need some sleep."

He had done the bulk of the driving.

Higgins and Gibbons noticed them now and joined them. Higgins filled them in. There'd been no word from the kidnappers and according to his wife Roger Dunphy was on a sales call but would be returning to Akron any time now.

"Did you call the pigs?" asked Tweedy.

"The what?" asked Higgins.

"The police."

"We decided to wait for Dunphy. It's his decision." Higgins pointed to Tweedy and Click. "You two go home and get some sleep."

"One question," said Tweedy to Higgins and Gibbons.

"Jack?" said Gibbons

"What imprisoned brothers are they talking about?"

"We have no idea."

While Boyd drove, Dunphy harangued Timmy who sat alone in the back seat.

"This is your fault, you know. You activated the magnet too soon. You gave yourself away. We practiced and practiced."

"I'm sorry, I was nervous."

Boyd felt bad for the boy. "He's only a kid," he said.

"Well, you ruined the whole thing," Dunphy said.

Timmy, who had been huddled in the back seat, suddenly shot up and scrambled over to the side reaching for the door handle. "I did not!" he cried out. "You did. I never wanted to be in that stupid derby and you know it. You made me!" He got the door open right before Roger turned around and reached over the seat back and grabbed Timmy with both hands.

"Hey," he shouted, holding on to the boy. "Are you crazy? Are you trying to kill yourself?"

"Maybe I am," Timmy said defiantly. He struggled to free himself from Roger's grip.

"Stay away from that door," Roger ordered. He released one hand from Timmy and closed the door. "Settle down."

Timmy struggled, then gave up and meekly slumped back in the seat.

"At least I got to meet Lorne Greene at the awards banquet," Timmy grumbled, "and Knucklehead Smiff."

Once they reached a suitably seedy, inconspicuous motel Boyd pulled into a parking slot in the back. While Dunphy and Timmy waited in the car Boyd checked in using a fake name. They went into the room and looked around.

"Keys," said Dunphy to Boyd.

Boyd handed over the car keys.

Before he closed the door behind him Dunphy said, "Remember, call me at the Sentinel tomorrow at noon. I gave you the number." He thought it best to quiz Boyd. "When?"

Boyd recited, "Noon o'clock. A.M. or P.M?"

"P.M.! Timmy, you remind Boyd when he has to call. And a word of advice: if you ever do want to learn to ski remember to always wear a helmet." He pointed to Boyd. "This guy didn't."

Thrusting his face within inches of Boyd's mug Dunphy growled, "And don't show Timmy's face outside this room until I get back."

"Right."

"Timmy, remember, I'm doing this for you."

Timmy muttered, "This place is even crummier than Jack Tweedy's house."

Dunphy heard the remark. "Look, Ellie Mae, we're not here to do a photo shoot for House Beautiful, okay?" He slammed the door on his way out.

Back on the highway Dunphy began practicing the sequence of looks he would use when informed of the kidnapping: first shock, then concern, then decisiveness. He wanted to get it right before he returned to the Mayflower. He flipped the sun visor down so he could look at his face in the little mirror. Shock – concern - decisiveness. Practice makes perfect. Shock – the eyes widens and the mouth opens and drops. Concern – the eyebrows knit, the mouth tightens. Decisiveness – fixed gaze, head erect and held high. Repeat.

Had Dunphy focused less on the vanity mirror and more on what could be seen in his rear view mirror he might have noticed the same Cadillac following him that had trailed him since he left the Mayflower Hotel.

"What do you make of all this?" Fletcher asked.

Dickie scratched his head, which served to aid him in thinking. "Well, look at what we've seen. We saw Roger Dunphy and some other guy grab Timmy Nolen. Then we saw an envelope being passed through a third party from Roger Dunphy to the newspaper people. It seems obvious to me what happened."

"Yeah? What?"

"The newspaper was holding Timmy for ransom. That's what the envelope contained – ransom money. Roger Dunphy paid the ransom and got Timmy back from the newspaper people. And Dunphy left Timmy at that motel with that guy for protection. He looks kind of like a guy you'd hire for muscle, don't you think?"

Fletcher said "Uh, huh", and thought for a minute. "Hmm, that does follow. So Roger Dunphy is a good guy?"

"I don't know." Dickie wasn't eager to draw that conclusion about the man who ruined the Derby.

Fletcher asked, "Is the Sentinel broke or something?"

"I don't think so," answered Dickie.

"If it isn't for the ransom money then why would the Sentinel kidnap the kid who cheated?" Fletcher asked. "To punish him? As a lesson to kids who are thinking of cheating in the next Derby?"

Dickie said, "I don't think so."

"To sell newspapers?" Fletcher offered.

Dickie was skeptical. "So they can get a headline that reads 'Sentinel kidnaps Derby Cheater for ransom?'. I don't think that would make the paper look so good."

Stumped, Fletch and Dickie went silent and continued to trail Dunphy. Estelle Yount wished Dickie would call. She wanted to tell him that the Derby Committee had telephoned; they had voted to fire Dickie.

CHAPTER 53

Jan was so busy working on the obituary of a woman named Teresita Hanley that she didn't notice that Tweedy was standing at her desk until he said "Ahem." Startled, she looked up from her computer.

"I'm sorry, Mr. Tweedy," she said. "Please let me get you a seat."

She jumped up and dragged a chair over to her desk. "I've been writing this obituary. The preliminary information I was given said that the deceased made beds, so I figured she was a chambermaid. But I just learned she was the President of a large firm that manufactures beds. Glad I caught that one in time. Whew!"

Tweedy smiled and held up a couple of pieces of paper. "We're overdue for your internship report. You've been with the paper over half a year. This is something the McNaughton Foundation insists on."

"Now?"

"Why don't I give you the questions. Some of them require you to go into detail, like question three – 'have you formed a guiding philosophy of newsgathering?' You can take some time to reply to those. The others we do together: I ask you questions, you answer and I respond to your answers."

Tweedy handed the sheets of paper to Jan. She examined them and whistled. "These are tough questions. There are no right or wrong answers."

Tweedy was preparing to stand up when Ned Edwards entered the newsroom, looked around timidly, and walked over to Jan's desk. She was astonished and momentarily speechless. Tweedy said 'hello'.

"Hello, Mr. Tweedy," Ned said. He was genuinely happy to see Tweedy. "Nice to see you again." To Ned's relief, Tweedy was running interference for him.

"I was just telling Jan here that I've missed seeing you around. Good to see you. Here, you take my seat. I've got to get back to whatever I've got to get back to. I'll leave you two young people." Tweedy got up and gave Ned a pat on the shoulder then left for his office.

Ned had tried to look nonchalant, but he didn't carry it off too well. "Hello."

Jan said hello. What she wanted to do was fling herself at Ned, wrap her arms around Ned, and nestle her head on Ned's chest, but, alas, this was, - after all, - her place of work. Also, she'd covered enough sports by this time to know that she 'couldn't read the play' yet.

Ned asked whether he might be allowed to sit.

"Of course," said Jan formally. "That's a nice coat."

Ned sounded distracted. "Oh, thanks." He paused then said, "Look, Jan, I could make up some bogus excuse and tell you I came to the paper to visit Mary Karnes, but it wouldn't be true. I came to see you. I've been miserable the last few weeks without you."

That clarified things nicely.

It took a superhuman effort to keep Jan from kissing Ned right then and there, Instead she began to cry.

A few of the newspaper staff were watching Jan and Ned out of the corners of their eyes.

"Could we go somewhere?" Ned asked.

Jan wiped her eyes and nodded. She grabbed her purse and coat and walked out of the newsroom smiling and sniffling. Ned followed. Once they got outside Jan threw her arms around Ned and they kissed at last. They held each other for a long time, slowly rocking side to side, and began walking with their arms around each other.

"Where are we headed?"

"I don't know. Just for a walk. It's a beautiful day."

In fact, it was kind of cold and overcast, but this wasn't something they had any intention of arguing about. They ended up at a coffee shop and sat and talked about this, that and the other.

Jan thought it best to avoid any discussion of the hospital internship scandal. But when Ned brought up the subject Jan said it was a closed case. "No harm, no foul, okay?"

"Okay," he said.

Finally, Jan asked whether Ned would go with her to West Virginia for Christmas.

"Definitely," he smiled.

CHAPTER 54

When Roger Dunphy finally made it to the Mayflower Hotel at six a.m. and learned about the kidnapping of Timmy by the PLA he ably demonstrated the range of expressions he had practiced so diligently. Vivie told him what she knew and told him that the Sentinel people had visited their hotel room the previous day.

His first question was not "Do you know if Timmy is okay?" It was "What are they going to put in the paper about this?"

Vivie shook her head. "They're not."

"What? Why not?" he cried out. This time he didn't have to pretend to look shocked, one of the three expressions he had spent so much time practicing.

"You'll have to ask them," was Vivie's response.

"We'll go there." Dunphy was exhausted from driving. He called the Sentinel, spoke to Higgins and said he and Vivie would be over as soon as he'd showered and shaved. He wanted to look good for the photographers.

After Dunphy hung up the phone Vivie asked, "Where's Boyd?"

"Sales call."

He got as spruced up as he could – trying to look camera-ready - and took the rental car to the newspaper. He and Vivie were greeted by a solemn Higgins and Gibbons. He was ushered into Higgins' office and shown the 'communique'.

"I think I should call a press conference," said Dunphy.

Higgins and Gibbons couldn't see a good reason for this. They emphasized that there shouldn't be any publicity, that Timmy's life was at stake.

Dunphy said, "Wait, I see what's going on here." He began to bob his head up and down as though that helped him make the picture clearer. "The kid was kidnapped right under the noses of your reporter and photographer. You were responsible for him and now you're afraid that the paper will look bad if you report it." He gave the appearance of being shocked and outraged.

He surreptitiously checked his watch. It was almost noon. Boyd had better call.

"You know, I could contact the Herald and the radio stations," Dunphy said.

Higgins shook his head. "I wouldn't recommend that."

Dunphy stormed around Higgins' office and then out onto the newsroom floor. Higgins and Gibbons and Vivie followed his random path as best they could. Dunphy kept moving around the room, trying to eat up the clock.

"Mr. Dunphy, please," they said over and over.

Finally, the news desk called out, "Telephone call for Roger Dunphy. Someone calling himself 'Avenger'."

(If someone at the paper had done his homework he would have discovered that the new line of plastic ski boots in Dunphy's catalog was the Avenger series. Vivie had come up with the name.)

Higgins, Gibbons, Dunphy and Vivie re-entered Higgins' office.

"Well," Dunphy said dramatically, "here we go - the kidnappers!"

"Are you sure? It could be the Nobel Prize Committee," Vivie said quietly to no one in particular. She was beginning to suspect that not everything about this kidnapping was on the up-and-up. Roger glared at her.

"Or maybe the Academy Awards people," she added.

"Quiet," ordered Dunphy. He composed himself and picked up the receiver. "Hello?"

"Boss, it's me, Captain America."

"Yes, this is Roger Dunphy."

Dunphy began nodding and saying, "Yes, yes" and "Right" and "Uh, huh". He took out his handkerchief and mopped his brow.

Timmy had gradually grown more talkative when he was with Click and Tweedy, but once the kidnapping began he had reverted to taciturn, sullen mode. But for some mysterious reason Timmy got a kick out of Boyd. Perhaps it was a recognition that he and Boyd were both the objects of Roger's contempt. While waiting to make the phone call Boyd and Timmy had concocted a scheme to have a little fun at Roger's expense.

As Roger was grunting his various "Uh, huh's" Boyd yelled out "Crank up the voltage!" He gave it his best version of a Gestapo agent accent.

Timmy screamed.

Vivie could hear the commotion through the phone and became concerned.

"Roger, are they torturing that little boy?"

Timmy shrieked.

"Tell him to shut up," Roger said crankily.

Vivie was alarmed. "Roger, did you just tell the kidnappers to shut Timmy up?"

Roger patted the air with his free hand to encourage Vivie to mind her own business."

He said, "Uh huh" a couple more times, then hung up the phone.

He stood there, struck a noble, decisive pose and declared, "I'll put up the ransom money and save my nephew. This gang that calls itself the People's Liberation Army underestimates my resolve. I'm Roger Dunphy, I'll not be defeated."

Vivie rolled her eyes. She didn't buy Roger's performance. Apparently, neither did Gibbons or Higgins. Experienced newsmen, they smelled a rat.

Regrettably, even though he was standing at the very heart of Akron's leading newspaper, there was no one there interested in memorializing his remarkable declaration.

With chest out and head high, Dunphy strode out of the newspaper office like General Douglas MacArthur wading ashore on the beach at Leyte, but without the soggy trousers. Vivie caught up with him and they returned to the Hotel. Vivie didn't say anything as they entered the lobby. Vivie kept shaking her head as she briskly walked to the elevator while Roger went to the branch bank in the hotel lobby and cashed a corporate check for twenty thousand dollars.

Without the press covering this breaking story and with only his wife there as witness, Roger felt he was wasting his time. Why, without the media present his actions were nothing but a charade. He returned to the hotel room, showed Vivie the twenty thousand dollars and said, "I'm off to rescue Timmy." Then, sadly he added, "You might call the newspaper and let them know."

"Don't forget to free Avenger's imprisoned brothers – Larry, Curly and Moe - while you're at it."

He slammed the door on his way out, took the elevator to the lobby, and looked around hoping there might be at least one member of the press there to witness history being made. Disappointed once again, Dunphy went to the parking lot, found his rental car and drove off to retrieve Timmy and Boyd.

Back at the Sentinel Gibbons and Higgins couldn't make heads or tails of what was going on.

"This has the makings of a great shaggy dog story," said Higgins.

"So where is Timmy? And has he really been kidnapped?" said Gibbons.

"Search me," said Higgins.

CHAPTER 55

After dropping Fletcher off at his rooming house, an exhausted Dickie Yount went home for a shower, a clean change of clothes and to learn that he'd been fired as General Manager of the Great Soap Box Derby, Inc. Estelle gave Dickie the news as he walked into the living room of their house.

"Dickie, you must have expected this," said Estelle Yount. "You assaulted Roger Dunphy. And the worst cheating scandal in the history of the Derby happened while you were General Manager. What did you expect - a raise?"

Estelle saw that her words stung. She put her arm on his shoulder and guided Dickie to an easy chair. "I'm really sorry, Dickie, but this might be a blessing in disguise. You could go back and work with your dad at the appliance store."

Dickie slumped into the easy chair. It had never occurred to him that he'd ever be fired. After all, he was Mr. Derby. Derby royalty. How do you go back to selling ovens and garbage disposals after you've been royalty?

"They needed a scapegoat," he said bitterly.

Estelle tried to tease him into a healthier state of mind. She climbed onto his lap, threw her arms around his neck and began to nuzzle him. This had always worked in the past, but it was having no good effect on Dickie this day. He jerked his head out of nuzzling range. He didn't want consolation. What he wanted at that moment was revenge.

This was all Roger Dunphy's fault.

Estelle knew that when Dickie was mad he was likely to do something foolish. She sat in his lap and stayed there until his resistance weakened. She took off his large aviator-style glasses and began twirling his hair around her index finger. His face and neck wandered into nuzzling territory.

"Honey, I just know this is going to turn out for the best," she assured him. "You can deal with Roger Dunphy later."

He grumbled. A consolation nuzzle was better than no nuzzle at all, he supposed.

She softly whispered, "I'm making meatloaf for dinner."

She knew his soft spot.

CHAPTER 56

In the living room of Little San Simeon Jan and Ned were sharing her couch. Each had an end; their feet met in the middle. Ned was reading <u>Arrowsmith,</u> by Sinclair Lewis. Jan had squared away the details of their upcoming trip home for Christmas and was now working on her fauxbituary. It was warm inside the little cottage. Mugs of cocoa rested on the coffee table.

Jan shook her head. She was unhappy about the progress she'd made on her obit.

"The way I describe my early years makes me sound like a cross between Pippie Longstockings and that woman who wrote <u>Little House on the Prairie</u>."

"Laura Ingalls Wilder."

"Right. I think of myself as a humble person and that's how I want to be thought of. I can see why Pell Newcomb wants me to do this. You shouldn't be responsible for writing other peoples' obituaries unless you can write your own. It helps if you're dead. You gain perspective."

Ned said, "By the same line of reasoning you shouldn't be allowed to deliver a baby unless you've had one yourself. That would rule out a career as an obstetrician for me."

"Hmm, I see that my thinking is flawed. Are you considering obstetrics?"

"I'm considering it."

Jan smiled at the thought of Ned and babies. She tickled his feet with her own.

"What if you had to write your own obituary?"

"I'd have to write about us."

Jan said in a teasing manner, "Oh, what would you say?"

"Well, remember when we were at the Derby Museum and you said you didn't want our relationship to be like a Soap Box Derby race – short and boring?"

Jan laughed. "Yes."

"There's another reason I don't want my life to be like a Soap Box Derby Race. Those races are won by whoever keeps his head down lowest. I want to be able to keep my head up and be proud of what I do. I want to contribute to my community, my church and my family."

"That's nice."

"And I think I can do that best if I have a partner."

"Oh?" Jan stretched out that single syllable to a fine point as if it were taffy. She got a sense from Ned's tentative way of speaking that an important moment was imminent.

"With you."

Jan sat up. She tilted her head to look at Ned who was still reclining.

"Jan, I think I'm asking you if you'd like to get married."

"You think?"

"I know. Yes, definitely."

"You're sure?"

"Jan, I'm sure!"

Jan said 'yes' and threw her arms around Ned.

CHAPTER 57

As he drove to the motel to pick up Timmy and Boyd, Dunphy went over his story which went something like this:

He'd been directed by the voice on the telephone to drive to Oilville, to the corner of Sanderson and Teller Streets where he would find a telephone booth. He was to wait for the phone to ring. He did so. The phone rang, he picked it up and the voice told him to walk two blocks east. He did so and met a tall man with permed brown hair and sunglasses who demanded the twenty thousand dollars cash. He handed it over and once the man determined that the entire twenty thou was there Dunphy was told that he would find Timmy in the boathouse by the lake in Strasbourg Park. "Power to the People," the man said as he walked away. Dunphy drove around until he saw a sign for Strasbourg Park. He made it to the park, located the little boathouse and found Timmy with his hands and feet bound. He released Timmy and they drove to Akron.

The actual series of events was that Dunphy drove to the motel. Once he'd given the proper knock on the door that he and Boyd had worked out (knock, fast knock, knock, pause, slow knock) he was allowed in the room.

"Come on, let's get out of here," said Dunphy.

"Don't you want a receipt?" asked Boyd.

"A receipt? For what?" asked Dunphy puzzled.

"For the ransom," answered Boyd.

Dunphy swiveled his head around to address Timmy. "Don't forget: wear a ski helmet every time you hit the slopes."

Timmy nodded. Some kids in his position might be seething with resentment; Timmy just went numb and quiet.

The trip to Akron was uneventful. Dunphy periodically reminded Timmy not to talk about the kidnapping to anyone. Dunphy was worried that Timmy might say the wrong thing.

"Leave it to me and we'll both come out of this looking good."

When they got back to the Mayflower Hotel it was after dark. The hotel staff recognized Timmy and were polite but reserved.

Dunphy was still being given the cold shoulder. Dunphy couldn't get used to it.

Boyd booked a room for himself while Timmy and Roger went to the Dunphy suite. Timmy was reunited with his Aunt Vivie who was relieved, but not surprised, to see him in one piece. Kidnappers recently had taken to sending little body parts to prove they were serious about doing serious harm to their victims. Vivie swept back Timmy's long hair to make sure that Timmy's ears were still attached.

"Safe and sound, Vivie. See, I rescued the boy," Dunphy boasted.

"Whatever you say, Roger."

CHAPTER 58

In the early 1970s, in the later stages of the Vietnam War, there was a popular saying that made its way onto posters and bumper stickers: "What if they gave a war and nobody came?" That slogan can be paraphrased here: "What if Roger Dunphy called a press conference and nobody came?"

Try as he might Dunphy could not get anybody to pay attention to him. He called a press conference for noon (that is, noon p.m.) the next day. He had booked the conference room at the hotel. He had even had Boyd pay a bunch of street people to show up in support. But the press conference didn't happen because what's a press conference without the press? Dunphy sat at the table and waited. After waiting for forty minutes, he gave up and returned to his suite. The street people were returned to the street by the security staff.

"Vivie, we're getting out of this tinhorn town," Dunphy bellowed when he entered the suite, slamming the door behind him. "Call down and book the next flight to Denver."

Timmy spoke up. "I want to go to my mother."

Dunphy had forgotten about Timmy. That was easy for him to do since he had never really paid much attention or had much use for the boy. To Dunphy Timmy was a pathetic loser who refused to "get with the program." The program included the flag football games Roger organized on the front lawn at home. In his estimation Timmy couldn't hold a candle to Roger Dunphy Jr. who had just returned from a summer spent with some of his classmates in Europe. Boarding school would be starting in a few weeks and Roger Dunphy Sr. was eager to spend a few weeks with Junior before shipping him off to Connecticut.

"I'm not sure that's possible," said Dunphy. Dunphy wasn't comfortable dealing with the issue of his sister, Timmy's mother. Dunphy was about vigor and health, not sickness. Sickness was for losers.

Timmy responded, "I can go with Click and Tweedy."

"Who?"

"The newspaper guy and the photographer." Timmy changed his tone to insinuate, "If you won't let me go with them I can tell them things you don't want them to know."

It looked as though the time Timmy had spent with Dunphy hadn't been a total waste. He'd learned how to make threats.

Dunphy thought a moment and agreed that sending Timmy to the Mayo Clinic with the newspaper crew was a good idea.

"We'll go to the newspaper tomorrow morning."

Once that was settled Dunphy settled into a few minutes of rest and relaxation until there was a knock on the door. It was Dickie Yount. Dunphy put up his hands in a defensive posture ready to be assaulted. "What do you want?" he asked.

"Can I talk to you?" Dickie asked.

"As long as you don't get violent." Dunphy pointed to the bedroom he shared with Vivie. "In there."

Dunphy walked behind Dickie and closed the bedroom door behind them.

"Okay, what do you want?" he asked unpleasantly.

Dickie remained standing. "I know all about the kidnapping." He waited for a response from Dunphy.

Dunphy froze for a few seconds, regained his composure and said, "Timmy is safe."

Dickie said, "I know."

"So what is it you want – money?"

"Mr. Dunphy, because of you I lost my job."

Dunphy was irritated. "Because of me? What are you talking about? You attacked me! I could have had you arrested." His eyes narrowed to unpleasant little slits.

Dickie became defensive. "I know and..."

"And what? Look, pal, you come in here and threaten to blackmail me? I'm not going to stand for that."

Dickie was confused. Why would he blackmail a guy who had just rescued his nephew from kidnappers? How could he? Dunphy must misunderstand. "No, that isn't what I..."

Dunphy broke in, "Okay, you're out of a job because of me. Stop whining. You want a job? You can work for me. What were you making?"

Dickie told him.

Dunphy said, "All right, I'll double it. You never mention the kidna..." Dunphy caught himself. "The business we just went through to anyone, you get twice what you were making. Good enough?"

Dunphy figured it was worth it to buy Dickie Yount's silence. Besides, Dunphy didn't think well of anyone who worked for him, so what was one more incompetent parasite?

And so Dickie and Estelle were bound for Denver, Colorado to work for the man who ruined the Great American Soap Box Derby.

And that is why the good people of Akron ended up despising Dickie Yount, the former Mr. Derby.

CHAPTER 59

"Have you been to the Mayflower Hotel?" asked Tweedy.

Jan said 'no'.

"We should go there," Tweedy said. "Grab your coat."

He and Jan were in his tiny office. He stood up and started toward the exit followed by Jan who grabbed her coat and bag.

They didn't have to walk far. The former Mayflower Hotel, once the grandest hotel in Akron, was around the block.

Tweedy stopped in front of a rundown building. The magnificent art deco portico fabricated of stainless steel was no longer there, replaced by a plastic and tin sign reading "Mayflower Tower."

"This is it," said Tweedy.

It was no wonder that Jan had walked past it many dozens of times without paying it any attention. It was now subsidized senior housing.

Jan followed Tweedy inside. The grand ballroom, site of countless testimonial dinners and where the annual Great Soap Box Derby banquets used to be held, was now broken up by partitions into three areas: one was a dining area; another a television area with tables for small group activities; and another that was deemed a 'multi-use' space, which meant nothing went on there.

The cracks in the terrazzo floor in the lobby had been carelessly repaired with cement. Tweedy stood in the shabby lobby furnished with cheap vinyl covered chairs and laminate tables and began a recitation:

"And on the pedestal, these words appear:

My name is Ozymandias, King of Kings;

Look on my Works, ye Mighty, and despair!

Nothing beside remains. Round the decay.

Of that colossal Wreck, boundless and bare

The lone and level sands stretch far away."

He had that faraway cast to his eyes Jan had seen before. Some of the seniors who were playing out their strings sitting in the lobby stared at Tweedy. Some looked annoyed at the disturbance. Some sat slumped and snoozed. Jan clapped.

"Shelley, my favorite author!" she said. It seemed unnecessary to mention that what she liked about Shelley was his middle name.

Tweedy said, "When I was in school we had to memorize lots of poetry. Schools don't make students do that anymore. By the way, how's the evaluation going?"

Jan said, "I admit I'm having a hard time with it. I have learned a huge amount, especially from you and Pell Newcomb, and I've enjoyed every minute of it."

Tweedy smiled. "That's good enough for me. Now put it in writing for the MacNaughton committee, please.

"Mr. Tweedy, would you like to hear me recite 'Hiawatha'?"

Tweedy seemed surprised and delighted. "Yes, please."

CHAPTER 60

Roger and Vivie Dunphy and Timmy took a cab to the offices of the Sentinel to meet with Tom Higgins and Sam Gibbons. They were ushered into Higgins' office.

"Well, what can we do for you?" asked Higgins. He didn't invite them to sit down so they all stood.

Before Dunphy could open his mouth Timmy said, "I want to go to see my mother and I want Click and Jack Tweedy to take me."

Nothing could have pleased Higgins and Gibbons more. Tweedy's dispatches from the road had boosted circulation. Lots of readers had been disappointed when they abruptly and mysteriously ended a few days ago.

"Well, if it's okay with Mr.Tweedy and Miss Gunderson then it's fine with me," said Higgins. He picked up the phone, dialed their extensions and asked them to come to his office. As soon as they walked in Timmy's face lit up. He went over and stood between them.

"Click, Jack, ready to hit the road again?" Higgins asked.

They were willing and almost ready. Jack hadn't unpacked his stuff so he was ready, but Click had been to her apartment, unpacked, laundered and put her things away. It would take a few minutes for her to gather her stuff and re-pack. She would have to collect the photographic equipment for the van again. Aside from that, she was ready.

Higgins wrote out a voucher for Tweedy to cash at the treasurer's office. They discussed the itinerary, including Timmy's flight from Minnesota to Baltimore, and ironed out a few details. Then it was time for goodbyes. Vivie hugged Timmy; Roger shook the boy's hand.

Roger leaned down and whispered, "Remember, mum's the word."

Timmy thought Roger was talking about his sister, Timmy's mom. Timmy nodded.

Roger and Vivie returned to their suite, packed and checked out of the Mayflower. Their trip back to Denver was not without incident, however. As they moved through the airport terminal at the airport Roger got into a scuffle with some Hare Krishnas who were soliciting funds and singing.

"Hare Krishna, Hare Krishna, Hare, Hare, Hare Krishna," the shave-headed Krishans sang. Catchy tune, but not Roger's cup of tea.

"Out of my way, parasitic insects," sang Roger. *Parasitic insects – now where have I heard that phrase before?* Vivie asked herself.

Roger pushed one and slugged another of the saffron robed Hare Krishnas. They went down in an orange jumble and Roger ended up getting detained by airport security. Fortunately for Roger, the head of security was an understanding sort of man who had little patience for the Hare Krishna people and was sick of their monotonous singing. He negotiated a modest cash donation to the Krishas in exchange for dropping any possible future charges against the ski mogul.

At the departure gate they were greeted by the District Attorney accompanied by three Akron police officers. The travel agency in the Mayflower Hotel had helpfully contacted the D.A.'s office.

"What do you want?" Roger snarled.

The District Attorney reminded Roger that he was prohibited from leaving Akron until the D.A.'s office had decided what charges to bring against him.

"What'll it take to let us get out of this burgh?" Roger asked.

The D.A. corrected Roger. "Not 'us' - you. Your wife is free to go."

Vivie was sorely tempted to climb the stairs to the awaiting plane by herself. She looked at Roger hopefully.

"I've got your ticket," he said, patting his jacket and sneering. Directing his attention to the D.A. Roger asked, "Okay, what'll it take for me to get on that plane?"

"We'll consider not bringing charges in exchange for a donation of $1,000 to the Police Athletic League."

Roger's lips tightened into a scowl as he yanked his checkbook out of his jacket. He scribbled on the check, tore it out and shoved it at the D.A. who examined it closely. The truth was, the City of Akron was so eager to be rid of Roger that it would have paid for his plane fare.

"Okay?" asked Roger.

The D.A. said, "Okay."

"Insects!" was Roger's parting word as he climbed up the mobile stairs to the airplane.

Boyd was three seats behind Vivie and Roger.

Their Akron adventure was over. Akron, Roger and Vivie breathed a collective sigh of relief.

CHAPTER 61

Christmas! Jan's all-time favorite holiday.

With Ned behind the wheel of his car, Jan climbed in. The entire back seat was filled with brightly wrapped gifts in all sizes and shapes.

"Santa, take this sleigh to West Virginia!"

This year Jan had enough money to buy the gifts she wanted for the members of her family. Ned had done the correct thing and bought a gift for his hostess. Fancy embroidered tea towels are always appreciated even if they end up unused in the linen closet.

It was a cold and sunny day as Jan and Ned wound their way to the Pancake farm. As they passed under the familiar sign 'Welcome to West Virginia – Wild and Wonderful" Jan became contemplative. She still thought of West Virginia as home – she had, after all, grown up there. But in the last three plus years she had spent only a few months in her home state. She wondered how much more time she'd spend at her parents' place, especially now that she was engaged to Ned.

They had agreed to keep their engagement a surprise, intending to reveal the news at Christmas dinner. Ned would tell his parents when they went to Hingham, Massachusetts for New Years. Jan was excited that Ned would finally meet the family. It was late afternoon when they got to the farm. As they drove into the Pancake's hollow and up the gravel driveway to the house the Pancake clan came out to greet them. There were her parents, sisters, grandparents, Sissy, Mary Lou, Josiah, a couple of aunts and uncles, some kids and Myrt.

"Big family," Ned gulped.

"Big enough," replied Jan. "Look, Myrt's here!"

Ned parked. As they emerged from the BMW they were engulfed by family chattering and hugging.

Jan raised her voice, "Everyone, this is Ned." Ned was inundated by a wave of friendliness.

Jan waded through the crowd to join Myrt. The two friends hugged.

"Well," said Myrt with a big smile.

"Well," said Jan.

They began laughing.

"You're letting your hair grow long," said Jan.

"Yes."

Jan was nearly bursting. Yes, she'd agreed not to spill the beans, but she couldn't help it. "Myrt, we're engaged!"

Myrt started squealing and jumping up and down. This wasn't Myrt's customary conduct, but this was a special occasion and, besides, Myrt had changed.

"Can I tell?" Myrt asked Jan.

Jan bobbed her head 'yes'. Myrt announced it to the assembly. They were all excited and wanted details.

"This is good news," her father, Charlie, said quietly.

"She's all about news," said Josiah, "aren't you, Sis?"

"All the news that's fit to print," said Jan.

Mrs. Pancake urged everyone to get inside the house before they caught their death of cold. They trooped inside and continued sharing news.

At dinner that night Jan learned that her second grade teacher, Mrs. Sterling, had died a few weeks before. Jan was hurt that no one had thought to call her with this information. She would have come back for the funeral. It made her feel that much more distant from her childhood and left out of the community.

Like the rest of the second graders, Jan loved Mrs. Sterling. To them her piano accompaniment to classroom singing was a marvel. The way she encouraged their artistic endeavors made each and every one of them feel special. She involved herself in their play and was inventive.

"She was a warm, lovely person," said Jan, not letting on that she felt a bit hurt. "I would have liked to have had the chance to write her obituary."

Myrt said, "You still can, can't you? Maybe put it in the local paper or the school newsletter?"

Jan said that maybe she'd do that, but she knew she wouldn't. It was too late.

Mrs. Pancake said that it had been a very nice funeral service.

"Marcia Midkiff was at the funeral. She's going to be having her first baby soon. Do you plan to see her while you're home? You haven't seen Marcia in at least a year, as I recollect."

Marcia had been one of Jan's best friends growing up; friends from first grade on. After graduation Marcia began working at the dollar store full-time and continued dating her high school boyfriend, Trevor, before marrying him over a year ago.

The last time Jan had visited with them Marcia and Trevor spent most of their time discussing the particulars of their daily life between themselves and, Jan thought, showed very little interest in the particulars of Jan's life in college. She ended the evening early, leaving shortly after the table had been cleared but before the dishes had even been washed and dried.

"I don't think I'll be seeing her, Mom," Jan said. "Our lives have taken different paths."

Mrs. Pancake nodded and said, "Uh, huh."

Ned was pretty quiet at the dinner table but was comfortable answering questions about his family and his internship. When Uncle Carl found out Ned was a doctor he was eager to show him a rash he was concerned about. His wife, Jenny, frowned at Carl and that was that. There would be no medical consultation.

After dinner Jan was in her old bedroom unpacking. Myrt knocked on the open door.

"Want some company?" Myrt asked.

Jan smiled. "Whew, it's been nothing but company since we got here."

Myrt may have misunderstood. "If you'd rather we talk some other time..."

"No, no, come in," said Jan. "Please, I didn't mean you. Sit." Jan moved her suitcase and made some sitting room on the bed for Myrt.

"Myrt, I feel strange coming home now. Look around this room. It's full of stuff from my childhood. And I still feel pretty childish. I mean, I don't feel all that different. But I'm engaged to be married. That's pretty weird, don't you think?"

"That's a pretty adult thing to do," agreed Myrt. "So, did he ask you or did you ask him?"

Jan described the events leading up to his proposal.

Myrt asked, "And the matter about the sex worker and the internship program?"

Jan said, "She was an escort."

Myrt said, "That's a euphemism for 'sex worker' which is a euphemism for..."

Jan interrupted. "Whatever. The point is we got past it." Jan didn't feel much like talking about the decision not to print her expose, or about Phil Abrams or Julia. It all seemed unimportant.

"What about you and Josiah?" Jan asked.

"Well," Myrt said slyly, "I've decided I might go to veterinary school instead of med school."

"Oh?"

"That way I can help Josiah with the farm."

Jan asked, "What are you saying?"

"I'm saying we may have a future together. It won't be for a while. I've got a few years yet."

Jan had to ask, "Do you love my brother?" Jan felt a little funny talking about her brother this way.

Jan just said, "Hmm."

"He's very loveable," Myrt said. "We'll see."

They sat there on the bed. Jan had no more clothes to put away.

In church Christmas day Ned and Jan held hands and shared a hymnal. Pastor Linger seemed to be looking directly at Jan when he said, "Christmas time is a special time not only because of the birth of our Lord Jesus Christ but because it brings back to us the special people in our lives." Jan was content in this church and so happy to be with her family. She looked around at all the familiar faces.

Jan and Ned drove back to the farm with Myrt and Josiah. Myrt sang "Will Jesus Wash the Bloodstains from Your Hands" an old Hazel Dickens tune.

Jan said, "That's a little gruesome, don't you think, Myrt?"

"Roots music, sister, roots music."

So much for Tuvan throat singing, thank goodness, thought Jan. Then she had another thought that made her laugh out loud. *Flo McCauley could get those bloodstains out.*

"What's so funny?" asked Myrt.

Jan just shook her head.

Christmas dinner brought out the Pancakes' good china. Mrs. Pancake exhausted herself cooking but declared afterwards that it was "worth it."

During dinner Jan told a story that her family had enjoyed for years:

The Church's youth groups traditionally staged tableaux for Christmas in the sanctuary after Celebration. When Josiah was nine years old his group was assigned staging the nativity scene. Josiah was given the role of a cow.

"Since he was raised on a farm that had cows it was good casting," said Mrs. Pancake.

Josiah sat back in his chair and smiled.

Jan continued the story: "In rehearsal Josiah did just fine holding up the cow's head. But when it came time for the actual performance the boy who was supposed to hold up the donkey's head didn't show up." Jan turned to Josiah. "That was Carl Bagley, wasn't it?"

Josiah nodded. "It was Carl; he showed up all right, but he puked because he was nervous and couldn't go on."

Jan continued: "Oh, well, there was no one else to hold up the donkey head so Mrs. Pennington asked Josiah to hold up both heads. And you know Josiah. He'll agree to anything."

Most everyone at the table nodded and chuckled. They knew what was coming.

"So, the curtains parted and there was the tableau. The sacred nativity scene. All was still...except the cow's head and the donkey's head kept bobbing up and down. First one person in the audience began laughing, then everyone began laughing. Mrs. Pennington had worked so hard on this tableau and everyone was laughing. She closed the curtains and began crying."

Everyone at the table looked toward Josiah, who couldn't help but laugh. "Those heads were paper mache and were heavy."

Myrt smiled and kissed Josiah on the cheek. "My hero!"

Charlie Pancake slowly shook his head and grinned. "With Josiah it was always one thing or another."

While Mrs. Pancake, Jan and Sissy were doing the dishes Mrs. Pancake remarked that Ned was a closed-mouth sort of fellow.

"Don't talk much, that's for sure," said Sissy.

Jan smiled. "He talks to me."

"Well, that's a blessing," said Mrs. Pancake, satisfied with Jan's answer.

The rest of the Christmas holiday passed too fast. Jan really didn't get to spend much time individually with her brother or sisters. Sissy and Mary Lou still hadn't been to visit Jan. They vowed to try to convince their parents to take them. And Josiah, well, he was so enchanted by Myrt that he could talk about little else.

Periodically, Jan would ask Ned, "You okay?"

His answer was always "Fine," accompanied by a smile or an arm around her waist. Ned was not an overly demonstrative person, so it came as a surprise when he surprised Jan by presenting her an engagement ring while everyone was around the Christmas tree exchanging gifts. Her response was like a special Christmas cookie recipe, a mixture of surprise, excitement and elation, with tears, hugs and kisses folded in.

And Ned liked his new sweater very much.

When they drove back to Akron the back seat was emptier, but their hearts were full.

CHAPTER 62

Once again, Timmy, Tweedy and Click embarked upon their odyssey to Rochester, Minnesota. Click would take pictures and Tweedy would write articles about Timmy's trip. Timmy's spirits were higher than they had been since the interruption of the trip by the kidnapping attempt. Tweedy had been told by Higgins that he was not to mention the kidnapping. It was as though the kidnapping never happened, which, in a sense, was the truth. Roger Dunphy thought that Timmy had agreed that "mum's the word" meant that he wouldn't tell anybody about his experience. Once again Roger was mistaken. How likely was it that he wouldn't talk? He was a thirteen-year-old boy who had experienced something very unusual. He shared the details of the kidnapping with Tweedy and Click. They agreed not to discuss it with others.

"I think you should have this van painted psychedelic," said Timmy.

Click, who was driving, said, "You mean like Ken Keysey's bus?"

"Yeah."

"Further," said Tweedy, "that was the name of the bus."

Tweedy said he would pass on Timmy's suggestion to management. He asked Timmy what he thought was wrong with the van's present color which was pearl gray.

"Well, it's kind of boring," said Timmy.

"What's wrong with that?" asked Tweedy. "Do you think it should be fire engine red?"

"As red as a cardinal?" asked Click.

"Yup, that'd be great!" said Timmy, before asking, "We're still going to your family farm, right?"

"It's up to you," said Tweedy.

Timmy asked, "Chickens, ducks, woodchucks, deer, bears even?"

"And lots of birds. We've got binoculars there."

This pleased Timmy.

Tweedy said that for decades the family farm was known by family members as The Gathering. Then a horror movie named The Gathering, based on a horror novel by the same name, was released.

"Completely spoiled the name for us. We've been looking for a better name ever since."

A minute passed. Click began, "How about…"

Tweedy interrupted her. "We don't want a pun. Puns get stale very fast."

"Oh," said Click.

"My Uncle Chuck named the back parlor "The Elbow Room" but it never caught on. He thought it was appropriate because going out to the farm gave people a chance to get away from their cramped lives."

"Nice sentiment," said Click

"Decent pun," said Tweedy.

They stayed at the same motel they stayed at the first time they passed this way and ate breakfast in the same coffee shop. This time, though, Timmy had something called 'pigs in a blanket'. The name tickled him and he repeated it over and over and laughed.

"Why is that so funny?" asked Click.

Timmy didn't know. It just did. For the next couple of days all Tweedy or Click had to say was 'pigs in a blanket' and Timmy would double over with laughter.

Timmy was sometimes very silly and sometimes very serious.

"Please don't call me Timmy anymore," he asked as they were motoring through Summerfield, Michigan.

Click asked, "What would you like us to call you? Tim?"

"My mother calls me Timothy."

Click and Tweedy agreed to call the boy Timothy from then on.

"And I'll call you 'Snap'," Timothy said, pointing to Click. "And you'll be…" he paused trying to come up with a funny name for Tweedy.

"How about 'Bruce'?" said Tweedy.

Timothy and Click both said "Bruce?" at the same time.

"Why Bruce?" asked Click.

"It's a very heroic name," said Tweedy.

Timothy didn't see Tweedy as a Bruce and decided that Tweedy's name should remain Tweedy. Click agreed. "You are a Tweedy kind of guy, you know," she said. This wasn't a taunt. She had grown fond of Tweedy.

Timothy asked whether they could make a slight detour so that they could pass through Greenville, Michigan.

"Why?" asked Click.

"When I was kidnapped Boyd and I were watching cable television. There was this Arts and History Channel show about hidden places in America. Did you know that James Dean is in a sanitarium in Greenville? He didn't really die in that car wreck. He survived but was horribly maimed and made crazy so they sneaked him out to Greenville where there's this sanitarium. He sits at a window there and waves at cars going by."

Tweedy asked, "This was a cable television show?"

Timothy said, "Uh, huh. And they showed pictures of the place. I know I can recognize it if we go by it. Maybe James Dean will wave at us."

Click and Tweedy looked at one another. Tweedy shrugged. "Why not? And Click can take a picture of James Dean waving at you. Front page stuff."

"You mean 'Snap'," corrected Timothy.

Click said, "We'll go there but you'll have to call me 'Click'. It was hard enough getting used to 'Click'."

Timothy asked, "What's your real name?"

"Marjorie."

Tweedy said, "That's a nice name."

"Thank you. Okay, Greenville, it is."

They drove to Greenville, population 533, but try as they might, they could not find a sanitarium. They found a barbershop and spied other cars with out-of-state license plates driving around looking in vain for the dead movie star. The detour was not a complete loss. At one point they got out of the car and Click took photos of Timothy searching for James Dean.

"Put your hand up to your eyebrow," Click directed Timothy. "No, not that way. You look like you're saluting. Try to look like Lewis and Clark. You're on a bluff overlooking the Columbia River scanning the horizon."

"Who is Lewis N. Clark? Are we supposed to know him?" Tweedy said with a twinkle in his eye."

Click lowered her camera and slowly shook her head side to side in mock consternation. "Tweedy, you are a very silly man." She explained to Timmy, "Lewis *and* Clark were explorers."

"What does the 'N.' stand for in Lewis N. Clark?" Timmy asked before breaking down in a case of the giggles.

"It stands for anything you want it to stand for, my good man," answered Tweedy, "or it stands for 'Nothing'."

"Timmy, you're as bad as Tweedy." Click stifled her own giggles as she scolded them. "Now come on, be serious."

Timmy nodded and assumed a more explorer-ish pose.

""Perfect," said Click. She took some shots.

They returned to the van and resumed traveling.

"Did you know that Lewis had a nervous breakdown?" asked Tweedy. "Ended up committing suicide."

Click asked, "Who, Meriwether Lewis the explorer or Lewis N. Clark the inventor of the whoopee cushion?"

"What's a whoopee cushion?" Timothy asked.

"I'll let you explain the whoopee cushion to him, Tweedy," said Click.

"Timmy, there is no explanation for the whoopee cushion. It speaks for itself."

"How'd Clark kill himself?" asked Timothy.

Tweedy said he didn't know.

On their way back to the highway Timothy called out "Stop!" Click slammed on the brakes.

"What?" she asked urgently. "Did you spot the sanitarium?"

"A turtle," said Timothy. He was craning his neck to look back at the side of the road they had just passed. "Back up."

It was a country road so there was no traffic. Click backed up until the van was abreast of a painted turtle that lay on the side of the tarmac. Timothy jumped out and knelt to inspect the turtle. The turtle, which was about 10 inches from head to tail, tucked his head into his shell which had been damaged by an automobile. The shell was cracked on the edge and a smear of blood marred his green skin. Click parked on the roadside. She and Tweedy joined Timothy who had picked up the turtle and inspected the injury.

"The carapace is fractured, but the plastron is fine."

Thank goodness for that.

"Do we have a box we can put him in?" he asked. "We can take him to your farm, can't we? We can release him there."

Tweedy worried that the turtle was in worse shape than Timothy thought.

"I guess so," Tweedy said reluctantly. He didn't want to disappoint the boy if the turtle were to die.

Click found a photographic paper box that was nearly empty. She emptied it and Timothy put the turtle in it.

Tweedy said, "Doesn't it need one of those little plastic palm trees?"

Click and Timothy ignored the joke. Click asked, "I have some red nail polish. Could you repair the shell with that?"

Timothy thought that might work. Click fished through her bag, found the polish and gave it to Timothy. Click took a couple of photographs of Timothy and the turtle. At the next opportunity she'd wire them to the Sentinel. They reassembled in the van and Click drove off.

"Do we have to get lettuce for him?" Tweedy asked.

"I don't know. He might be in shock. He might not want to eat," said Timothy who kept his eye on the turtle.

Click teased Tweedy. "You know, they eat flies. Jack, keep your mouth open and when you catch a fly close your mouth real quick."

Timothy added, "Make sure not to swallow. It's best if they're still alive."

"Ha, ha," said Tweedy.

The next day they reached Jack Tweedy's family farm. To get there they had to drive about a mile through woods.

"We have to watch out for deer and my sister Aggie," said Tweedy.

"Who's going to be there?" asked Timothy.

"You never know," said Tweedy. "The farm is owned by all the members of the family. So there is family there all the time during the summer. We have fun there all summer and during the winter the place gets vandalized. My cousins Arthur and Larry should be there now. And my cousin Denny. And Aggie. You'll like her. She's the family hippie with all sorts of nutty ideas, but very kind. Some of my cousins all have kids so they'll be there."

Ten days earlier Tweedy had written letters to Arthur and Larry and some other family members asking them to please not bring up the topic of the Great Soap Box Derby during their sojourn.

Eventually the road looped around in front of a sprawling green Victorian farmhouse with wraparound porches on the ground floor and two sleeping porches on the second floor. Nearby was a barn.

"There's Arthur," said Tweedy. He seemed excited to see his cousin. The van stopped and Click and Timothy slid out onto the ground. Arthur saw Tweedy and raced up to the van to embrace Tweedy. Tweedy introduced Click and Timothy, then did the same when Arthur's brother Larry strolled over.

"What's happening?" asked Tweedy.

"The usual," said Arthur.

That sounded pretty good to Tweedy, Click and Timothy.

"Where's the best place to release a painted turtle around here?" Timothy asked.

Larry asked, "You've got a painted turtle?"

Timothy nodded.

"Lake Shorty," Larry and Arthur said at the same time.

"Hey, Audrey! Come over here, please," Arthur called to one of the kids playing nearby. Audrey, Arthur's ten year old, stopped playing and ran over, pigtails flying.

"Would you show Timothy the way to Lake Shorty, please?"

Audrey said, "Sure."

Arthur introduced Timothy and Click to his daughter. She already knew Tweedy, who she called Uncle Jack.

"Come on," Audrey said, and called a couple of kids to tag along. Timothy said he had to get his painted turtle. Audrey and the other kids followed Timothy to the van, which they all thought was cool. They took the box with the painted turtle and headed into the woods.

Arthur confided to Tweedy that he'd often tried to find Lake Shorty as an adult and failed. The farm had a couple of hundred acres, much of it wooded, so Lake Shorty – more of a large pond, really – would be easy to misplace.

Tweedy said, "I remember tons of bullfrogs."

Arthur and Larry remembered the bullfrogs, too.

"Maybe Lake Shorty is one of those magical places that only kids can see," Tweedy speculated.

Larry scoffed. "There you go again, Jack, always romanticizing things. The fact is Lake Shorty is small but it's still big enough to be seen by satellite."

Larry worked in Naval Intelligence so he would know.

The farm more-or-less paid for itself by leasing out acreage to local farmers for cattle grazing, growing asparagus, and by the careful harvesting of lumber. That paid for the utilities and upkeep. Even though the farmhouse was located within 100 acres of field and forest vandals managed to find the place during the two seasons it was usually unoccupied. Some years the vandalism was worse than others. Jack's sister Aggie was convinced the vandalism followed lunar cycles.

The farm was otherwise run along the lines of a commune. There were plenty of chores for everyone. There was always cooking and laundry to do. Cousin Arthur enjoyed mowing the grass. His wife, Miriam, enjoyed gardening, as did Tweedy's sister Aggie. Fortunately, more than one of the relatives was handy using tools. Even the children were given suitable tasks.

"Is Aggie here?" asked Tweedy.

He'd barely gotten the words out when a large woman in a bright caftan and head scarf came charging out of the house.

"Jack, you made it!"

Aggie wrapped her arms around Tweedy, squeezing him so tight she almost lifted him off his feet.

"Hi, Aggie," Tweedy squeaked.

Aggie released him so that she could welcome Click and Timothy. Aggie gave Timothy a big hug.

"Well, let's get you settled," said Aggie, taking charge. "You're just in time for dinner."

"Great, we're hungry," said Tweedy.

Aggie laughed. "No, Jack, you're just in time to help make dinner."

That evening it was warm and dry so dinner was served outside as it usually was. People sat and ate wherever they wanted – on the porches, at the picnic benches or on blankets on the ground. Tweedy was put in charge of getting tableware onto the tables. Timothy was kept busy helping around the kitchen then when outside to play. Click, her sleeves rolled up and her hair in a kerchief, had quickly become part of the family cooking crew and had made friends.

Tweedy watched her with admiration. Tweedy wished he made friends that easily.

"You know," he said when Click stepped out onto the porch for a break, "you're a good egg."

Click knew this was a high compliment. She wiped the sweat from her forehead, smiled and thanked him. "I'm having fun. Coming here was a good idea. Look at Timmy, sorry, Timothy."

Timothy was goofing around with the other kids. Later after it got dark he would join in with the others in a game of flashlight tag. Click noticed that Timothy was no longer picking at his cuticles.

"You know I invented flashlight tag," said Larry to everyone within earshot.

This wasn't so, but no one could be bothered to argue. Larry was extremely competitive. At the ping pong table he crushed anyone who challenged him. He was so overly serious about the game that after a while it wasn't fun anymore and no one would play with him.

When it got dark Click and Tweedy sat on the porch and watched the fireflies. It was late in the season so there wasn't the abundance there had been in July.

"Most of the fireflies have found their partners. Those guys," Tweedy pointed to the few blinking bugs out in the field, "they're the loners, the ones who couldn't find a mate."

Click said, "Maybe they were too choosey. They lose out."

Tweedy offered, "Let that be a lesson to you, Click. Don't be too choosey. Remember, I'm still available. You just have to lower your standards." He raised his eyebrows to assure her that he was joking.

"Hmmm," said Click noncommittally. "By the way, where are we sleeping tonight?"

Tweedy acted shocked. "I said I was available; I didn't say I was easy."

"Tweedy!"

"Well, there are bunks in the barn. There are beds on the sleeping porches of the Manse and I'm sure there must be an available bed in what they call the girls' dorm – that's up in the attic. Timothy can have the room I reserve for myself every year. Okay?"

CHAPTER 63

Mornings at the farm were not greeted as was often the case by a rooster's crowing. The farm was only used a few months of the year by the family so animals couldn't be raised there. One of the local farmers leased pastureland from the family and cattle could be heard in the distance. The family made do with a cowbell hanging from the porch outside the kitchen that was rung to announce mealtime.

Their second day at the farm found Tweedy, Click and Timmy following the lead of the rest of the family by relaxing. The only one who found it impossible to relax was Cousin Larry. As he did every year he tried to assemble a group to go hunting with him. And as usual he failed. He stood on the front porch wearing his camouflage pants and shirt, holding his rifle and calling out to everyone he saw "Say, want to do a little hunting?" They all shook their heads. They'd gone through this before. Every summer Larry brought his gun to the farm. Every summer he'd ask if anyone wanted to be his shooting buddy. Every year everyone said 'no'.

"This is a family of gatherers, Larry," said Cousin Bette, "not hunters. That's why we gather here every summer."

This was extremely frustrating for Larry. There were so many deer in the woods surrounding the farm and many of them taunted Larry by moseying up to the farm at dusk. Larry lived and worked in Washington, D.C. where hunting wildlife was discouraged.

"What about the kids?" groused Larry. "You shouldn't speak for them."

Cousin Fred answered, "Don't be ridiculous, Larry. Of course we speak for them. They're our children."

Aunt Martha, Larry's mother, smiled and said, "Larry, why don't you help us pick blueberries?"

Larry gave up, shook his head and plopped down on a wicker chair on the porch. He set his sights on Tweedy and Timmy. "What about you two?"

Tweedy shook his head. "No, thanks, Larry, but can I make a suggestion?"

"Sure."

"Instead of that camouflage outfit why not try disguising yourself as a Pontiac or a Chevrolet? Cars don't seem to have any trouble bagging deer."

"Ha, ha," Larry said sarcastically.

Timmy asked Larry, "Can I see your gun?"

That was the opening Larry needed. "Sure!" he said enthusiastically.

Timothy looked at Tweedy for approval. "Can I?"

Tweedy shrugged his shoulders and followed Timothy to where Larry sat. He began explaining that "this is a Tarpon 336."

"Is that a good gun?" asked Timothy.

"It's chambered for .30 -.30 Winchester or .35 Remington cartridges. It'll get the job done," Larry said firmly.

"Where do the batteries go?" asked Tweedy.

Larry squinted at him trying to figure out whether Tweedy was trying to pull his leg or not. Tweedy wasn't. "Jack, do you see the name 'Mattel' anywhere on this rifle?"

Tweedy was embarrassed.

Larry said, "Let me explain," in that superior way he had.

He proceeded to show Timothy and Tweedy how the rifle operated. Timothy and Tweedy were both impressed with the engineering that made the rifle operate. Tweedy conceded that it was a "clever bit of machinery'. He was still surprised that no batteries were required. Timothy admired the quality of the finish on the wooden stock.

Once he was finished explaining things Larry asked, "So, want to do a little hunting?"

Timothy said, "Kill animals? Uh, uh, no way."

Tweedy smiled. "Larry, we're going to go hunt wild blueberries. We'll bring you back a big one...maybe even the legendary Big Blue." He led Timothy off the porch and towards some family members, each of whom was carrying a pail or basket.

"Wimps," muttered Larry.

Tweedy heard Larry's remark. He called back over his shoulder, "You won't say that when you're eating your blueberry pancakes at breakfast tomorrow."

"That's telling him," said Timothy.

"Come on, let's get some buckets. It's man versus blueberry and may the best blueberry win."

Larry stood on the porch with his legs spread wide and his hands on his hips, shaking his head in disgust.

CHAPTER 64

The following day Tweedy drove to Guelph, the nearest town that had telephone service to call in his dispatch to the newspaper. He learned from Higgins that Vivie Dunphy had called a press conference in Aspen and announced that she would be filing for divorce from Roger. Her press conference had much higher attendance than Roger's press conference. That comparison is not really fair, though, because Vivie was a popular socialite in Aspen's fashionable circles whereas Roger had been the most despised person in the eyes of all Akron.

Tweedy wondered what effect this would have on Timothy's situation. He figured on asking Click, who had a better grasp of these things. After picking up the local newspaper he drove back to the farm. He pulled up and watched as Timothy was teaching the entire family how to do the Teaberry Shuffle, a dance step made popular by a chewing gum commercial. From inside the van Tweedy laughed along with everyone else. He watched Click as she snapped photographs.

Tweedy got out of the van and walked across the lawn to where Click was standing. "How did this happen?" Tweedy asked.

Click had to laugh. "I have no idea! Your sister is getting her cassette player so we can all do the twist. That includes you." She could see him wince. "Now don't be an old stick-in-the-mud."

"I'm not," insisted Tweedy. "I'm a stuffed shirt."

But when his sister returned with the cassette player Tweedy twisted along with everyone else. He declared it a "blast," a word he had never used before. Talking to Timothy about the divorce could definitely wait.

Later that afternoon Timothy decided to see how the painted turtle was making out. He thought he'd better inform Tweedy and Click, who were both sitting on the side porch.

"Can we come?" asked Tweedy.

"Sure."

Some other little kids asked whether they could join the party so off they went to Lake Shorty. Click insisted that everyone apply insect repellent. The little kids, being little kids, raced ahead on the path. Timothy hung back with Click and Tweedy, pointing out some of the more noteworthy birds, trees and other vegetation as they walked on the trail.

"You see that? That's a ladyslipper. And that's a mugwort." Further along the trail he pointed out a blue mistflower.

Click said, "That mistflower is very pretty. You're a real naturalist. Is that what you want to do?"

Timothy replied, "Maybe."

When Timothy spotted a pretty purple flower he bent over and broke the flower off at the stem. When he thought that Tweedy wasn't looking he shyly offered it to Click.

"Thank you, Timothy," she said. "You are most gallant." She gave him a smile.

Timothy smiled back, a little bit embarrassed, and raced to catch up to the little kids.

Tweedy, who had observed the exchange, said, "Click, I do believe that boy has a crush on you."

Click nodded.

Tweedy said, "He's not the only one."

Click sighed. "Oh, Tweedy."

"Why, what's wrong with me?" Tweedy asked. "I'm not such a bad looking guy."

"No, Jack, you're not."

"Then what?" Tweedy pressed."

"Jack, can't we just enjoy this walk; being outside on a beautiful day?"

"Sorry if I'm spoiling things," Tweedy said.

"Oh, Jack."

After a while Lake Shorty revealed itself. There were bullfrogs everywhere, and small fish, and turtles basking in the sun on logs.

"There's a snapping turtle," yelled one child.

"It's so ugly," said another.

"Stay clear of it," warned Tweedy.

It was large, greenish and mossy looking with a pointy little snout, feet with huge claws and a bad disposition. The derogatory things the children said about the snapping turtle might account for its attitude. One child picked up a long stick and began to poke at it. Timothy grabbed the stick and tossed it in the woods.

"It's one of God's creatures," he said simply. "Leave it alone."

The child resented being scolded by another child. "It's ugly."

Timothy didn't respond.

The band scouted around the little lake. Someone spotted Timothy's painted turtle resting on the bank. It was easy to spot because of its shiny coat of nail polish on one edge of its shell.

"He'll be happy here," said Click. "This is a good place for him."

"Are you sure it's a 'he'?" asked Tweedy. "After all, it's wearing nail polish."

"Oh, Tweedy."

That evening's dinner was barbeque, except for Aggie who made a lentil and quinoa loaf for herself and anyone else willing to risk a case of gastritis. It weighed approximately fourteen pounds. Dinner conversation at the table ran the usual gamut from politics, the environment, and the next day's weather. At Tweedy's end of the table his sister Aggie talked about UFOs and alien abductions. Aggie had wild red hair that looked like the tangle of wire coat hangers you find on the floor of your closet. She wore baggy dresses that looked like Indian wall hangings. Her feet were shod in big clunky earth shoes. Whenever she saw Tweedy she'd hug him and tell him he needed to get Rolfed.

"I'm not getting Rolfed," Tweedy always said, "and I'm not joining an encounter group. Not now, not ever."

Aggie had a new audience in Timothy. She started off by hugging him. Aggie had become a big hugger ever since she took some courses in mind control taught by Fernando Silva. She dove into her shoulder bag that may have been made from remnants of the same Indian bedspread her dress was made from, only with little mirrors sewn on. She pulled out a yellow smiley button and tried to pin it on Timmy.

"You need to smile more," she said.

Timmy shrank back and refused her button. "Smiley buttons? They're so 1960s," he said. "This is 1973."

Aggie shook her head. *An unhappy boy*, she thought.

After dinner Aggie tracked Timothy to the porch where he was sitting on a glider with Tweedy. She sat down beside Timothy. "You know about the hollow earth theory, right?" she whispered. She said this with the same conspiratorial glee that she demonstrated when the truth about Area 54 was first revealed to her.

Timothy shook his head which was Aggie's signal to launch into theories about the Bermuda Triangle, the hollow earth, UFOs, demonic possession, and voodoo. She showed Timothy an amulet she wore around her neck.

"See this? This was given to me by Marie Levay, the voodoo priestess. Very strong magic."

"Aggie, stop trying to fill this boy's head with nonsense," Tweedy admonished his sister. "He's got enough things to deal with. Let him digest his dinner in peace."

"But I want to hear, Tweedy," said Timothy.

Tweedy gave up. "All right, Aggie, let 'er rip."

For the next hour or so Aggie filled Timothy's head up with late night AM talk radio nonsense. His conclusion?

"Aggie's a very interesting person."

Tweedy said, "Timothy, I think you might have a future in the diplomatic corps."

CHAPTER 65

Every Thursday evening during the summer movies were shown in the barn. The projector was old and so were the movies, but the popcorn that came from the kitchen was fresh and hot. This evening's film was <u>The Babe Ruth Story</u>, starring William Bendix.

"I've watched that movie every summer," said Tweedy. "It portrays Babe Ruth's life with the same veracity that Beetle Bailey deals with the war in Vietnam. I say we skip it."

After a review like that Click agreed not to go the movie. Timothy went along with Tweedy and Click. So, instead of watching this cinematic gem they sat on the back porch, listening to an owl and the other nocturnal birds and the mechanical whir of the cicadas, and watching the stars.

Tweedy said, "Timothy, do you think we ought to leave tomorrow to go see your mother?"

"Aren't you having fun?" Timothy asked.

"Well, yes, of course, but...don't you want to get to where your mother is?" Tweedy hated to say 'the hospital'.

"I guess."

Click asked, "You're a little afraid."

Timothy nodded and lowered his head.

The adults would have liked to say something along the lines of "I'm sure your mother would like to see you," but they weren't entirely sure of the condition of Timothy's mother.

Click said gently, "I think it's time we go."

"Tomorrow morning," said Tweedy. He made it sound like a question, hoping to be challenged.

"Let's stay one more day," said Timothy.

"You make a very formidable argument, young man," said Tweedy. "Your logic is unassailable. I vote for staying another day. Click?"

Click laughed. "Oh, heck, why not?"

The next morning Click was involved in making breakfast for everyone. When Tweedy entered the kitchen and saw Click making flapjacks he began thinking what it might be like to live with Click. To have Click making breakfast just for him. Tweedy may have gotten used to eating food prepared by Swanson's but that didn't mean that he couldn't get used to food that didn't come frozen in small partitioned aluminum trays. Tweedy left the kitchen and puttered around the farmhouse informing family members that his group would be leaving the following day. When his sister heard this she sought out Timothy and took him aside in the front parlor.

She whispered to him conspiratorially, "Timothy, I'm going to give you something, but don't tell my brother." She removed the amulet from around her neck and held it in both hands the way you would a newborn chick.

"Now when you get to your mother's you take this and hide it in a place as close to her as you can. Maybe hide it under her mattress; that's a good place."

She removed a candle, a feather and a piece of paper from the big fabric bag embroidered with little mirrors and elephants that was slung over her shoulder. "Every evening you light this candle, blow on this feather and say this prayer." She poked at the words written on the piece of paper. Your mother will get well."

Tweedy had walked into the parlor and heard Aggie.

"Aggie, is this black magic?" Tweedy asked.

Aggie hissed impatiently. "Timothy, don't listen to him."

"No, it's not black magic," she answered Tweedy. "That would be evil. This is white magic."

Turning back to Timothy she entreated him. "Will you do this?"

Timothy assured her he would.

"Swear. Spit on your palm and swear."

Timothy spat. "I swear I'll do it."

Aggie said "Good," gave Timothy a hug and glided away towards the dining room to enlist some adults and children to participate in some "New Games".

"The New Game movement aims to orient people away from competitive sports and toward cooperative games," she announced to a curious audience of flapjack eaters.

"You see, deep within you is a superb athlete with fantastic abilities. But society has undermined and suppressed those abilities."

"Where are you coming from, Aggie? Nobody ever suppressed my ability. I just wasn't any good," said Old Jack Lydecker. "Have you ever seen me actually hit a baseball? No one else has either."

Aggie shook her head. "Jack, think back to the memories of past humiliations you felt when you were playing sports. Remember how disappointed your parents were when you didn't excel on the playing field?"

Jack was a good-natured guy. "Aggie, I wasn't any good. That's all there was to it." He laughed.

Jack's brother, Ed, piped up, "He's telling the truth: he was terrible."

"Yup, but you were even worse," answered Jack.

They both broke out laughing.

"You have untapped ability," insisted Aggie.

"No, Aggie, I'm tapped; I'm plenty tapped," said Old Jack. "But you tell us about your games," he said, a mite patronizing.

"Well, I took a workshop at Esalen on game theory and it all made a lot of sense. Traditional sports are macho and embed aggressive behaviors that become a lifelong pattern. We can break that pattern by substituting noncompetitive games that foster cooperation."

A couple of the women nodded. It made sense to them.

"So, this afternoon we're going to play some new games that everyone can participate in. There'll be no hard and fast rules. It'll be us playing together to achieve a goal of harmony and understanding."

"And enlightenment," added Click.

"Anyone who wants to join in meet at the front lawn at eleven," said Aggie, "and be prepared to have fun."

"What's wrong with softball?" grumbled Larry.

"Badminton is fun," said Tweedy.

At eleven about fifteen members of the family, children and adults, showed up in the front lawn for Aggie's games. Larry was wearing a track suit and carrying his cleats, just in case he needed them.

"Aggie, what did you do to your face?" Tweedy shrank back in mock horror at the sight of his sister, her face painted in garish colors and glistening from lots of glitter.

"Games are supposed to be fun and I thought I should look funny." Aggie was wearing tie-dyed coveralls "You'll notice I don't have a whistle around my neck. There are no hard and fast rules to any of the games. No off-sides, no out of bounds. Just fun."

"Well you look a fright," said Tweedy. He'd always razzed his sister; no reason to stop now. "Next thing I expect you'll be sporting tattoos."

Aggie shook her head. "Tattoos? No, the only people you'll ever see with tattoos will be sailors and convicts, same as always."

"Whatever you say, Sis."

The first game was Gorpball, a game that was meant to blur male/female inequalities leading to a oneness of all and an appreciation of the specialness of our differences, according to Aggie.

Tweedy groaned as he pushed the gigantic water-filled gorpball.

"You know, Aggie, this human potential movement of yours will fail not because of its ideas but because of the gibberish you use to explain those ideas."

Gorpball involved pushing against the gigantic ball and moving it past various lines laid out in the grass. Because it was so heavy it required cooperation. When one side appeared to be winning they were encouraged to join the losing side and help out.

Larry was lost. "I don't understand the point of this at all," he griped.

Aggie explained. "Larry, competition is good, but winning and losing is not."

"Then what's the point?"

Aggie spoke to Larry as though he were a kindergartner. "The point is human transformation."

Timothy, who was pushing the ball on the winning/losing side said, "I want to be transformed into a turtle."

Tweedy laughed. "I want to be transformed into a duck. Quack, quack!"

Larry didn't laugh. "So what team am I on?"

"No team, Larry," said Aggie. "Join the side you want to join. Switch sides if you want. We're about inclusion here, not exclusion."

Once about ten people were involved in Gorpball (or were thoroughly confused) Aggie moved to the meadow and started a new game called Human Knot. Human Knot was a version of the commercial board game Twister that was introduced in 1969. Tweedy joined this game because he saw Click getting involved. Human Knot was a physical game requiring players to connect their hands and feet to other players' hands and feet according to the directions of the "facilitator." The game was a good stretching exercise and a way to get very close to other people very quickly.

Aggie assigned the role of facilitator to their cousin, Will. Will called out the moves: "Okay, left hand over your neighbor's right leg", etc. Though he tried to get in a position close to Click Tweedy ended up in ultra-close contact with his hefty Aunt Hazel. It was much too uncomfortable for Tweedy – he had known Hazel his entire life in an entirely different way and had no intention of knowing her any other way - so he called out, "I lost it in the sun" as though he were a baseball outfielder. He broke the wrestling position he was in with Hazel and scurried off to join the Gorpballers.

I'll never be able to look Aunt Hazel in the eye again, Tweedy thought. *And I'll get back at Cousin Will, too.*

Timothy was really into Gorpball and was joining sides willy-nilly. Tweedy hoped Timothy had broken out of his depression once and for all.

Coaching from the sideline (though there were no actual sidelines) was Aggie.

"Move the ball with your chi, Timothy," she called out. "Your chi."

Larry rolled his eyes. "Spare me."

During a break Timothy was standing bent over with his hands on his knees, catching his breath. Tweedy asked, "How's it going, Sport?"

Timothy quickly shook his head. "Whew! It's going good."

After a few hours of play everyone was exhausted but fulfilled. They appeared to have their mind/body orientations in holistic shape; their ying and yangs all sharpened up, so it was time for the communal lunch.

"This place is turning into a commune," complained Larry. "It's communism!"

"Right on, Brother," said Arthur in jest.

Tweedy saw that Timmy was lying on his back enjoying the warmth of the sun.

At dinner Aggie awarded all the players blue ribbons. Then she awarded the people who didn't participate identical blue ribbons. Because people were eating in the dining room and kitchen and living room Aggie had to raise her voice when she congratulated everybody. "These are life games and the goal is enlightenment. We're on our way!"

After dark the game of choice was good old-fashioned flashlight tag. This was the game that everyone delighted in. Larry, dressed all in black, entered what he called his 'stealth mode'. From all over the grounds you could see flashes of light, laughter, and squeals of "Gotcha!"

After flashlight tag was over Tweedy thought it was time for Timothy to turn in for the night. He was unable to find him. He hunted down Click who was sitting at the kitchen table chatting with some other women. Tweedy whispered to Click. She looked concerned.

"Anything wrong?" asked Tweedy's cousin Abigail.

"We seem to have misplaced Timothy," Tweedy said. "I'm sure he's around," trying to sound casual.

Click got up and excused herself. She and Tweedy grabbed flashlights and went out in search of the boy. They fanned out as well as two people can and kept calling Timothy's name. He didn't answer. It took about fifteen minutes before Tweedy found him huddled in a sitting position with his arms around his knees under a tree at the edge of the meadow. Tweedy called out to Click then sat down next to Timothy.

"What's wrong?" he asked.

Timothy didn't say anything. It reminded Tweedy of the first time he found Timothy huddled in the dark tunnel under the Derby grandstand

Click made her way over to them. "Thank goodness," she said in relief. She stood looking at Timothy and Tweedy. "Everything okay?"

Tweedy looked up at Click. "Everything will be." He put his hand on Timothy's shoulder. "Right?"

Timothy nodded. "You know, I didn't mean to cheat," he said quietly.

"We know that. Hey, hasn't it been a good day," Tweedy said enthusiastically, getting to his feet. "Let's turn in."

Timothy got up. Click took his hand and the three of them made their way back to the house.

When they reached the house Timothy asked, "Can I go see Red before we go?"

"Who's Red?" asked Tweedy.

"My turtle," said Timothy.

"Of course you can. Tomorrow morning," said Click. "And maybe we'll be here next summer and you can spend more time with Red. How about that?"

Hearing that got Tweedy's hopes up.

Next year…me…Click.

Tweedy and Click saw Timothy to bed then returned to the front porch. They sat quietly on a faded blue wicker settee enjoying the night sounds. The noise the cicadas made was so loud it made Tweedy giddy. Click looked at Tweedy smiling and asked, "What?"

Tweedy answered, "Nothing. I'm enjoying myself. Aren't you?"

Click nodded. "Uh huh."

"I've never asked. Why do you like photography? You do like photography?"

Click laughed. "Yes." She thought a moment before responding. "You may have noticed I'm not the most touchy-feely kind of person." She expected a response.

Tweedy waited for her to continue.

"Well, it's true, I'm not. I think it's because my parents were kind of remote. They loved me, I'm sure; they just weren't very, - what's the word? – demonstrative. I think that's why I sometimes keep people at a distance." She leaned the slightest bit toward Tweedy so she could make her point. "But photography lets me be at a distance from people and still get up close to them. Thanks to my lenses I can get closer to a person I'm photographing – even a perfect stranger - than I would ever get without my camera. Do you understand?"

Tweedy did. He had a strong urge to lean close to Click, maybe even close enough to maybe kiss her. He reached over towards that end when Cousin Larry barged out of the house and flopped onto a wicker chair. The romantic moment was spoiled.

"So, how was the hunting?" asked Tweedy sardonically.

Larry grunted. "Not good. Say, I've been thinking about Timothy. Everybody here's treating him with kid gloves, acting like he didn't do anything wrong, like he's the victim."

Tweedy and Click sensed what was coming.

"Why not call it like it is: he's a cheater and he got caught. The victim was the Soap Box Derby."

Larry shook his head. "He's a cheater. He knew what he was doing. Don't give me this 'his uncle pressured him'. He's thirteen and he knew what he was doing. He made the choice to cheat. Well, he got caught. Everybody here's pussyfooting around it. When I was his age I was working in my dad's drugstore after school. So was Arthur. If I screwed up I took responsibility for it. I learned to accept the consequences of my actions. That's what's wrong with kids these days. Stop babying him."

Click put her hands over her ears. "I don't want to listen to this," she exclaimed.

Tweedy turned to face Larry.

"Larry, you were a bully when you were little and you're still a bully. I know how you used to pick on Arthur. I remember when you locked him out of the house that winter. What was he, eight years old?"

Larry looked a little sheepish. "Yeah, well…"

"And you demanded that he call you 'The Big Shot' or you'd beat him up. What kind of a kid wants to be known as The Big Shot?"

Larry scoffed. "We're not talking about me. We're talking about Timothy. He's a wimp and you're just encouraging him by condoning his cheating."

Click said fiercely, "We're not condoning anything. Where's your sensitivity, for Pete's sake?"

For a minute none of the three said anything. The single long spring on the old wooden screen door creaked slightly. They turned and caught a fragmentary view of Timothy as he withdrew from the door. They heard sobbing as he pounded up the stairs back to the bedroom.

"He was listening," said Click. "We'd better see if he's okay."

"I didn't know," Larry said defensively.

Tweedy and Click ignored him and went into the house to comfort Timothy.

Larry sat, then said aloud, "I think I'll walk the perimeter." He stood up and walked down the porch steps onto the path that lead to the front gate.

Timothy was in bed staring at the ceiling when Click and Tweedy entered the bedroom. He was expressionless. When asked whether he was okay he nodded.

Tweedy said, "Look, I don't know how much you heard out there but Larry's wrong. Just wrong. Nothing he said is right, understand?"

Timothy didn't respond. Tweedy looked at Click helplessly. Click smoothed the bedsheets, smoothed Timothy's hair and kissed him on the forehead. Tweedy held the door open for Click then began closing it quietly. Click put her hand on Tweedy's and shook her head.

"Better keep the door open," she said.

They returned to the porch and to the settee. The noise of the cicadas was the same, as was the moon. But the mood had changed. Tweedy began telling Click his plans for getting out of the financial rut he was in when an explosive blast rang in their ears. The jumped up from the settee and ran into the house. For a moment the cicadas stopped their fiddling. Tweedy preceded Click up the stairs, their hearts racing. Taking two steps at a time Tweedy slipped and bumped into Click before regaining his footing. As doors began to open in the hallway Tweedy and Click burst into the room to momentarily behold the remains of Timothy before averting their eyes from the gruesome sight. Click clutched at Tweedy, burying her face in his chest. Timothy lay sprawled on the bed, Cousin Larry's rifle beside him. Clutch fell to her knees at the side of the bed and began to cry. Tweedy staggered out of the room and slowly descended the stairs. He found his way to the living room where he collapsed into an old rocking chair. He didn't rock; he sat still, staring out the window.

Shortly thereafter, family members, some in bathrobe or pajamas, huddled around the bedroom door peering in before quickly retreating. This was going to be a busy night at the farm and few would get much sleep.

When Larry heard the gunshot he had raced back to the farmhouse. He thought that as a member of the military that he should take charge but there was little for him to do.

Cousin Arthur volunteered to drive to the Sheriff's office. His wife, Miriam, put herself in charge of comforting Click who sat stunned on the floor next to Timothy's bed. As a news photographer Click had covered a few violent deaths but neither Click nor Tweedy had ever covered anything this awful or personal. At first Click shrugged off Miriam's attempt to coax her from the bedroom, but Miriam persisted and helped Click to her feet. Circling one arm around Click's shoulder Miriam calmly urged her to vacate the bedroom. Click nodded and allowed Miriam to guide her out of the room. Miriam closed the door behind her.

"I think I'll make some tea for us," Miriam said simply.

Everyone knew that the gun belonged to Larry. Family members who already had no fond feelings for him now took to shunning at him as he sat in the living room.

"Damn fool," muttered Uncle Sal. "All these children around and he doesn't keep his gun locked up. Tsk."

"A troubled young man," Larry said to no one in particular.

No one responded so Larry asked Tweedy, "Don't you think so?"

Tweedy didn't answer.

The Sheriff's Department car, followed by Arthur's car, eventually arrived around ten o'clock. Sheriff Thompson and his deputy briskly climbed the front porch stairs two at a time and entered the house. The Sheriff asked to be taken to the scene of the crime. Cousin Larry identified himself by rank and guided the Sheriff to the bedroom. Sheriff Thompson ordered everyone, including Larry, to please stay on the first floor. After visiting the bedroom the Sheriff slowly clunked down the stairs shaking his head. "An awful thing," he said to no one in particular when he reached the front hallway. He asked to speak to Click Gunderson and Jack Tweedy. He requested a quiet room. Miriam, showed him to a room everyone called the back parlor. He found it acceptable and asked Miriam to have Tweedy brought to him. He was sitting in a rocker with his notebook on a table he'd moved in front of him when Tweedy entered.

Until he was asked to talk to the Sheriff Tweedy had not spoken a word since the gunshot. Now he sat in a rocking chair facing the Sheriff and answered Sheriff Thompson's questions so quietly and tersely that he could hardly be heard. He sat staring down at his hands which were clasped resting in his lap.

Sheriff Thompson had been County Sheriff for many decades. The reason he was routinely reelected in this rural county was due to his kindly disposition and his good manners. He was level-headed and as polite as the people he'd meet at the local gun shows his department policed. (People who go to gun shows are unusually well-mannered.)

When he was finished asking Tweedy questions he thanked him and asked to see Click. Tweedy nodded, left and fetched Click, then left the room again. Click sat in the rocking chair vacated by Tweedy.

"We don't get this sort of situation very often," Thompson said sadly. "Why don't you tell me what you know, please." He put his elbows on the table and steepled his hands.

Click filled him in with as much of the story as she could. When she was through Sheriff Thompson sat back in the rocker for a minute or so, then quietly averred that he doubted that there would be an inquest.

"Such a young boy," he said, shaking his head in sorrow. "I'll be talking to the coroner. I see no reason not to rule this unfortunate event an accidental death."

After getting statements from Tweedy, Click and Larry, the Sheriff left to telephone the coroner. There was no telephone service at the farm. The family members who were still up weren't sure whether the Sheriff would be back that evening.

"He'd better be," said the Deputy. "He's my ride home."

That settled, they waited downstairs for the coroner and the return of Sheriff Thompson. The kitchen table seemed to be the hub where family members found comfort. The farmhouse returned to the normal sounds of the summer. Old plumbing, creaking floorboards, occasional throat clearing and allergic sneezes. After warning the family members who were still up to stay away from the "scene of the crime" bedroom the Deputy went outside to sit on the glider and wait for the Sheriff's return.

Inside the kitchen Click asked, "Is it really a crime scene? Did Timothy commit a crime in the eyes of the law?"

Miriam didn't know. Neither did Larry or his brother. Tweedy was unresponsive.

"Maybe the Church thinks so," Miriam said after thinking about the question a while.

"Even if he's just a boy and not an adult?" Click asked.

"Maybe there's a dispensation, if Timothy was Catholic? Was he?"

Click didn't know the answer to that. And Tweedy wasn't talking.

"I think he didn't know what else to call it," said Miriam.

CHAPTER 66

The morning found families packing up, bundling their kids into station wagons, and leaving, some before breakfast. Cousin Arthur said that it reminded him of how tiny grey field mice scurry in every direction when he mows the tall grass for the first time each season. Aggie stayed as did Cousin Will and his wife. The coroner's visit the previous night allowed the local funeral home to proceed with the removal of Timothy's remains. Mr. Collins, owner of the funeral home, went over the steps that would be required over the next few days. He was admirably discreet in ascertaining who would be paying for his services.

"Roger Dunphy," Tweedy said.

"That was Timothy's current guardian," Click explained. "I'll get you his telephone number and address." Click left the room to fetch that information.

"We'll need his signature to release Timothy's remains. I assume he'll want to have Timothy shipped for burial?"

No one knew.

Sheriff Thompson was just arriving as Cousin Larry was driving past the front gate. The Sheriff turned on the gumball that rested on the patrol car's roof and used the car's loudspeaker to order Larry to stop his car. Sheriff Thompson got out of the car and approached Larry's car.

"Yes?" asked Larry, leaning out of his window.

"Are you leaving, Mr. Wakefield?" asked the Sheriff.

"Yes, I am. And it's Colonel Wakefield."

"Sorry," Sheriff bowed his head a tiny bit as he corrected himself, "Colonel Wakefield." He'd dealt with men like this before.

"I have to leave. Important meeting at the Pentagon. Naval intelligence, you know. I don't think we'd want to interfere with that, would we?"

"I see. No, we wouldn't. Well, your rifle will be returned to you once any inquest has been completed. My deputy gave you a receipt for the rifle?"

"Yes."

"I'd appreciate it if you would make yourself available if there is a formal inquest."

Larry nodded. He was proud of being a stickler for procedure.

The Sheriff gave a sort of two finger salute. "Then my sympathies on this sorrowful occasion, Colonel. Have a safe trip."

Larry nodded and drove off. He didn't get to ask Tweedy if he'd play one last game of ping-pong with him - "one for the road." He usually did and Tweedy usually declined. Tweedy and Click both weren't around when Larry left. The other family members were a little stiff when they said farewell to Larry. The family was always polite to one another but this event, now being called "the death of Timothy", made everyone uncomfortable. Nobody was pointing fingers, of course, but they all knew Larry and knew how he was.

CHAPTER 67

"See you in the funny papers!" this was Cousin Arthur's traditional way of saying farewell to Tweedy. But the jape fell flat the morning after the tragedy. Tweedy and Click, having packed everything in the van, were saying their goodbyes. Tweedy wouldn't see most of these relatives again until the next summer. Arthur, his wife Miriam and their daughter, Audrey, would be staying on, along with about a half dozen others. Some who had left might be returning in a week or so; other late season family members would appear over the next few weeks. The summer rituals would go on. Flashlight tag and flag football would continue. But for now a pall had been cast over the farm.

Aggie came over to the van holding something she had pulled out of her slouch bag. It was a big yellow smile button. She hugged her brother, Jack, and asked whether she could pin the button on him. Tweedy didn't resist.

"You know," Aggie said, "I wanted to give Timothy one, but he refused it. Called it 'tacky'."

Tweedy gave a wry smile. "It is tacky; but isn't that the point?" He shrugged and allowed her to pin the button on his shirt.

Aggie hugged him again, this time tighter. "You take care of yourself, brother. And smile more."

Tweedy fingered the smile button then wiggled it at her the way Oliver Hardy used to fiddle with his tie. He left Aggie and went to the van where Click was waiting. They climbed into the van and drove off.

"Well," said Click with a great sigh, turning to face Tweedy. Somehow that one word seemed to wrap up the events of the last couple of days.

"Look, I'm sorry," said Tweedy.

Click was driving. "I've told you: it wasn't your fault. It wasn't anyone's fault."

Tweedy responded, "All I know is: before he knew me Timothy was alive. After I entered his life he was dead."

Click abruptly swerved to the side of the road and yanked the hand brake. She didn't turn off the engine which probably meant this would be a short conversation, but you never know.

"Jack, we've agreed to go see Timothy's mother. I don't want you telling this dying woman that you were responsible for the death of her son. Do you understand?"

Tweedy nodded so Click released the brake and returned to the road.

"Now stop feeling sorry for yourself," Click ordered.

A minute later Click swerved to the shoulder of the road again. Again she applied the hand brake. She turned to Tweedy and put her hand on his arm.

"Look, I'm sorry I snapped at you. I know you're in shock. We both are. But if we're going to make this trip we've got to be kind to one other…and to ourselves. Okay?"

Tweedy nodded. Click disengaged the hand brake and returned to the road.

Click and Tweedy had decided that the proper thing to do would be for them to break the news of Timothy's death to his mother in person. Sheriff Thompson thought this was a very good idea. This would relieve him of the duty of calling her himself. This was a task which he always dreaded. Mrs. Nolen had been moved to a hospice near the Mayo Clinic. If everything went well it would take them a day to drive there.

CHAPTER 68

Jan was in her customary seat facing Jack Tweedy in his little office.

"Mr. Tweedy, I was going over my notes last night and I have a question: what was an 'encounter group'? You talked about Aggie trying to get you involved in an encounter group. And I don't know what Rolfing is."

Getting no response, Jan looked up from her notes to find Tweedy's head drooping, chin on chest. At first Jan was alarmed and was about to rush out of Tweedy's tiny office to alert the newsroom. But she saw that while Tweedy's eyes were shut his breathing was regular. He was drowsing. Jan sat back down in the chair and looked closely at Tweedy. His hands, which were resting on the front of his sweater vest, had skin like soft parchment, almost translucent, mottled with brown spots, and a fine tracery of veins. His hands were so different from her grandfather's which had been gnarled, hard and scarred from work in the mines and her father's. Tweedy's were almost delicate.

She sat for a while there while Tweedy napped, taking this opportunity to think back upon her trip with Ned to his family's home in Hingham, Massachusetts, for New Years. It was a short trip of only two days. She liked his family which was close knit. His sister worked at Harvard as an archivist at the Fogg Art Museum. His parents were retired physicians who kept busy with hobbies and travel. Hingham was a beautiful old colonial town by the ocean. Ned's family lived in a large early nineteenth century house that had been passed down to them. They seemed to like her.

Tweedy woke up, looked up, composed himself and smiled. "Did I nod off there for a while?" he asked.

"Yes. Can I get you something? Water? Or would you like me to leave you alone?"

"No, no, we must continue paddling down the stream of history. Now, where were we? Oh, yes, the trip to the hospice." Tweedy paused and prepared to launch his narrative. But before he could begin Jan said, "You know, when you were talking about looking for Timothy at the farm that night? It reminded me of something that sometimes happens at the farm. There's a condition called scourse that can strike newborn animals, especially lambs. It's a diarrhea; it causes dehydration. My brother Josiah always has to be very watchful with newborn lambs because it isn't obvious. A lamb will go off by itself and lie down and Josiah won't even notice that it's gone. By the time he finds it the lamb won't eat and is often near death."

"Does the lamb die?" Tweedy asked.

"Sometimes. Depends on whether Josiah finds it early enough."

"Interesting," Tweedy said quietly.

Tweedy and Jan sat without saying anything for a while. Tweedy said, "Well, where were we?"

Jan shook her head. "I'm sorry, I interrupted you. You were talking about the trip to the hospice."

"Ah, yes. The trip was uneventful, at least compared to other legs of the journey."

Tweedy went quiet. He looked across his desk at Jan. "Maybe we should break for lunch?"

"It's only ten o'clock."

"I notice that you're wearing an engagement ring," Tweedy said.

"Yes," said Jan, "I showed it to you last week, remember?"

"Yes." Tweedy was fidgeting in his chair.

"What happened when you reached the hospice?"

Tweedy scowled. Jan sensed that his mood had darkened.

"You must have some work to do," he asked.

"I'm sorry, Mr. Tweedy," said Jan. "I'm bugging you. We can pick this up, maybe tomorrow?" She stood up so that Tweedy didn't have to answer. She smiled and said, "You're right. I do have an obituary I have to write. I'll see you later. Thanks."

CHAPTER 69

Jan had to finish an obituary for Big Mike Fusco, owner of the Karate Garage martial arts studio. Far from being a 98 pound weakling when he embarked on a physical fitness regimen, Big Mike was carrying 450 pounds on his five foot four inch frame when he started exercising. He brought his weight down to 180 well-chiseled muscle and became a black belt karate expert famous for breaking coconuts with his head. His brother would be dropping off before-and-after photographs of Big Mike later in the afternoon.

Why coconuts? Jan wondered. This thought was interrupted by a telephone call from Myrt. She seemed concerned.

"Jan, do you have a minute?" Myrt didn't wait for an answer. "Last weekend I went to your family's farm."

"Is something wrong?" asked Jan, concerned.

"No, everything's fine. Except…let me tell you what happened. I was with Josiah and he decided to pull a prank on your father."

"Which he is known to do."

"Right. This time he moved a mountain of manure in the pasture about ten feet from where it was. Charlie was in town while Josiah did this. He used that thing – what's it called? It's yellow."

"The front loader?"

"Right. He did an excellent job and covered up where the manure pile was, so you couldn't tell. After Charlie came back from town we made a point to be at the pasture when he came out. We watched. It was hilarious. He sort of looked, took off his ballcap and scratched the back of his neck and shook his head a couple of times. He could tell something was different, but he couldn't tell what. Perfect cognitive dissonance. It was all I could do to keep from breaking out laughing."

"Okay. Good gag. So?" Jan asked.

"In a week or so Josiah plans to move the manure pile slightly somewhere else. Anyway, when he and I were laughing about it later Josiah talked about how much he loved the farm. We were lying back on a pile of hay…"

Jan interrupted. "You're sure it was hay?"

"Ha, ha. Yes, it was hay. We were in the barn. Anyway, he made a real point to tell me how important the farm was to him." Here's where Myrt's voice took on a plaintive tone. "Jan, he's never going to leave the farm, is he? He knows it. I know it."

Jan said, "I pretty much told you that, didn't I."

Myrt sighed. "Yeah."

Jan felt bad for Myrt. There wasn't more she could say.

Jan had a craving for Chinese food so she went off to The Imperial Golden Jade Dragon Gate for its buffet lunch. She didn't open her fortune cookie figuring she'd give it to Tweedy as a peace offering. She felt she had annoyed him. She returned to the Herald-Sentinel building and headed towards the stairs as usual when the receptionist called out, "Oh, Ms. Pancake?" Jan walked over to the counter.

"I thought you ought to know," the receptionist said in a low voice, "Mr. Tweedy was taken out of here about twenty minutes ago."

Huh? Jan wondered what Tweedy could have done. The receptionist saw Jan's puzzled expression and explained, "He's dead. He died."

Shocked, Jan raced up the stairs to the newsroom. Just looking around at the look on peoples' faces confirmed what the receptionist had just told her. Jan went over to Pell Newcomb's desk. Newcomb looked grim.

"Jack died. We think it was a heart attack. You'll write the obituary, okay? He wanted you to."

"What do you mean?"

"Weeks ago Jack came to me. Told me he wanted you when the time came."

Jan nodded.

"There was only one stipulation," Newcomb said. "He wanted it to have a happy ending."

Jan stood there.

"Well," Newcomb said, "better hop to it."

Jan plodded over to her desk and dropped into the seat. Write Jack Tweedy's obituary? She hadn't even finished her own. And now she was being told to write the obituary of a man she might have been responsible for killing. At least, that's how she felt. She had pushed Tweedy to recounts things about the death of Timmy Nolen he clearly didn't want to tell. Had she pushed him because she was ambitious, too eager to get "the story"? And now she wondered whether she could even finish "the story." Was it right to worry about that? There it was again - that ambition and conceit that Philippians warned against, enjoining one to "count others more significant than yourself."

There seemed to be an awful lot of death in the life of a woman this young. Dickie Yount, Timmy Nolen, now Jack Tweedy. All those obituaries. Jan began to sob. It may have revealed her lack of objectivity, her lack professionalism, but she didn't care. She sobbed and no one came over to console her. Then she stopped sobbing. Others – others who knew Tweedy longer and were closer – they probably felt worse, she thought. Maybe she could provide some consolation? She joined a group of people who were standing on the newsroom floor talking about the death of Tweedy, expressing their shock and sadness. The one thing they could all agreed on – that seemed to comfort them all - was that he was old, though no one was quite sure just how old. After a while Jerry Murphy, the Managing Editor, came out of his office and addressed this group.

"People, we have a newspaper to get out. There are deadlines. We'll have to grieve for Tweedy later."

And that was that. The staff went back to work. When Jan returned to her desk she opened her handbag to get a handkerchief and noticed the fortune cookie she had brought back for Tweedy. She tore the cellophane wrapper and cracked open the cookie. The little slip of paper read: "You will get good news soon."

That evening she had dinner with Ned at Mercy Hospital and told him about Tweedy. She began to tear up.

"I think I may have contributed to his death, Ned," she said sighing. She explained how she had pushed Tweedy to talk about Timmy Nolen's death long after he was showing signs of discomfort. She groaned.

Ned could see that Jan was upset and didn't make light of her fear. "There's no way of knowing, of course, but it's not likely."

It might have allayed Jan's fear more had he said that it was impossible, but Ned was a man of science.

CHAPTER 70

In the future Jan would be able to look back and wonder why she was so uncomfortable interviewing Jerry Murphy. In the future she'd think nothing of getting up to the dais at a testimonial dinner for Jerry Murphy and relate anecdotes and crack jokes at Murphy's expense. But on this day she was collecting information for Jack Tweedy's obituary and Murphy was on her list of people to talk to. She had already visited Personnel and the Morgue (in this case the newspaper archive) and so was armed with questions. She made an appointment to see Murphy.

Murphy ushered Jan into his office and offered her a seat.

"Jerry, Gloria (Head of Personnel) told me that Mr. Tweedy officially retired six years ago." She said this as though asking a question.

"I think that's about right," said Murphy.

"But he's been working here."

Murphy smiled. "Working unofficially."

Jan waited for an explanation.

"You see, about eight years ago Jack's doctor ordered him to retire. He had a heart condition, you know. That's what kept him out of Vietnam."

What a relief! Jan may not have been responsible for Tweedy's death.

"Jack had no life outside the S-H and his church. So when his retirement came we just ignored it. We liked having him around and with the reductions in force that we've experienced the last few years, well, there was room for him. Tweedy was like a connection to the old days of the S-H."

"The glory years?" Jan asked.

Murphy smiled. "No, the glory years are to come. Right?"

"Right!" Jan said with forced enthusiasm.

"Tweedy helped make the Sentinel-Herald what it is. And, for better or worse, the S-H helped make Tweedy what he was. The things that happened to him – like the nervous breakdown or whatever it was

– happened here, or at least because of us. So, we always felt responsible for him."

This was the first Jan had heard about a nervous breakdown, but it certainly wouldn't go into an obituary, so it wasn't any of her business.

Murphy smiled in reflection. "Jack was a darned good reporter in his day."

"But what has he done since he retired?" Jan had to ask.

"Well…" Murphy said, drawing out the word so that it might better be spelled 'Welllll', "he was in charge of the internship program. And he wrote occasional thought pieces, which we paid him for. But those came less and less frequently."

"And?"

"And we let him do what he wanted," Murphy said, somewhat annoyed. "The paper takes care of its own."

Jan smiled. "That's nice."

She had other questions but decided to end the interview here.

CHAPTER 71

Jan wrote an obituary for Tweedy that was respectful, stuck to the facts, and with just enough excerpts from particularly good articles he had written years before to make it interesting. There were laudatory quotes from fellow news people: for example, he was called "a newspaperman's newspaperman" by one, and "the soul of the Sentinel-Herald" by another. The obituary went into the paper on Monday and the funeral was to be held Friday at eleven o'clock.

On a sunny Friday in April Jan and Ned went to Jack Tweedy's graveside funeral service. There were around six dozen people in attendance.

Jan and Ned were probably the youngest people in attendance. Jan spotted many of the newspaper staff, including Mary Karnes and her husband, Pell Newcomb and Jeremiah Murphy. Jan spotted old Mrs. MacNaughton standing next to Murphy. Jan held Ned's hand and walked over to stand next to Newcomb. Newcomb nodded his head and gave them a twitch smile. Mary gave a little wave which Jan returned. Jan tried to identify some of the people she figured might be Tweedy's relatives. Could that be Larry? Will? Arthur and his wife, Miriam? And that middle-aged woman with them – could that be their daughter Audrey?

When eleven o'clock came and went and it was obvious that there would be no more mourners the minister, Father DiOrio, began the ceremony.

After the grayish days of winter, Jan couldn't help but be distracted by the abundance of life emerging all around her this spring day. Grass that had been pretty beat up the last few months was making a comeback. There were tiny insects hopping and jumping around her feet. A bluebird was chattering in the branches of a tree and squirrels were racing around after one another. Jan could hear the drone of traffic on West Market Street in the distance. She was finding it hard to concentrate on what Father DiOrio was saying.

Concentrate, Jan, this is Tweedy's funeral.

Jan tried to ignore nature. She looked at Ned. *How handsome he looks,* she thought. *That's a nice suit, but I'm not wild about that tie. I'll have to get him a new tie.*

Concentrate!

Nope, looking at Ned is too distracting. That's not going to work.

I should be paying attention!

Father DiOrio was saying some interesting things about Tweedy whom he had known as long as he'd been here in Akron. He had taken over his parish from Father Hudnut who had helped Tweedy during Tweedy's difficult period. He made reference to Tweedy's struggles and how, through the grace of God, Tweedy had faced his difficulties and overcome them. Father DiOrio was, thankfully, vague in some of his allusions but firm in his belief that Tweedy triumphed because of his faith in Jesus. He quickly moved on to Tweedy's role in the community and the Sentinel-Herald.

Jan thought that DiOrio was doing a nice job of organizing the information of Tweedy's life. Not a pyramid; not an upside down pyramid; more of a ziggurat. He covered a lot of territory. But Jan wondered whether a life should be summarized so easily.

A couple of prayers were said then Father DiOrio asked the mourners to join him in singing Amazing Grace.

After that Tweedy was interred. It had been a nice ceremony. People chatted for a while before they began to make their ways back to the road where cars were parked. Jan and Ned, still holding hands, followed the mourners down the slight hill. Their progress was halted when they heard a cry and saw a commotion back nearer the grave site. They trotted back to where they found a group of the mourners huddled around old Mrs. MacNaughton who was lying on the ground, her right leg awkwardly folded under. She had fallen, having tripped over one of those grave markers that are flush with the turf so as to allow lawn mowers to ride over them. Ned kneeled down and asked her, "Can you move your leg?"

Mrs. MacNaughton, in obvious pain, replied that she thought she could, but that it hurt a great deal.

"Just plant me here," she said, not in misery but in irony. She was annoyed at herself.

"I'm a doctor, ma'am. Do you mind if I look at it?" Ned asked.

Mrs. MacNaughton nodded her assent, so Ned took off her right shoe and felt around the ankle. When he applied some pressure from one angle she grimaced in pain. Ned apologized.

Someone in the huddle asked whether he should call an ambulance.

"Nonsense," said Mrs. MacNaughton. "I was clumsy and wasn't looking where I was going and there you are." Then she looked at Ned. "Well, young man, what do you think?"

"I think it's a bad sprain. It doesn't appear to be broken."

That diagnosis led a few observers to withdraw from the huddle and speed walk as inconspicuously as they could to their cars. Were they disappointed that it was only a sprain?

But a sprain on an old ankle can be a serious thing, can't it?

Father DiOrio, a well-groomed middle-aged man, was aware of the prominent position Mrs. MacNaughton held in the Akron community and was very solicitous. "If there's anything I can do, Mrs. MacNaughton…"

Ned looked at Jan for assistance. "Ma'am, we're going to try to get you up on your good leg, if you can," said Ned. Mrs. MacNaughton allowed Ned and Jan to raise her up on her right leg. Jan held her on one side and Ned put his arm around the other side. "Don't walk on that foot. We'll take you to Mercy General to get you x-rayed and bandaged, okay?"

Mrs. MacNaughton gave a pained smile of assent. She looked over to another elderly woman. "Clairsie, you'll go along without me."

Her friend Claire nodded. "Call me."

"I will. You may have to give me a ride home from the hospital." Mrs. MacNaughton turned to Jan. "Just give me my shoe," Mrs. MacNaughton ordered.

Jan reached down and snagged her shoe, and then she and Ned began to help Mrs. MacNaughton hobble towards their car.

"Stop!" Mrs. MacNaughton ordered.

"What's wrong?" asked Jan.

"I want to know who I tripped over. Phil, go see who tripped me up."

A man named Phil walked over and knelt at the offending little bronze grave marker. "Dennis Xander," he read.

"Xander? I don't know that name. What kind of a name is that?" Mrs. MacNaughton asked.

Jan said, "I think it's a fairly common name in West Virginia."

Mrs. MacNaughton sniffed. "Well, this one came to Akron just so he could trip me up. A bad lot, I'd say."

Jan had to smile.

They knew they had a challenge once they got to Ned's BMW.

"You expect me to get into that little thing? I couldn't get into that with two good ankles," Mrs. MacNaughton said. Ned wasn't sure whether she was pretending to be aghast or whether she really was aghast. The smart move was to apologize. He did. Then he did the best he could to maneuver her into the back seat.

"I'm sorry you had so much trouble getting into my car, ma'am."

"What is this car?" she asked.

"A BMW."

Mrs. MacNaughton made a sound that could be translated as "harrumph" as she folded into the bucket seat.

"I feel like a cheap pocket knife," she complained.

Ned apologized. Jan climbed into the front seat and Ned jumped in and drove off as though in search of a restroom.

"You're going to have to use the Jaws of Life to get me out of this vehicle," Mrs. MacNaughton said. She was getting less cranky.

"You look familiar," said Mrs. MacNaughton to Jan.

"I'm Jan Pancake. We met last summer at that luncheon for the interns? I'm one of the MacNaughton interns at the Sentinel-Herald."

"I remember. The girl from West Virginia."

"Right," said Jan.

Even though she was in some pain, Mrs. MacNaughton brightened and warmed up to Jan.

When they reached the hospital Ned parked in front of the emergency entrance, hopped out and commandeered a wheelchair. A hospital attendant helped him spring Mrs. MacNaughton loose from the BMW and Jan wheeled her into the hospital. Instead of sitting in the emergency room waiting area like the rest of the miserable wretches, Mrs. MacNaughton was wheeled directly into an examining room, x-rays were taken, a painkiller was dispensed, and the ankle was bandaged up in short order.

Now in much better spirits, Mrs. MacNaughton was happy to have Ned and Jan take her home accompanied by a prescription for painkillers and a pair of state-of-the-art crutches (which weren't – to be honest – all that different from plain old crutches).

Jan took note of the deferential manner everyone showed toward Mrs. MacNaughton. It might have been her impeccable conduct under difficult circumstances. Or it could have been her advanced age. More likely it was her name engraved on one of the larger bronze plaques on the wall in the hospital lobby.

Chapter 72

On a scale of homes ranging from Randolph Hearst's San Simeon (100) to Jan Pancake's Little San Simeon (1) Mrs. MacNaughton's house would rate a 90. It was a large brick, limestone and stucco pile that was built before radio and television cut into newspapers' domination of the media. It was before the term 'mass media' became common. It was built by Mrs. MacNaughton's father-in-law a so-called 'newspaper baron'.

Mrs. MacNaughton was met at the front door by her housekeeper, Bernice, who immediately made a fuss when she saw her boss with crutches. Mrs. MacNaughton told Bernice to shush and ushered Jan and Ned into the living room. Bernice tried to help Mrs. MacNaughton navigate to a sofa but was brushed off with "I've got to get good with these things because I'm going to be on them for a few weeks yet." She nodded toward Ned. "That's according to my new personal physician. But you can bring me that footstool and fetch us some tea."

Once she got settled, Mrs. MacNaughton talked about her late husband and the role she played as publisher after his death.

"I miss a great deal about not being at the paper every day. Every day was exciting. I miss the people. I made a point of having every new employee come to meet me in my office. I think it was important."

She talked about Jack Tweedy and asked Jan questions about her interests and her experiences at the paper. She wasn't just being polite. It was clear she was seriously interested.

After a while, - and long after the last of the cookies were polished off, - it was clear that Mrs. MacNaughton was tiring. She said that it was time for her nap. "I've enjoyed our chat. I want you to know that I'm going to keep an eye on you," she said to Jan with a smile.

Ned asked how she would get to a bedroom and learned that the house had an elevator. Ned was impressed until Mrs. MacNaughton said, "It's a small elevator."

Jan smiled. *Why are people apologetic about elevators?* she wondered.

"Bernice," Mrs. MacNaughton called out, "please see these lovely young people out."

After they all shook hands and said goodbye, Bernice escorted them out of the house.

Ned drove Jan to the front of the Sentinel-Herald building and said he'd see her later for dinner.

"Do you want to go out somewhere? Maybe a movie?" he asked as Jan was climbing out of the car.

Jan shook her head. "Don't think so. Let's have a nice quiet evening. I'll make something."

She kissed him goodbye and headed for the entrance.

Back at her desk she found a pink while-you-were-out note telling her that she'd missed a telephone call. The little box that indicated that she was to call back was checked. A telephone number and a name were handwritten: Marjorie Gunderson.

Marjorie Gunderson? Jan thought for a minute. Why, that must be Click Gunderson. She picked up the phone and dialed. The woman who answered sounded nothing like the perky young woman Jan had imagined for Click. No, it sounded like a crabby old lady.

Jan identified herself.

Click said, "I see that Jack Tweedy died. I was told you might know if there's to be a smoker for Tweedy."

"Smoker?" Jan asked.

"You know, a crepe party," she said impatiently. A gathering to celebrate Tweedy's life. A wake."

"Oh," Jan said, finally understanding. "Yes, Sunday night at Jeremiah Murphy's house. Can you come?"

"I'll be there."

Jan asked where she'd be coming from. When the answer was Chicago Jan asked whether she would need a ride. Click said she wouldn't mind getting picked up at the airport. She'd be coming from Chicago and would email Jan with details as soon as she had them.

"Ms. Gunderson, may I call you 'Click'?"

"No, but you may call me Marjorie."

After hanging up the phone Jan found Jerry Murphy and told him to expect one more person at his 'smoker'.

"My what?"

"Your gathering to celebrate Mr. Tweedy's life. Your smoker. Marjorie Gunderson is coming."

"My goodness," said Murphy.

Jack Tweedy never had the chance to talk to Jan about Click Gunderson's post-Akron career. There was no need: Gunderson was something of a legend around the S-H. Gunderson was the only staff member of the Sentinel-Herald to win two Pulitzer Prizes for her news photography. The S-H couldn't claim any credit, though, because Click won them while working for the Chicago Examiner. It could be argued that she honed her skills in Akron but this wasn't an argument anyone wanted to take up. When Murphy said "My goodness" it meant that a celebrity would be coming to his smoker. When Jan told him she'd be picking her up at the airport Murphy seemed a little jealous.

He needn't have been. Gunderson's flight was almost two hours late so Jan had to hang around Akron Canton Airport until Gunderson showed up. When she did Jan didn't complain about her wait, but Gunderson definitely complained about hers. Jan had hardly gotten to introduce herself before Gunderson said, "Damn, what an awful flight!"

Jan commiserated and asked Gunderson whether she had any luggage other than carryon. She hadn't. Jan tried to help Gunderson by taking her carryon luggage but Gunderson resisted.

"I may be old and lame but I can still wheel my luggage around, thank you," she said curtly.

She was, indeed, lame. She walked with a limp. After Jerry Murphy told her about Click's illustrious career, Jan went online and read an interview in which Gunderson discussed how she came to have that limp. On assignment for National Geographic she antagonized a band of Watusi warriors. One expressed his hostility with a spear that caught Gunderson in the thigh. She ended up with a limp and her first Pulitzer. "Wasn't even a chief," Gunderson complained to the interviewer. "It was simply a faulty translation of the word 'uulmaka' that lead to the misunderstanding," Gunderson explained to the interviewer.

As they walked down the hallway and lobby to the exit Jan sized up her guest. Gunderson still had the corkscrew hair that Tweedy had thought was so pretty but now it was white. Her face was lined, especially around her mouth. Probably a smoker, Jan surmised, too much time in the sun and not enough sun block. She was dressed in baggy khaki pants, a wrinkled shirt and wore a silk scarf around her neck.

Jan asked her whether she'd like to be dropped off at her hotel. (Under her breath Jan muttered "or from the hotel roof?")

Gunderson said she'd appreciate being dropped off at the hotel. As they drove through the city Gunderson looked around.

"Ugh, Akron," she sneered.

Jan made sure not to go over the speed limit. Still, she deposited Gunderson at the hotel in great time and arranged to pick her up around eight o'clock for the smoker. She didn't ask whether Gunderson had dinner plans. Gunderson said she wanted to take a nap.

CHAPTER 73

The benefits of a good nap cannot be overstated. When eight o'clock rolled around Jan wasn't eager to pick up her passenger but she made it to the hotel on time. Out from the entrance came a woman Jan hardly recognized. Gunderson had transformed herself into a fashion wonder. Her hair had been beautifully styled and her makeup was expert. Her smile was radiant.

"Thank you ever so much for doing this for me," she gushed.

And she'd had a personality re-do. Those wrinkles Jan had noticed? Fine lines, signs of character and a life well spent.

"Look, these things don't start warming up until around nine. What say we have a drink? I don't know a thing about you," said Gunderson, taking Jan's arm and propelling her into the hotel towards the cocktail lounge before Jan had a chance to answer.

The fact is Jan had never been in a bar before. She reluctantly allowed Gunderson to drag her into the lounge.

"This place is darker than my old darkroom," said Gunderson. "You can't see yourself think. It's perfect."

Before their eyes had a chance to adjust Gunderson steered Jan to a booth. They sat down and Gunderson crooked a finger at a waiter who hustled over to the booth.

"I'll have a martini," said Gunderson. Turning to Jan she asked, "What'll you have?"

Jan timidly said that she didn't drink alcohol.

Gunderson, taken aback, said, "Hardly something to be ashamed of. Would you rather we went to the coffee bar?"

Jan didn't want to make a fuss.

"Would you like a cup of tea or coffee?" Gunderson asked.

Jan ordered a cup of tea. When the waiter went away Gunderson said, "Well, a newspaper person who doesn't drink. That's refreshing. Newspaper people drink entirely too much, but maybe that's changing. There've been so many changes."

After a few minutes the waiter returned with their beverages. When he left Gunderson lowered her voice. "I must apologize for my attitude when you picked me up at the airport. Flying always makes me a little crazy. You must think I'm a monster."

Jan smiled and didn't say anything.

"Pancake, that's a West Virginian name. That's where you're from?" Gunderson asked.

Jan was surprised. She said yes.

Gunderson said, "Tell me about yourself."

So Jan did. She covered a lot of the ground that she had written about in the obituary that Pell Newcomb asked her to write. But when she was writing about herself she thought it sounded so boring she felt embarrassed. But Marjorie Gunderson seemed to find it very interesting. This made no sense. Gunderson was a Pulitzer Prize winner, a celebrated photographer who'd been all over the world covering important events. Jan covered public library puppet shows and City Council meetings. And wrote obituaries.

"Obituaries are a good start," said Gunderson, "but you won't make a name for yourself by writing obituaries. You do want to make a name for yourself, don't you?"

Jan said yes, but she didn't say it with as much enthusiasm as Gunderson was looking for. "Don't be ashamed of being ambitious. You've come this far by having ambition."

"You were ambitious?" asked Jan.

"You bet I was. And things were tougher then because I was up against a lot of men who didn't think too much of women."

"Still, you became a huge success," said Jan.

Some people would be self-deprecating at such talk. Not Gunderson. She smiled and said, "Yes, I did. I'm not embarrassed to say it. I'm proud of what I accomplished. As you get more experienced, I'm sure you'll get more confident. And never run down your accomplishments. There are too many jealous people who'll be happy to do that for you. Don't be timid. That was Tweedy's greatest failing. Too timid. That and gambling. You can't be timid! Would you like another cup of tea?"

Jan said that she would. While they waited for their drinks Gunderson asked whether many of Tweedy's family were at the funeral. Jan said that she thought that Cousins Arthur and Will were there. But she didn't think she saw Cousin Larry.

"You wouldn't. Tweedy would never speak to him after that night. What about Aggie? That woman was a hoot."

Jan said that she didn't see anyone there who might be Tweedy's sister.

"If she were there you would have known it," said Gunderson. "That gal was something. I suppose she must be dead by now."

Gunderson sighed. "Poor Jack, I'm surprised he lasted as long as he did. I think it must have been his faith and his simplicity that saw him through. He didn't talk about his religious beliefs but they were there. A lovely man. And a good writer; a good stylist. Not such a good reporter – too timid. I hope you learned from him. He could teach you a lot about writing."

Gunderson ordered another cup of tea for Jan and another martini for herself.

Jan told Marjorie that Tweedy had been a good mentor. She talked about her thesis and how Tweedy was describing the Soapbox Derby events up to the time of his death.

"Newspapers always call someone's death 'untimely'. Maybe Native Americans know when it's a good time to die, but I'm sure I won't."

Jan asked whether Marjorie could finish Tweedy's narrative.

A sad look came over Gunderson's face but she slowly nodded her head a couple of times. "Where did he leave off?"

"The two of you were setting off to see Timmy's mother."

"Oh, yes." Gunderson gave a slight groan and shook her head. "Well, it took us a day to drive to Mrs. Nolen's hospice. When we got there I couldn't get Tweedy to get out of the car. He just kept shaking his head and whimpering. He got into what I'd describe as a fetal position. It was terrible. He felt so bad about how things turned out and blamed himself for what had happened. It wasn't his fault and I kept telling him that. It didn't make any difference.

"Anyway, I went into the hospice by myself and was taken to Mrs. Nolen's room. I tried to explain who I was and what had happened to her son, but she was so groggy from the painkillers that I doubt that she grasped what I was trying to tell her." Gunderson sighed. "I think about that poor little boy often. He and Tweedy were a lot alike. Both very sensitive, very sweet and moody."

Jan asked, "What happened after you went to the hospice?"

"It was awful. Poor Tweedy was inconsolable. He felt so guilty. He kept talking about how he'd let Timmy down. I've never known a man so unhappy and I've known quite a few unhappy men. We walked around that town for hours. When we finally got back to Akron he fell apart. Completely unmoored. Started drinking and would show up for work in the worst condition. That's when he did show up. Frequently he didn't. You can't have that at a newspaper. Tom Higgins and Sam Gibbons were patient men but after a while they had to let him go. For a couple of years there Tweedy was a lost soul."

Jan looked stricken. "Poor Mr. Tweedy. And I was making him talk about the worst period in his life. I feel awful." She wrung her hands.

Gunderson patted Jan's hands. "Don't. I'm sure he viewed it as ancient history."

"Yes, he said that a few times – that it was history. So what happened?"

Gunderson laughed. "Like all good newspaper people you do like a good story, don't you. The people at the paper didn't give up on him. Higgins especially saw him through. Took him to AA meetings and had Tweedy move into his house. Mrs. Higgins was a saint. Every Sunday they'd take him to church with them. After a while Tweedy straightened himself out. Got his old job back. Moved out of Higgins' house. Those were some good people at that paper. It was the paper that saved him. That and his faith, I guess."

Jan was enjoying being with this woman and didn't want the conversation to end. She nodded and said, "Hmm." She looked around the cocktail lounge. She sort of liked this place. It was oddly cozy.

"Did you or Mr. Tweedy ever think that the press was responsible for Timmy's death? Did you talk about it?"

Gunderson put her martini down and picked up the cocktail napkin. She slowly folded it in quarters.

"Tweedy did. I didn't," she said firmly.

Jan didn't want to press her but she wanted to know. "At any time did you wonder whether you were exploiting Timmy?"

"Did you ask Tweedy that?" Gunderson said sharply.

Jan shook her head.

"Good," Gunderson said. "You're young." Then she paused and shook her head. "No, that's not it. I'm sorry, I'm being patronizing. Sometimes there are situations where the ethics involved are murky and you simply keep going. It's a matter of momentum, understand?" She unfolded the little cocktail napkin. "At the time we wanted to reunite Timmy and his mother. And we had the opportunity to cover a good story and sell newspapers." Here Gunderson made her point by tapping each word out on the table with her fingernail. "Which…was…our…job."

They were silent for a while.

Gunderson thought of something. "Look, don't get the idea that work is everything. It isn't."

"What is?"

"I don't have the answer to that. Nothing is everything. Working hard at something you think is worthwhile is a part. I'd tell you that you have to give back, help others, but I don't want to sound like a sanctimonious old biddy."

No one is going to mistake you for an old biddy," Jan said and laughed. "I'm sorry, I interrupted." And then she interrupted herself. "Incidentally, the phrase 'old biddy' is redundant."

"Oh?" asked Gunderson.

"A biddy is an old hen."

Gunderson laughed. "Takes a West Virginian farm girl to know that. Well, I was just going to say that you should work hard, help others and serve your God – how's that? And if you're lucky enough to have a family…" she said wistfully.

Jan asked, "Why did you come today? You haven't seen Tweedy in how long?"

"How long?" She thought for a minute. "At least twenty years. Why did I come?" She threw her head back and laughed. "I don't know. Tweedy and I went through so much together. I had to come. I don't know why. There isn't a good answer for everything." She looked at her watch. "Say, we'd better get over to Jerry Murphy's house." She started to rise. "Jan, I've enjoyed this. I'm going to keep an eye on you; follow your career."

Jan thought to herself, *Someone else who's going to keep an eye on me!*

As they were leaving the hotel Gunderson said, "Jan, I want you to call me Marjorie at this party. That'll be good for your reputation. Wait, better yet call me Click. I don't like it but it'll look like we're old chums." As they headed for Jan's car Gunderson wove her arm through Jan's arm. "You know what? We are old chums! At least, I am."

They got to Jerry Murphy's house. Gunderson was right: the party was just getting started. Ordinarily, Jan hated to go to parties by herself, but this time she was with Marjorie Gunderson. She found herself within the orbit of the center of attention. She wished Ned were there but he was on duty at the hospital. She'd see him tomorrow when they went to Mrs. MacNaughton's house to check on her ankle. She'd bake a strudel for Mrs. MacNaughton made from apples from Sunset Farms and Mrs. MacNaughton would call her a 'dear girl' and make her feel special. Click Gunderson made her feel special, too. Not the same way that Ned made her feel special, of course. He made her feel special in a special way: special and desired.

Jan's musings were interrupted by someone calling for a toast to Jack Tweedy.

"Pipe down," he ordered.

Everyone's mood turned momentarily somber. Pell raised his glass of beer and said, "To Jack Tweedy, we'll miss you."

Some in the group said, "To Jack." Others said, "To Tweedy."

Jan knew she would miss him.

The hubbub returned to its previous sound level. Jan heard someone ask Marjorie Gunderson for some advice. Her response was "Speak quietly and carry a high quality camera."

This witticism probably didn't deserve the appreciative reaction it got, but that's what happens when you're a celebrity.

Jan was at the drinks table picking up a bottle of water when Pell Newcomb said, "I've got something for you."

"Hi, Pell."

Pell, fishing around in his pocket, said, "We had to go through Jack's desk this afternoon. I found something. Jack had put your name on it." Newcomb pulled out a two inch diameter button from his pocket and handed it to Jan. "I guess he wanted you to have this."

It was the yellow smiley face button that Aggie had given him at the farm in 1973.

Jan took it and hugged it to her chest.

"So, it means something?" Newcomb asked.

Jan could only nod and smile.

Marjorie Gunderson seemed to be having such a terrific time that Jan was reluctant to interrupt her conversation, but she was tired and wanted to go home. She waited until Gunderson noticed her.

"Yes, Jan, my good friend."

"Click, do you think you could get another ride to your hotel? I'm tired and want to go home."

Gunderson got at least five immediate offers. She hugged Jan and said, "We'll be in touch."

Jan left the party and drove to Dobbins Doggy Lodge. It was after eleven but Jan felt like being with…she didn't know. She didn't change out of her dress; she just changed her shoes and wandered over to the kennel.

"Hello, Lucy, old girl." Jan flopped on the straw next to Lucy.

Lucy the blind Sheltie flapped her tail and lifted her chin. Jan scratched her behind her ears. Lucy liked being scratched there.

For the time being, they were content.

The end

Made in the USA
Middletown, DE
19 July 2021